Sunshine & Safety

An Oak River County Novel

Danielle Redman

Published by: Delightful Day Publishing
Cover design by: Danielle Redman
Edited by: Megan Harris
Interior formatting by: Danielle Redman

ISBN: 979-8-9953876-0-2

*For my husband, who is my best friend and
my safe place.
I love you.*

The next page contains trigger warnings.

Please skip if you wish to avoid any plot spoilers.

Content Warnings

Dear Reader,

Please note that Sunshine & Safety contains the following material that may be triggering for some readers: mentions of death by car accident, past sexual assault (off page but discussed), references to a past emotionally and psychologically abusive relationship, on page panic attack, on page violence and injury, threatening, stalking and harassment from a former partner, an abduction, on page sexual content, and some explicit language.

If you are sensitive to any of these subjects, please use this warning to make an informed decision about whether or not to proceed reading this story.

As always, take care of yourself. Your mental health matters.

Danielle

Prologue

Rae Whitaker

Moonlight streaked across the floor of the living room, casting an eerie glow around me as I carefully walked across the room. I made sure to avoid the spots that creaked so I didn't wake him up. I had successfully snuck out of our room before without waking him, and I could do it again this time. However, this time, I did not plan on walking back into this house. I took a few steps and then stopped and listened to his breathing. He was still snoring.

The nightmares, the constant fear of "what if," led me to this choice, and there is no way in hell I would change my mind this time. I took a few more steps and my breath caught when I did not hear him snoring. I stopped. My heart beat so hard, I was sure the sound of it could almost wake him. Thirty seconds or so passed and he started snoring again. I let out a quiet breath of relief and continued moving to the front door.

I passed by the wall of photos I had hung up, good memories, even great ones, with people who I love, and someone I thought loved me. I shook my head as if that would help erase the thought from my brain and continued to tiptoe to the front door.

I had stashed a duffel bag under the kitchen sink after work, with only a few things in it that I had bought at the store and a few essentials that I figured he would not notice were missing. I then called my mom and asked her if I could come stay with her and dad for a few weeks. She said they were out of town, but I was welcome to stay as long as I needed to. She sounded concerned even though I attempted to sound as cheerful as possible. I did not want to ruin their vacation, or make them come home early, so I figured I would tell them only what was necessary later. No sense in them worrying since I was leaving anyway. I quietly removed the bag from its hiding place and moved swiftly to the front door.

I paused at the door, wondering if I was making the right choice by leaving. It's not been all bad. Some days were better than others. I turned from the front door to look back towards the living room and kitchen, and memories started to flood my head. The first time we walked in the house, when my best friend brought her kids over for the first time and they took their first steps in the hallway. But just like the good memories, the bad ones came flooding in as well. I shook my head to try and clear the bad memories, then rolled my eyes as I realized how stupid that thought was. I crept back over to grab the photo of my best friend and I, along with one of me and my parents.

I paused again by the front door to quickly put the photos in my duffel bag and turned to open it, but then I froze when I heard movement coming from the direction of the bedroom. Movement followed by him quietly calling out "Rae? You in the kitchen?" I froze, forcing myself to breathe through the fear that welled up inside. At that moment I decided this was the only chance I had, and I flung open the front door and ran out, not caring about any noise I made in the process.

I ran to my car, opened the door, threw my bag in, and hopped in as swiftly as possible. Before I could shut the car door, I heard him calling my name and yelling something indecipherable. Shutting the car door at least muffled his voice. As I went to start the car, a light came on inside the house. My hands were shaking so badly but somehow, I managed to turn the key and bring the engine to life. I quickly backed out of the driveway and as I pulled onto the street he stood on the front porch staring at the car as I drove away. For now at least, I could breathe and was safe.

Chapter 1
Caleb Walker

"I'll be right back, Duke. I'm just running to the store to get more apples for the horses." I patted the soft, fuzzy block-like head of my new best friend. He looked up at me with the saddest puppy dog eyes, begging me to take him with me, like I had been doing most days since I brought him home. However, the weather would probably warm up, and I did not want to leave him in the truck while I went into the grocery store.

"Okay, how about a treat to make it up to you?" I dug into the treat jar by the front door and tossed one to him. Duke walked forward, watching the treat midair. However, he walked a little too far, and it landed on his back, startling him and making him dart across the room to find a place to hide. I laughed as I bent down to pick up the treat and walked it over to Duke, who was now shaking under the kitchen table. As I offered the treat, by hand this time, he investigated it to make sure it would not try and get him again.

"Don't worry, boy. It won't get you. I'll try and remember you aren't great at fetch yet, too." I scratched under his chin after he took the treat. I made a mental note to myself to pick up a couple more toys at the store to help him learn to catch, something we had been working on since I brought him home.

The shelter had only given me limited information: "approximately 10 months old, American Staffordshire Terrier. Male." Knowing staffies were among the list of breeds most people avoided adopting, and after seeing that this pup was the only staffie there, I had chosen the little underweight pup and named him Duke. Over the last few weeks, Duke had put on weight, come out of his shell, and had shown me he was the silliest, happiest, most loyal pup ever. Unlike what many people thought about the breed, Duke was the most loving and snuggly dog, and also a scaredy-cat.

Before I stood up, I scratched behind Duke's ears again and gave him a gentle hug, then walked to the front door, reassuring him I would be back soon.

The air outside felt warm but thankfully not sweltering like it would be during the summer months. Stepping off the porch, I saw my neighbor Jenny as she passed by with one of the horses. I had hired Jenny for part-time help around the farm after her home caught fire a few months ago. She needed the extra cash for the home repairs, and I needed the help once my brother had moved. It was the best decision I had made in a long time considering not only that it helped a dear friend, but I did not have to admit to someone I barely knew I was struggling to do everything by myself while working full-time at the sheriff's office. Jenny had been my neighbor since we were in grade school together, and unlike most of our friends, she went to a local college.

As I raised my hand to wave at Jenny to say good morning, Luke walked out of the barn with another horse.

Just like always, Jenny's focus shifted the moment Luke appeared. I laughed to myself as I hopped in my truck, wondering when either of them would realize they were in love with each other and not just best friends. I started the engine of my truck and began driving away from the house, looking in the rear-view mirror and seeing Luke help Jenny into the saddle. He had been helping rebuild her house for only the cost of materials and came over to spend time with her any day she worked on the farm. Seeing them together, despite them not admitting they loved each other, reminded me of...

No. I can't think of that right now.

"Gosh, the town is busy today," I whispered while I peered through the windshield. I should have known it would be bustling as people were getting ready for Memorial Day events and get-togethers, but I had put off this trip long enough.

I walked into the grocery store and grabbed the last basket available. It would not hold much, but thankfully I did not need much more than apples, carrots, and dog toys.

I picked up the needed things and decided to buy blueberries for Duke to see if he liked them, so I walked back to the produce aisle. As I rounded the corner, I spotted a familiar face up ahead that made me stop dead in my tracks, someone I had not seen or even spoken to for several years: Rae Whitaker. She was the one I had a crush on from the moment I met her, and I considered her to be the one that got away. We had stayed in touch as best as possible after she had left for college but drifted apart in her last year. She had been coming home during spring and summer breaks, but to my knowledge, she did not come home during that last year. I had not seen her or even heard from her since. It had been roughly five years since I had last seen her, and somehow, she was more beautiful than back then, if that was even possible.

I watched her at the opposite end of the aisle, debating if I should go say hi. We had been best friends with Jenny and Luke in high school, but I did not know why we stopped talking. I did not want to make her feel uncomfortable if she did not want to talk to me.

Gosh, she was breathtakingly beautiful, her long light auburn hair that looked redder in the sunlight, her gorgeous green eyes, her curves that drove me wild.

She turned from the shelf to put something in her basket and glanced at her phone. While she still had not seen me, I could see her face better, and noticed a touch of sadness in her eyes. She pushed the bridge of her glasses farther up her nose as they slipped down a bit. Her body language did not seem the same as the confident and vibrant Rae I had been friends with all those years ago.

She reached back to the shelf to pick up another item when glass shattered somewhere across the store. I saw her flinch and freeze before slowly looking around, checking her surroundings. She seemed spooked but took a couple deep breaths and then reached back to the shelf to grab another item. Her hands seemed to be shaking a bit. Her movements and that reaction reminded me of things I had seen many times in my line of work.

She still had not seen me, but if something was bothering her, maybe seeing an old friend would help. I started to walk in her direction at the same time she began walking towards me, steadying her hands on the handle of the cart. She had a faraway look in her eyes. I started to open my mouth to say hi when a kid ran out from another aisle and plowed into her legs, making her lose her balance. I moved as fast as possible and caught her before she hit the ground. She covered her face with her hands for a brief moment, but then slowly moved them away as the kid who knocked her over said, "Sorry, lady!"

"Oh my gosh! Thank you for catching me. I'm so sorry. I wasn't paying attention to—wait." She looked up at my face and stared for a brief moment before standing up completely. She looked at me with her beautiful green eyes that I remembered—the ones with brown and gold flecks in them that made her eyes shine in the sunlight. "Caleb? Caleb Walker?"

"Hi, Rae."

Chapter 2

Rae

Coming to the store was so far not a horrible idea. With my parents out of town, I needed to get some perishables that they did not have. It was nice to be back in town. It had not changed too much since I had last visited.

My phone buzzed in my purse and when I opened it, I saw a text from Ethan begging me to come home. This wasn't the first text like this that I had received since leaving. I should just block his number, but...

Something crashed and glass shattered somewhere behind me, and I jumped. *Shoot, he found me and he's angry,* I thought as I stood there, frozen. It felt like an eternity before I heard a mom tell her kid to be more careful and apologize to the employee. I tried to settle my nerves. Taking a few deep breaths, while glancing behind me, I realized I was safe. So why were my hands still shaking so much?

I need to just keep moving. I need the rest of my groceries and then I can go home. Taking a couple more deep breaths, I moved towards the other end of the aisle which was stocked with produce.

Suddenly, something slammed against the backs of my legs, causing me to lose my balance and start to fall. Strong arms caught and wrapped around me, but I was so scared I felt like I couldn't see anything. *Oh no, this cannot be happening,* I thought, covering my face, as if that would keep me safe if he found me.

"Sorry, lady!" a little voice said, and I realized a child had run into me, not Ethan coming after me. I slowly uncovered my face and looked up at the man who caught me. Realizing that it was also not Ethan, I stood up as fast as possible and apologized, feeling so deeply embarrassed when...

Caleb. I'd know those deep blue eyes anywhere.

"Hi, Rae." The deep rumble of his voice carried a smile, rich and warm enough to settle my nerves in an instant.

He looked the same as he did in high school—those piercing blue eyes that I used to get lost in, that smile, his bald head because he started shaving it as a teen, and his beloved cowboy hat he always wore because his dad gave it to him. But he looked bigger than I remember. He was always muscular in high school, but now...Wow. He had a couple of tattoos on his arms now. My eyes wandered and I noticed he'd also grown his beard out since I last saw him. His deep red beard was now peppered with gray, somehow making him look more handsome than I found him the last time we had seen each other.

I quickly realized I had not replied to him yet and felt my face flush. "Hi, um...Thanks for helping me out there." I gave him a small smile, trying to hide my embarrassment.

Chancing a glance back up at him, he flashed me the smile that made me feel like putty. "Anytime. I didn't know you were coming back to town. Last time I spoke with your parents, your mom said they were going out of town on vacation."

"Oh, um. Yeah, I wanted to get out of the city for a bit and figured I'd come stay here while they're out."

"That makes sense. How long are you in town for? We could meet up for coffee or dinner, or you could come to the farm and I can cook for you—catch up, talk about 'the good old days.'" His laugh was like whisky laced with sunlight—smooth, bright, and it made my unsteady heart beat hard in my chest.

"Yeah, that sounds nice. I'd like that. I'm not sure how long I'm in town for, to be honest."

"Oh, well, maybe if you're in town long enough, you and I could meet up more than once." He gave me that smile again. Back in the day, I was a dorky teen, though, and now, I felt broken. No one in their right mind would want to be with me.

"Yeah, that would be great." I tried to sound as upbeat as possible. However, I didn't know if I was convincing enough. My nerves were still shot since the glass broke.

Caleb pulled his phone out of his pocket and passed it to me. "Here, type your number in if you want." I did and passed the phone back to him. "I'll text you so you have my..." He looked at it for a brief moment. He must have seen the sun icon next to my name. He smiled at me. "You remembered."

For a brief moment, it felt like "the good old days." He had called me Sunshine from the day he met me. He'd said my name being "Rae" fit because my personality was like a ray of sunshine, and I always brightened his days. If I only felt now how I used to feel.

"I did, Ranger," I smiled back at him.

At the end of the aisle, a tall male resembling Ethan passed by, and a wave of anxiety went through me. My legs started shaking and soon my hands were as well. The world around me felt like it was closing in on me, and I knew I had to get out of here, to safety.

"Hey, Rae, you okay?" Caleb said, and it sounded like he was miles away despite standing next to me. "I, um, I have to go."

"You okay? You look like you've seen a ghost." Caleb sounded so concerned.

"S-something like that. It was good to see you." I abandoned my cart and briskly walked out the door before I collapsed or embarrassed myself more. As soon as I was in my car, I locked the doors and started the engine, the keys jingling in my shaking hands. In my rearview mirror was the man I'd seen inside the store, not Ethan. He looked like him but thank goodness it wasn't him.

I thankfully never gave Ethan my hometown nor parents' address. He just knew I grew up in Missouri and my last name which was not the same last name as my parents' or my mom's maiden name. My biological father had not been in the picture since my fifth birthday, but they'd chosen to give me his last name on my birth certificate, and when my mom remarried, we just never changed it. Thankfully.

My mom's new husband was my dad, even if we were not blood related. I had wanted to change my last name to his for years, but I just never thought about it when I had time, and now I am thankful I hadn't yet.

While Ethan could do some research and find information eventually, I was hoping he would just stop caring at some point.

I took a few deep breaths and pulled out of the parking lot. Grocery shopping would have to wait, but at least I felt safe.

Chapter 3

Rae

My phone buzzed and a text notification popped up. Clicking on the notification, I saw a message from Caleb.

> *Caleb: You didn't have time to finish shopping so I bought what you had in your cart, added a few things, and dropped it off. It's in a cooler bag, so it should be good for a few minutes. Seemed like something was wrong. Hope everything is okay. If you need anything, call me. Anytime.*

This man is still watching out for me after all these years. I smiled as I stood up from the couch where I'd found myself after coming home from the store. I had needed a bit to wind down after my nerves were wound so tight.

I opened the front door and looked around but didn't see anyone around. I brought the groceries inside and began putting them away. Caleb had added a lot more to the cart than I'd had in my basket when I left. Things I'd had on my list as well. *Did I leave it behind?* I walked over to my purse and found my shopping list crumpled inside.

In awe of how he knew a part of what I'd needed, I resumed putting the groceries away. In the last bag were my favorite mint cookies and my favorite tea that you can only buy from the corner store. I smiled at how sweet this gesture was. He went out of his way to buy my favorite things for me, but what was even sweeter than that, he remembered—after almost five years.

I perched on the couch with my phone in hand and texted Caleb.

Me: I got the groceries. That was so kind of you, I'll pay you back, if you let me know how much it was. I couldn't find the receipt. Also, how did you know the extra things I needed when you didn't have the list - and my favorite cookies and tea? You remembered.

I tapped the "send button" and almost immediately the little bubbles popped up, meaning he was replying. A small smile crossed my face as his reply appeared on the screen.

Caleb: No need for paying me back, unless you let me take you to coffee. I'll accept that as payment, if you want. Oh, and the cookies and tea, you're not one to forget, Sunshine.

That text sent a tingling feeling throughout my entire body. I read the last line again.

"You're not one to forget."

I smiled again as I replied.

Me: Okay, Ranger. Deal. Coffee sounds nice.

I set my phone down, still smiling at the thought of going to coffee with him. The feeling caught me off guard. Happiness. It felt foreign, like something that couldn't possibly last, yet it was here, plain as day.

Chapter 4

Caleb

"She remembered, you guys. She remembered what I called her in high school, and she put it as part of her contact in my phone. Sunshine." I sat across from Jenny and Luke at dinner a few short hours later and told them who I'd run into at the store.

"I knew you liked her!" Jenny hit the table. "You denied it all those years ago, but I knew it!"

"I did, back then, but according to her parents, she's now got a boyfriend. Plus, so far, she's only visiting." A wave of disappointment overcame me as I thought about the reality of reconnecting with her. "We lost touch for a long time, and I bet you when she goes home, it will be the same. She won't contact anyone."

"Okay, I have a question. If her nickname is Sunshine, shouldn't yours be Rain Cloud? Because you're being super negative about possibly reconnecting with her." Luke finally joined in the conversation, giving me a half grin.

I let out a half-hearted chuckle as I ran my hand down my face. He may have been joking, but he was also right. I missed her all those years she was gone.

"Sorry, guys. I really hope this time is different. We all used to be really close, but she was really special to me, and when she moved—"

"You missed her because you love her," Jenny teased me, but she wasn't wrong. "Oh, and Luke, 'Rae,' like 'ray of sunshine.' Caleb also thought she lit up his life, like sunshine brightens a day." Her teasing tone made me laugh and I started to open my mouth to say something, but she continued, her voice with an extra edge of teasing to it. "And Ranger is her nickname for him because his dad gave him that cowboy hat on his eighteenth birthday and he never takes it off, unless he has to." She shot me a grin, knowing that Luke remembered my nickname, but now was her chance to tease me.

"Oh that's right! Sorry, it's been years." Luke gave Jenny a sly look, picking up on her teasing. "Also, Caleb, this might be your chance, man. I mean, she was the one that got away, after all." Luke glanced at me and then looked at Jenny as he gave a goofy grin.

I laughed. "Shut up." But they were not wrong. I fell for her all those years ago, and running into her today re-ignited those feelings. Feelings I hoped would be easy to push away this time when she left.

Chapter 5

Rae

Caleb had called me to plan a time to have coffee together, and we chose to meet up after his next rotation at work. It had been five days since we'd seen each other at the grocery store. Today was the day.

I paced the living room while waiting for the time he said he'd arrive. I stopped and looked at the clock—five minutes left—then resumed pacing and trying to talk myself down from the ledge my anxiety put me on.

"I've known about this for four days now, so why am I freaking out about it? Caleb has always been good to me," I began to ramble to myself while spiraling. "What if I make a fool out of myself though and need to leave immediately, but he's the one driving? Should I drive? Should I call and cancel? No, that would be even worse. It will be fine. If anything happens, I can just tell him I'm sick or something and he can bring me home."

A knock at the door made me jump. Caleb. I opened the door, and he stood in front of me dressed in a pair of blue jeans that were not tight but somehow hugged him in all the right places and a black shirt that made the muscles in his arms look downright sinful. His boots and favorite cowboy hat tied his look together. This trip to get coffee together would be interesting. I'd have to make sure I didn't stare at him the entire time.

"Hey, Sunshine," he said as he flashed me the biggest smile—the one that made my knees weak in high school and apparently still had that effect on me.

I smiled back at him and then realized what he had in his hands. "Oh my gosh, you didn't have to bring me flowers!"

"Well, I know how much you love flowers, but while these are from me, this one is not." He passed me the bouquet he brought, then a mysterious single white rose with a ribbon around the stem.

"Oh. That's weird. I wonder who left that. I didn't hear anyone on the porch." I had a weird feeling about it but pushed the thought away. There was no way he could have found me that fast, right? Plus, if he had found me, why would he not have made his presence known? No, he hadn't found me, I was—

"Maybe we should get you security cameras." Caleb's voice interrupted my thoughts, and I was so thankful for it, yet he sounded like he was trying to laugh off the worry in his voice.

"Yeah, we can do that. I'll ask my parents about it. It would probably be a good idea for them to have it anyway." I wanted to quickly change the subject because if he was worried, then I would worry more. "Ready to go?"

"I've been ready for the last five years, at a minimum." He flashed me a grin that sent goosebumps all over my body and opened the door.

We were silent on the drive to the coffee shop, the kind of easy quiet between two people who had known each other for years, but it was more than that. When

Ethan had cut me off from most of my friends and family, it probably left Caleb with a bunch of questions.

When we first got to the coffee shop, I reached for the truck door but Caleb put his hand on my arm. "Hold on. Don't move." He got out, put his cowboy hat on and walked around to my side of the truck.

"Such a gentleman. Thank you." I flashed him a nervous smile as he held out his hand to help me out of the truck. As I moved so the truck door could be closed, he placed a gentle hand on the small of my back, causing me to slightly tense up. *It's Caleb. It's Caleb. He is safe.*

Caleb opened his mouth to say something but quickly closed it. I couldn't help but wonder if he picked up on my nerves. If he did, he hadn't said anything yet, and for that, I was thankful.

Caleb walked beside me but made sure he was two steps ahead of me when we got to the door. He opened the door to the coffee shop and gave me a smile as he motioned for me to walk in first. He asked me to order first, and I ordered something that felt familiar, a hot vanilla latte with oat milk. He insisted on paying for my coffee and us getting breakfast as well. He recommended an egg white breakfast sandwich and asked them to remove the cheese from mine.

I gave him a confused look, but he smiled warmly in return. "How did you—" I stopped mid-sentence when his smile widened, causing a sudden feeling of butterflies in my stomach.

"Your groceries were all dairy free, and you got oat milk in your latte just now." He winked at me as they gave him the table number, and he pointed at an open table by the window. That wink. I gave him a smile as we walked to the table.

"This spot okay? I figured you would like the view."

I nodded and he set the table number down. Before I had time to move at all, he pulled out my chair for me and waited for me to get settled, before sitting across from me. I sat in the chair and adjusted my purse in my lap, focusing on the little number card on the table. I wished my heart would calm down, even just a little.

Caleb was just being Caleb. The guy who I grew up with and had carried my books in the hall just because he could. He was the one who always made sure I made it to my car safely or would walk me to my door. He'd done this back when we first became friends. This wasn't new, but somehow, it felt different.

Ethan was the reason these simple moments with Caleb felt different. I knew that, so why could I not shake the negative thoughts?

"You okay?" Caleb interrupted my thoughts, obviously picking up on my nervousness. His voice was warm, not judgmental or annoyed. Instantly, my face felt hot. I had to be a deep shade of red now, so I did not look directly at him for a few seconds.

"Mhm. Yeah, I'm fine." I nodded quickly.

He looked towards the counter to see if our order was ready. He didn't push the conversation, just offered a smile. I followed his gaze, but my mind was wrapped up in the thoughts of everything Caleb had done so far—the flowers, the doors, the chair, and paying for the food.

It was thoughtful and sweet, but it scared me.

Ethan was kind at first, too. Over time, he changed. He had used kindness like bait. Even though I knew Caleb was not anything like my ex—not even a little bit—my heart hadn't picked up the message yet. My brain hadn't settled.

The second the coffee cup hit the table, I wrapped my nervous, cold hands around it, trying to steady myself. I realized I had been twirling the strap of my bag around my fingers. The coffee somewhat solved both of those problems.

Caleb looked at me again, then smiled—calm, patient, not even a hint of frustration in his eyes about my silence.

I knew I had to say something, or he may think I didn't want to be here. "Thank you for inviting me to coffee today. I know it's just coffee, but.."

"It's not *just* anything," he said simply. His eyes were soft and his voice kind. He reached out and touched his fingertips to the back of my hand. I subconsciously flinched. Caleb pulled his hand back and just looked at me with that same steady, patient look in his eyes. "I - I'm sorry."

"No, don't be. I'm sorry I startled you."

I started to say something but couldn't find the words. Instead, I gave a small smile and took a sip of coffee while the quiet settled between us again.

As if he knew something was bothering me, he leaned back, giving me room to breathe. I let myself breathe. Just for now. Just for a moment.

22

Chapter 6

Caleb

I was sitting across from the most beautiful woman in the world. The way her cheeks tinged pink when she got embarrassed, the shine her hair had when the sunlight shone through the window, even the small smile she gave me after I winked at her. Something was different now, though, from the last time we saw each other. Something changed in her that made her seem to hesitate trusting me. She was jumpy and didn't seem like she could relax. I wanted her to be comfortable with me again, even if our friendship couldn't pick up where we left off five years ago.

"So, what's your favorite thing about where you live?" I tried breaking the tension with the first question that popped into my mind.

"What?" Rae snapped out of whatever daze she was in. Something was definitely different with her, and while I didn't want to pry, I wanted to know what had changed.

"Do you have a favorite thing about where you live? Is there somewhere you like to eat? People you like?"

"Oh. Umm..." She bit her lip as she thought about her answer. "This may sound silly, but it was this little bagel shop. It was run by a family, and they had every type of bagel you could imagine. They made sandwiches, smoothies—it was a pretty popular place people would hang out after class or some weekend mornings."

"Oh, nice. I bet you didn't have a small business coffee shop like this one, though."

"Oh no, not at all. There were coffee shops, sure, but nothing like this one. The coffee from here will never be beat." She was right. This shop had been around since we were in middle school, and the coffee here was the best around.

"So is your boyfriend coming to visit while you're staying here?" As soon as I asked the question, I regretted it. Rae had just taken a sip of coffee and started to choke.

"Oh my gosh, are you okay, Rae?" I pushed back my chair and knelt beside her, placing my hand on her arm.

She gave me a thumbs up and then held a finger up as if she was saying "yes, just a minute."

"Sorry about that. Umm...Let's not talk about him, if you don't mind." She grabbed her coffee cup again and began to pick at the cardboard sleeve around it. I nodded and gave her an apologetic smile. "What about you? What are you doing for work now? I know you said we could meet up after your next rotation but didn't give details." Her words tumbled out almost too fast, as if she was nervous.

I thought about what she said, "Let's not talk about him." Maybe they broke up and that's why she was here.

I then realized I still had not answered her question. "So, I work for the Oak River Sheriff's Office now. Been there a couple years. Some of the work is scary or sad, but most of it is really fun—cool stuff."

"That's really neat. I didn't realize you wanted to be an officer."

"I didn't really know until four years ago when my parents died. My brother and I were in the back of the car, on the way back from dinner with our parents, when the accident happened. The first officer at the scene was there for us. He waited at my window and talked to us until the firemen could get my parents out. The paramedics were trying to help save my parents."

I let out a shaky breath. Talking about my parents was easier now, but the accident...that would probably never get easier. "More officers arrived, and none of them let us see anything after we were pulled from the car. Somehow, we were unharmed. They distracted us by talking about school stuff—what we were learning, just normal stuff. Obviously, we were really worried, but they tried to keep us focused. My dad's best friend was the captain still, and he was there as soon as he heard about the accident. I found out later that one of the officers heard the paramedic say something about my dad not having a pulse for a bit..."

My voice came out sounding like I had swallowed gravel. I took a sip of my coffee and cleared my throat, chancing a look at Rae. Her eyes were glossed over, and she was fighting off tears. I hadn't meant to tell the whole story right now, but something about talking to her just made the words flow. I cleared my throat again before continuing.

"Then they stayed with us at the hospital as we waited to hear if my parents made it. Cap and one of the other officers stayed with us at the hospital, even well after we were told my parents had not made it. After we finished up at the hospital, they drove us home. They both stayed with us while we called Jenny's family to come be with us. At some point, Cap went out and bought food for us for the next few days in case we would be hungry. I was twenty-three, so I could be my brother's guardian until he turned eighteen a few months later, but they still didn't want to just leave us high and dry. I was going to school full time and working part time, but I needed to find a full-time job as fast as possible to pay the bills. After my parents' services, I talked to Cap about becoming an officer. The way he and the other officers helped my brother and I on the worst day of our lives...it meant something to me. He pulled some strings to get me started in the jail as a corrections officer, and then..." I cleared my throat again. "Then he paid for my academy tuition."

I heard her sniffle. Gosh, I had made her cry, but Rae deserved to know. She used to spend so much time at the farm with me, and my parents had treated her like she was their daughter. She had loved them, and the feeling had been mutual. However, that day still burned badly for me so I was hoping for a change in topic.

I chanced a glance up again and she had tears threatening to fall. "Oh, Caleb, I'm so sorry about your loss. I did not know how to bring it up since...I wasn't able to text you since I, umm, lost your number. You know I loved your parents so much. If I had been able to, I would have been there for you. I am really sorry, though. And for not being able to reach out." Hesitation shone in her eyes but she reached her hand out. I took it in mine and gave her a small smile.

26

"Nah, don't mention it." My voice sounded slightly choked up still, so I cleared my throat again. Her fingers felt cold and her hand was shaking slightly. Was she nervous? I gave her hand a gentle squeeze, and she looked at our hands briefly before nervously pulling hers from mine. She looked embarrassed so in order to not keep focus on it, I continued talking. "Honestly, I wasn't in the greatest head space at that time, so I ignored a lot of calls and texts for a bit. Your parents were pretty great, too, though. Jenny's family and yours. They all helped out with taking care of the farm until I could manage it better."

"Jenny from down the road?" I picked up a slight sense of jealousy in her voice, and it made me smile. Rae, Jenny, Luke, and I had all been best friends from day one of freshman year, but there was not a day I was not teased about the possibility of Rae wanting to be more than friends. I wanted that, but I did not think she did. While we were all really close—inseparable even—Jenny and Luke were closest to each other, and Rae and I had a special bond of our own. Before leaving for college, Rae had admitted to me that she was sad she was the only one moving. I had applied to the same school, but unlike her, I didn't get accepted.

"Yup. That Jenny. I told her and Luke I ran into you at the grocery store the other day. They would love to see you, if you wanted to meet up with them." This conversation was a welcome relief from the conversation about my parents.

She nodded and smiled. "I would love to see them. Did they ever get together?"

I immediately began to laugh. "No, they still won't admit to themselves or each other that they are in love. We all know it, but they still don't see it. Jenny's parents decided they wanted to move into a smaller house, so they gave her the house and moved. A brush fire started while she was at work one day, and it moved too fast. Caught the house on fire. It was pretty badly damaged but not a total loss. Once she was able to, she hired Luke to do the repairs. He refused to let her pay him, so she is only paying for materials. She is actually working a few hours here and there to help me out on the farm since my brother moved. She needed the extra cash, but having her around to help out with that, even for a few short hours on her days off, I think it helps me out more."

"Oh, wow. That's a lot of information to unpack." She let out a breathy giggle.

We both laughed, and I was happy to see her starting to relax. She didn't have a death grip on her coffee cup anymore which made me smile even more.

Our conversation blossomed into one of memories from high school. I watched her across the table from me as she giggled more and more during our conversation. She picked at her breakfast sandwich until she finished it. There were times her hands shook or her mind seemed to wander when she looked around, but I was glad that, for the most part, she seemed to be a bit more comfortable. Something had happened that brought her home suddenly. I was sure of it. However, I was happy to see her smile, and I would not take any moment with her for granted again.

Rae's phone buzzed and, after barely glancing at it, her posture stiffened immediately. She reached for her phone and turned it over.

"Everything okay?"

"Oh yeah, it's nothing." She gave me a half grin that didn't meet her eyes. She crossed her arms and rubbed her hands on them as if she was cold while not making eye contact with me.

"Alright," I said softly. "Just—if it does ever turn into something, or if you ever want to talk, you can. You can come to me for anything. I mean it."

Her eyes lifted to meet mine. I saw something flicker in her eyes. Sadness? Fear? Whatever it was, she was holding it all in. She gave a restrained smile. "Thank you."

I let the silence settle between us for a moment. "You ready to head out?" I would never tire of being around her, but I could tell she was done for now.

"Yeah, sure. Sorry. Thanks for the coffee, by the way. I really had a good time hanging out with you."

"Anytime, Sunshine."

Chapter 7

Rae

As I shut the door behind me, I started to crumble. I had such a nice time with Caleb, talking like we used to, until Ethan texted me. I had just briefly looked at the text and immediately shut down. Caleb was the exact opposite of everything Ethan was, and he was nice company to have, but the chance of him being willing to hang out again was slim. I knew that. I ruined it. Like I ruin everything else.

I ran a hand over my face. "Good going, Rae. You really knocked that one out of the park."

I changed into a pair of leggings and a giant sweatshirt and sat on the couch, across the room from where my phone was. I needed comfort and to calm down a bit before I did anything else. I hadn't even fully read his text yet. That could wait, right? It wasn't going anywhere.

A buzz came from across the room as my phone vibrated on the table. I looked over at it like Ethan could jump out of it at any moment and hurt me again. Another buzz of the phone sounded.

Sighing, I stood and walked over to where it sat. As I turned on the screen, a sense of relief washed over me at two new messages from Caleb and only the one from Ethan.

Walking back to the couch, I opened the text from Ethan. *Better to rip off the Band-Aid, I guess.*

A shiver went through me as I closed Ethan's message and switched to the messages from Caleb.

I set my phone down for a moment and ran my fingers through my hair as I let out a huge sigh. "No pressure" versus "I need you to text me now." Sure, he may be concerned and wanting to know I'm okay, but probably not. Caleb, though, was not wanting to pressure me into anything.

"What did I ever see in Ethan?" I grumbled angrily.

I picked up my phone, opened the message from Caleb, and sent him a reply.

I set my phone down, feeling a bit lighter after his text.

At least I've got a good friend in Caleb.

Chapter 8

Rae

I woke up to the sound of crunching rocks outside my bedroom window in the flower bed my mom put in. I lay in bed, listening, and the sound stopped. *I did hear that, right?* I put my glasses on just in time to see a shadow pass by as the crunching sounds resumed. I sucked in a breath and held it.

Did I lock the front door? I quickly looked around, realizing I was not really sure what I was looking for.

I slowly and quietly threw back the covers and walked to the front door, gripping my phone so tight.

Oh, thank goodness it's locked. I held my hand over my pounding heart as I let out the breath I had been holding. The back door from where I stood looked locked as well.

Was I imagining things or dreaming? Not wanting to chance it, I went to my room and peeked out the window to double check the front yard. I didn't see anything, so maybe it was a dream.

Just as that thought popped into my head, the knob of the back door jiggled and then I heard faint footsteps.

I froze, then dialed 911.

"Oak River County 911, what is the address of your emergency?" The woman's voice was calm, and I wished she could pass that feeling through the phone.

"521 Meadow Lane. I saw a shadow at my front window and then heard the back doorknob move—heard footsteps on both sides of the house."

"Okay, what's your name?"

My voice and hands were shaking now. "Rae."

I heard the dispatcher telling officers the needed information as I looked down at my hand that wasn't holding the phone. I was shaking so bad, so I shoved it under my other arm, trying to steady it somehow.

"Hi Rae, we have officers on their way to you right now. Is there somewhere you can hide to be safe in case the person does get inside?"

"Behind the clothes in my closet maybe?" My voice was shaking noticeably, too.

"Okay, dear. Go hide and officers will let you know it's them when they arrive. Stay on the phone with me."

A sound of agreement was all I could manage now. I crawled in the closet, shifting things aside as much as possible. I thought I heard the front doorknob jiggle again, but I did not know if it was my imagination or not. Either way, I was moving faster than before. After I hid in the closet, I heard footsteps at the front side of the house again. This time, I knew I wasn't imagining things.

"I think the person is right outside the window of my room again." The pure terror in my voice sent shivers up my own spine.

"Alright, Rae, let me know if that changes but try and be really quiet so they don't possibly hear you, okay?"

Within seconds that felt like hours, I heard sirens approaching the house.

"Rae, officers are on scene. Are you still hiding?"

"Yes." My voice was barely above a whisper—so low I almost couldn't hear myself.

"Okay. Deputy Walker will let you know when it's safe to come out. I'm going to end the call now since they're there."

"Th-thank you." I breathed a sigh of relief knowing Caleb was out there, then glanced at the time on the screen as I tapped it to end the call.

I looked at the clock on my phone which read 5:30 a.m. I then checked the call history—5:21. Resting my head against the closet wall, I closed my eyes and breathed. It had been only nine minutes, but I was already feeling exhausted, even though I had just woken up.

Thank goodness Caleb was at work today. A few minutes passed and I heard movement outside the house. I froze as I heard footsteps on my porch, but then a calming voice broke the silence.

"Hey, Rae? It's Caleb. You can come out. It's safe." His voice was the most comforting thing I'd heard in a long time. Like a breath of fresh air.

Crawling out of the closet, I got to my feet and went to the front door where I found Caleb waiting for me.

A sense of relief and heat went through me as I saw him standing in front of my door in his gear.

"Hey, Rae."

Chapter 9

Caleb

Calm washed over me when Rae opened the door. She was wearing leggings that made her beautiful curves stand out and a giant sweatshirt over them, and her hair was a mess but in the cutest way. My pulse raced and I wished I could take her inside and make her forget about the situation. Quickly I shove that thought away, feeling guilty, as I noticed the fear in her eyes.

Rae had opened the door very carefully and peeked out at first to make sure it was really me out here. It had only been a few seconds since she'd opened the door, but she hadn't said anything. However, I could see tears welling in her eyes.

"Rae, whoever it was, they're gone." I motioned over towards the other two squad cars, parked in front of the house. "We've canvased your backyard and the entire neighborhood at this point, and there's no sign of anyone. Sadly, they probably heard the sirens and got out of here."

"You—believe me?" Rae's voice was soaked in tears but none had fallen yet.

I reached up and switched off my body camera, trying to keep my voice as tender as possible when I spoke. "Of course I do. Why wouldn't I?" Genuine confusion must have crossed my face because the next words she spoke rushed out as if she was trying to vouch for herself—trying to find the words to make me believe her.

"Because I could have been dreaming and there's no one here to prove otherwise. I was probably dreaming, it's what makes sense. I'm so sorry to have called and had you all come out. I swore I heard—"

With as gentle a voice as I could use, I attempted to calm the chaos in her mind. "Whoa, hey, Rae. No, I believe you. We believe you. Plus, come look at this." I pointed to the flower bed near her window.

As she walked with me, she started to smooth her hair. I noticed she was trying to be sneaky about it and not bring attention to herself.

"Hey, you look really cute. Don't worry about your hair." I gently placed my hand on the back of her arm while trying to quietly reassure her. She blushed and looked away.

Okay, Caleb, change the subject. Now.

"We took photos of these spots where the gravel was very disturbed, and we're writing an informational report to send out to the squads. We're also going to make sure someone adds your street to the list of extra drive-bys." I pointed at a spot in the rocks where a couple of boot sized divots were. A portion of the rocks were compressed so deep and rocks had been scattered that you could see the soil underneath it.

"Rae, this is the second time someone has been on your property that we're aware of."

"Second time?"

"The white rose I found. I had a concern the other day after I found it on your porch."

36

Rae looked startled. Not like how she had looked in the grocery store before she left her groceries but still startled. "Do you think it's the same person?"

"There's no real way to know since there is no evidence we could find that they left behind." I paused, not knowing if those words were scary to her or reassuring. "However, I want to pick up security cameras for you as soon as possible. If you're okay with it, I'll pick some up after my shift and bring them by to install them. Or something that would make me feel better about your safety is...I have a spare room you could stay in until your parents come back."

"What? No, I can't. I..." She looked...actually, I didn't know how to read the look on her face.

"Okay. Okay. I won't fight you on that, for now, but if something like this happens again, I will bring it up again. I want you safe. What do you think about the cameras, though?"

Rae wrapped her arms around herself and nodded.

We walked back to her front door where my partner stood. "Is this your girl, Walker?" Santana asked excitedly. I had probably spoken about Rae a few times a month prior to her return to town. Since she had come back, though, Rae was one of the only things my crew had heard about.

"Yep. This is Rae." I tried to hide the small smile on my face as I glanced at Rae, who wore a puzzled look.

"Hi, I'm Deputy Santana. Elena. I work on Caleb's squad and live right up the road." She pointed ahead, past Rae and me.

"While I think you should probably stay with Walker here for a bit, if you decide against it, my work number is on the front, and my personal number is on the back. Day or night, you call. Anyone that's important to Walker is important to us." She passed Rae her business card, and I shot her a quick grin as thanks.

Rae hesitated but then reached to take the card. She said a small "thank you" and her voice shook but smiled slightly. Santana smiled and nodded before walking back down the driveway. In high school, Rae had been one of those people who liked animals more than humans, and I had seen how she would act around other people, when I was not by her side. However, when I was with her, she would typically be a social butterfly. Something about being around each other had given us the confidence or boost we needed. This Rae was not like the one I knew all those years ago. It concerned me that she was so shut down.

"She's really nice." Rae's voice sounded so small. Gosh, if my crew was not here, I would offer Rae a hug, but if I did that, I would be teased for all eternity. Did I care? No. Rae did not seem in the mood for a hug, though.

"Yeah. She's pretty great. We've been through a lot together while on duty." Rae was listening intently. Interested in what I could mean by that, or jealous? I was so curious. "She chased a suspect for me a while back when I was seconds later than her to a call I was supposed to be going to. I had just finished with a really tough motor vehicle accident and needed a few minutes. She was just running radar down the street, so she attached herself to the call until I could get there to back her or take over. The suspect ended up running and Santana's foot got stuck in a hole in the grass, causing her to fall and dislocate her shoulder." I chuckled at my next thought. "To repay her for that, I took a knife to the arm for her about a year later." I lifted the bottom of my shirt sleeve and showed her the scar I had. "I hear the ladies like scars," I teased as I winked at her.

So many emotions ran across her face all at once. She seemed to not know if she should be shocked at my story, still scared at what had happened, or if she should be shy and embarrassed because I very obviously flirted with her.

"Don't worry, we're good. Typically, it's just us telling people they can't trespass, running traffic—just normal stuff." A call started to come out on the radio, and I knew I would probably have to back whoever took the call, but I needed to try and convince Rae about staying with me one more time first.

"However, this possible stalker stuff worries me. I want you safe. Will you please consider staying with me? I have a spare room."

"I'll...think about it." She bit the inside of her bottom lip. The nervous energy in her eyes was back. She could tell I had to leave.

Satisfied with that answer, I reached out to touch her arm briefly, attempting to give some comfort. She tensed but just as quickly relaxed.

I told her I would be back after work with cameras and waited for her to walk inside and lock the door. Once she was inside, I went back to my car.

In my car, I let out a long sigh and rubbed a hand over my face. Whoever was scaring my girl did not know what they were getting themselves into.

Chapter 10

Rae

I was tired but too nervous to go back to sleep this morning, and now, Caleb would arrive at any moment. I made him food, did laundry, and cleaned the house. The only thing I had not done yet was rest. We were having chicken, rice, and veggies for dinner. I just hoped he liked it.

I jumped when I heard the chime of the doorbell. After checking to make sure it was Caleb, I let him in. We caught up while we ate dinner. He said he really enjoyed it, and to say I was relieved would be an understatement. Watching him across the table from me, talking about his day at work, reminded me of what I had hoped for back when I was in high school. I quickly realized something. It was what I longed for now. Maybe not this exact moment, but one day. Having him around was nice.

Caleb shifted in his chair, making me snap out of the thoughts in my head. "Can I help at all?" I asked.

"While I would say yes typically, you made me dinner and that was already so helpful."

The smile he gave me made my entire body feel warm. No guy has smiled at me with such sincerity since...

I have to stop thinking of Ethan.

I stood up from the chair, feeling kind of woozy now that I had been sitting for a bit and ate actual food. *Gosh, I can't believe how tired I am.* "Are you sure? I can pass you stuff when you need it." I stifled a yawn and rolled my eyes because it was like my own body betrayed me.

"Did you go back to sleep after I left?" he asked as he reached out to gently touch my arm, the same comforting way he had this morning. I flinched slightly, but only a tiny bit before I forced myself to relax some. *This is Caleb. He wouldn't hurt me. Right? No, he never would.*

I fully relaxed and realized his hand was still on my arm. Gentle.

Caleb pulled me into a hug. Again, I froze but forced myself to calm down. Caleb was a friend, a great one, and he would not hurt me.

"Rae, how much sleep did you get?" he whispered into my hair. His entire body was so warm, and it made me feel like I was melting some.

"I went to bed late since I was reading. I couldn't sleep at first, so maybe four hours? I had planned on sleeping in a bit." I was still pressed against his chest, listening to his heartbeat. *Am I too tired to worry, or do I actually feel safe with him?*

He pulled back only enough to look me in the eyes, his arms still around me, "Rae...Sunshine. Why don't you go sleep while I'm out there? I won't let anything happen to you." His voice was gentle and protective. He leaned in again and brushed a gentle kiss on my head. My body betrayed me again and I stiffened and had to force myself to calm down. Dang, this was aggravating.

Once I calmed down, though, I realized how warm I felt. I was fully wrapped in his arms again and I hadn't noticed or flinched. He kissed me. It was my head, but still, what did that mean?

I leaned back to look at him and studied his face for a moment. I knew my face had to be extremely red, but I didn't care. Gosh, he was so handsome, somehow more attractive than when we were in high school, if that is even possible. His blue eyes watched me as I looked at him. They were the kindest eyes I had ever seen. Suddenly, I realized he was talking to me. Had he asked me a question? Oh gosh, did I ever answer his last question?

I stared at him blankly and felt my face turn a deeper shade of red. "I'm so sorry, I must have zoned out." My brain told me to prepare for anger and a fight, but I was only met with a smile.

He reached up and gently pushed a hair out of my face. "I suggested you sleep while I am installing the cameras. I will make sure you're safe."

I nodded and gave him a small smile. Satisfied with that answer, he pulled back from the hug. I immediately missed him, his warmth.

As Caleb grabbed the things he needed, I found a blanket and curled up on the couch to try and rest. "Hey, Ranger?" I already sounded sleepy.

"Yeah, Sunshine?" I saw a small smile on his face before my eyes started to close.

"Thank you." Before he could even answer, I dozed off.

Chapter 11

Caleb

I had already finished installing the cameras on the back and sides of the house. I hoped that the sound of the drill wasn't keeping Rae up as I moved to the front where I'd left her sleeping on the couch. She looked so tired, but I needed to get this done if she was not willing to stay at my place just yet. These cameras would have to do for now.

I climbed the ladder and made marks where I wanted the camera to be when I heard a sound behind me and looked down. A delivery driver stood near the bottom of the ladder.

He wore the typical blue vest and a baseball cap with the company name on it, shaggy blonde hair sticking out from under it.

"Hey! Just dropping off a couple packages." He waved up at me with a big smile on his face, a thin scar running through his bottom lip.

I didn't even hear him drive up. "Hey." I waved back as I looked out at the road and then back at the man. "Did you walk here?" I asked when I didn't see a vehicle.

"Yeah, just parked a couple houses down, but this is the last house on the street before I turn around, so I fig-ured I'd walk it."

"Oh, okay…have a great night." I gave the delivery driver a nod. He lifted a hand in a quick wave before heading back down the drive.

Through the branches of the trees surrounding Rae's parents' place, I caught a glimpse of the front of his vehicle as he climbed in and drove off. Something about it didn't sit right with me. Maybe it was just my nerves wound tight from worrying over Rae's safety. I forced myself to shake it off. Just a delivery driver in the same uniform they all wear. He was gone. Not hanging around.

I went back to the camera installation, trying to push the feeling away. He'd had a company logo on his hat, packages in his hands—everything lined up. Still, the unease clung to me. Something about that guy felt…wrong.

A while later, I walked inside to find Rae asleep on the couch still. She looked so peaceful. She had the blanket curled up under her chin, her mouth was open slightly, and I could hear the faintest snore.

I got myself a glass of water and walked to the wall of photos Rae's mom had hung up. I figured I would wait a bit longer and avoid waking her. I scanned the photos on the wall and remembered Rae loved taking pictures more than being in them. My favorites, though, were the ones she was in. Her smile had been so bright.

My gaze landed on a photo of the two of us. It was taken right before she moved away roughly nine years ago. I smiled at the memory of growing up with her. She had been the best person to have come into my life. Every moment I'd been able to spend with her had been the highlights of high school. I wish I'd told her how much she meant to me back then because maybe whatever is haunting her now, to keep that bright smile off her face, wouldn't have happened.

Behind me, Rae started to stir. She opened her eyes just enough to see me, gave me a small, sleepy smile, and then closed them again. "Hey, Ranger," she said sleepily, a tiny smile still on her face.

"Hey, Sunshine." I crossed the room and sat on the floor next to the couch near where her head was. I noticed that she held her breath as I scooted closer to her, but she didn't move away, and after a moment, she started breathing normally again.

"How long was I out for?"

I couldn't help but smile at the sleepy sound in her voice. "About three hours. Do you feel better?"

She nodded. "Thank you for putting the cameras up and letting me rest. I'm so sorry I didn't help, though."

"Hey, don't apologize. I wanted you to sleep." I reached up and brushed a hair out of her face. She sat up suddenly, her face turning a shade of pink. She didn't look at me right away. Did I catch her off guard, or did I startle her this time? "Rae, I'm sor—"

She cut me off. "I need to get my phone to pay you for the cameras, and so you can show me how they work." She shifted the blanket off her lap and swung her feet off the couch, each movement displaying the nervous energy coursing through her.

"First, you're not paying me for anything." I laughed when she looked like she was about to try and argue with

46

me. She lay back down with a look I knew all too well. She knew if she argued with me that I would win, so she gave up and gave me a goofy, fake, frustrated look. It was good to see that was something that had not changed.

One of her hands was resting by the pillow, and I took a chance and reached up to hold it gently. It was a risky move, but I had a feeling someone had hurt her, and I wanted her to feel safe with me. I hoped with the small things I did that she would soon see that if she hadn't already. She didn't flinch or pull away. Inwardly, I cheered.

"Rae, don't argue with me on this. I wanted to do this for you. Your parents, too. Also, if you're okay with it, I'll monitor it for the next couple of days while I finish my rotation at work. Once I verify that everything works properly, I will add it to your phone."

Rae nodded and I gave her hand a gentle squeeze, then released it so I could stand up.

"I should probably go, though, so I can get sleep for my shift tomorrow. Are you sure you don't want to stay with me for a bit? I could even sleep here, on your couch, if that would help you feel safe."

Rae sat up again. "I really appreciate that, but I don't want to be a burden, so I'll stay here. I have the cameras now, so at least we may be able to see who it is if they come back tonight."

I nodded and sighed, trying to think of what to say so she knew I cared, but at the same time avoiding scaring her away or making her uncomfortable.

"Caleb, are you—are you mad at me? Did I say something wrong?" When I turned to look at her, she stood slumped over as if defeated with tears in her eyes.

"Oh my gosh, no." I took her shaking hands in mine. "I'm sorry I made you think that. I just wish you wouldn't think of yourself as a burden. I was trying to think of a way to tell you that."

Rae looked at the ground, and I saw a single tear fall.

"Woah, hey, this—this is not my Sunshine. This is not the girl I lo— knew back in high school. Come here." I led her across the room to the wall of photos. "See this smile? I've not seen it since you came back to town, and I'm curious, who took it from you? Who hurt you, Rae?"

She stared at the photo for what felt like an eternity. "Just...life" The tears in her eyes were gone when she looked away from the photo and to me instead.

"Okay. When you're ready to tell me, I'm here. No judgment, no pressure. But one thing I know for sure—" I hesitated but nudged her chin up so I knew she was locked in. I gently brushed my fingers under her chin while looking into her beautiful green eyes. "I'm determined to get my girl back." Much to my surprise, she did not move away.

We stayed like that for a moment, my hand gently on her chin, barely touching it, and our eyes locked, like I was trying to read her mind—searching her soul for answers.

My phone buzzed across the room, breaking our focus from each other. I walked over to it and unlocked the screen. I couldn't help but let out a laugh. "Well, at least we know the cameras are working!" I turned the screen towards her and Rae giggled as she saw a chicken on the porch.

"What's it pecking at?"

"Oh, that's right. A delivery person brought two small packages up while I was out front." I opened the door and walked onto the front porch. "Hey, chicken, I'm gonna need those packages, please." Rae stood in the doorway giggling while watching chicken peck me. "Maybe you don't need cameras after all. All you need is a guard chicken."

Still giggling, Rae walked onto the porch and picked up the chicken. She spoke sweetly to it while running her fingers over its soft feathers. She then walked into the yard and placed it under the tree. I watched her the entire time, smiling at this sweet moment I had the honor of witnessing. "Okay, Miss Animal Whisperer." We both laughed as I carried the packages inside for her.

Our hands brushed against each other as I passed her the boxes, and a blush appeared immediately on her face that she tried to hide by looking down at the shipping labels.

"Oh, great! This is my shampoo and body wash! The store was out of my favorite scents so I had to order them online. I've been using a different scent that I wasn't a big fan of since I got home." She opened the bottle and took a deep breath while smelling the body wash. "Here, smell this."

I stepped closer to her, smelled the familiar scent, and then looked at her. "That smells good. Peaches?"

A small glimmer of happiness appeared on her face. Smelling her favorite body wash brought her joy. Maybe it was the sense of normalcy it brought. Seeing her like this, finding the joy in something so simple, made her happy and turned me on.

It smelled how her favorite perfume smelled when we were in high school. She always liked the light fruity scents. The smell of the body wash lingered and my mind wandered to the idea of her being in the shower, getting out and wrapping herself in a towel, her hair wet—.

I immediately hated myself for that thought. She has obviously been uncomfortable a few times tonight, and while I was sure it wasn't because of me, I couldn't be so selfish. "Yup. It's called 'Peaches and Sunshine.'" Her words broke up my thoughts.

I let out a chuckle. I attempted to quickly shove the thought that was just in my head away and stood behind a kitchen chair, hoping she had not noticed the crack in my composure.

"That name is fitting for you." I smiled at her, and my smile only got bigger when she smiled back.

We both looked at the clock at the same time. "I should probably get some sleep," I said. "I'm sorry. Offer is still open if you want to come stay with me."

"Thank you. I think I'll be okay. Thanks again for everything, Ranger." She took a step towards me and immediately looked shy. Did she want a hug but didn't feel comfortable asking for one?

She glanced up at me very briefly, and then down at the floor again before she began to take a step backwards.

50

I couldn't let that happen, so I extended my arms, offering a hug. She quickly stepped forward and placed her hands on my chest as I wrapped my arms around her.

"If you need anything, you call me. Anything at all. Okay?" I felt her nod and then she wrapped her arms around me. "I will always be there for you if you want me to be."

She pulled back and whispered her thanks. I smiled at her and stepped out onto the porch. "Please lock up before I step off this porch. I'll be watching the cameras. Goodnight, Rae."

She thanked me again and smiled. This one finally reached her eyes. She then shut the door and locked it. Only then did I leave the porch and walk to my car.

I scanned the street to look for anything that stood out, looked back at the window and caught Rae peeking out at me. I smiled and waved, then got in and started the engine.

In the safety the darkness of the car brought, I let out a huge breath, willing the heat she'd caused when she hugged me to simmer down. As I drove home, the thought of Rae, even just being in her presence, drove me wild. *Gosh, I don't know what she has been going through, but she does not need this from me.*

Another thought quickly rushed through my mind. *Something had changed in her. Something had scared her.* The thought of anyone hurting her infuriated me, and I just knew I had to help her feel safe again. Somehow.

Chapter 12

Rae

My thoughts were going everywhere as I watched Caleb drive off.

When he said "my girl," my heart started racing. I immediately knew he hadn't meant it the way my heart thought, though. We'd been friends for years, so he probably meant "my friend" instead. But even at just the thought of him calling me "his girl," how he took time to put the cameras up and care for me—also how protective he sounded when he asked "who hurt you?" it turned me on.

I can trust Caleb, right? He's never hurt me, and he doesn't have a reason to, so why would he? I mean, unless I make him mad, maybe. I used to always make Ethan mad by messing up. I thought they were minor things—like not having dinner completely ready for him when he got home, or asking him for help with bringing groceries in. But those were the things that started his frustration. After that, anything could make him mad.

What if I do the same to Caleb?

I let out a frustrated sigh.

What if I ask for too much, or need him too often? I'll push him away or make him upset with me. Ethan made me feel like I was nothing but a burden, like I was annoying just for needing anything at all.

No, Caleb isn't like that. I know that. He's patient, he's kind, and he's never once made me feel like I was in the way. I wished this stupid voice in my head would just shut up or tell me what the truth is! Because I thought I was safe with Ethan once, too…*and look how that turned out.*

I covered my face in frustration as I groaned at how exhausted my thoughts made me. *Now I'm angry with myself. Great.*

However, as I started to get ready for bed, I found myself continuing to think about Caleb. I picked up my toothbrush and mindlessly went through the motions of brushing my teeth while my thoughts were on other things.

Our faces had been inches from each other when he tilted my chin up. His hands were never rough with me, just gentle. My mind flashed to how close he was after I woke up when he brushed my hair out of my face. I heard my phone buzz in the other room and snapped out of my thoughts. I realized I was standing in the bathroom, leaning my hip against the sink with my toothbrush tucked into the corner of my mouth.

"Why am I getting myself all worked up over a guy who would never like me?" I groaned while glaring at myself in the mirror.

I went into the living room and found my phone. A few new text messages had come in. I opened the app and immediately, any ounce of happiness I had was now gone.

Ethan: I need to know that you're safe.

Ethan: Answer me back, dammit!

Ethan had texted again.

Chapter 13

Caleb

Over the last couple of days, I'd received notifications on the camera app when Rae went outside to water the plants or get the mail. We'd text each other a bit, but not nearly as much as I would have liked. I would never get tired of talking to her, but I didn't want to push, if she didn't feel the same way. At least I had work to distract me during the last two days. However, today, I would have to keep myself busy around the farm. I'd been up since before sunrise feeding the animals, watering the garden, and cleaning the barn, but nothing could help keep my mind off her.

I ran a hand over my face and sighed. *Jenny is right. I do still love Rae.*

I didn't know why I tried to lie to myself, like it was any feeling other than that. She had been the one for me back in high school, and I was too young and too scared of losing my best friend to tell her how I felt. And now, she seemed uninterested in anything romantic with me, almost scared of being touched or having someone close to her.

Gosh, Caleb, how could you be so stupid to let her go?

I needed to focus, and sitting there thinking about her was not going to help that. I needed to help her get comfortable with being my friend again, just being happy again, and whatever I was doing right now was not helping.

Duke came up and put a big paw on my knee. "You want to go out in the field, bud? Let's go!" Duke tilted his huge block head to the side and barked. We both walked to the barn to get the horses.

"Hey guys." I greeted each horse as I passed by them before I prepped my horse's saddle. I adopted my horse Boone about a month after my parents died. Boone's first family had to move due to the family's dad's job transfer. Sadly, they were unable to take him with them, but I gave him a loving home, and he'd been a great addition to the family. We'd both lost something, and it was like Boone knew I was mourning someone.

After opening the stall doors for the other horses, I mounted my horse and led the others out of the barn. All the horses walked, keeping pace with Boone and myself, while Duke ran ahead. As soon as we were in the middle of the field, I got off Boone, took the saddle off, and they all ran free.

I pulled a blanket out of one of the saddlebags and spread it out on the grass. I sat and watched the horses run free. Duke ran behind them, thankfully smart enough to not get underfoot.

My mind was immediately back on Rae, thinking about how beautiful she was, how much I missed her while she was gone, and what the hell changed her while she was away. I ran a hand through my beard and let out a huge sigh.

Coming out with the horses was supposed to help me clear my mind, not make me think about her more. However, the more I tried to not think about her, the more she was in my thoughts.

Frustrated, I lay back on the blanket and stared up at the clouds. Duke ran over and plopped down next to me, soaking up the warm sun. I gave him some water and, after drinking, he rolled over on his back, belly up without a care in the world. Duke's feet wiggling in the air made me chuckle.

Laying back on the blanket again, I remembered how my parents would bring me out to the middle of the field to try and help me clear my mind when I was little. We would look at the clouds together, watch birds fly by— just spend time together as a family. Stress as a child was so different from the stress an adult feels, but something about being in nature really helped center me, helped me clear my mind.

The memories calmed my mind for once.

I woke to the sound of stomping hooves and snorting horses. Opening my eyes, I realized I'd subconsciously put my hat over my face. Removing it, I saw two of my horses standing over me and the others close by.

I let out a laugh. "Okay, okay. I'm up! You guys ready to go back?" I reached for the saddle and the horses whinnied. Duke jumped up, looking happy as could be, like always. I looked at my phone, checking the time. I wasn't out for long, thank goodness, but was relieved when I saw there were no camera notifications I had missed.

When we got back to the barn, I gave the horses fresh food and water, then divided up the last of the apples.

"I'm going to go to the store to get y'all more treats."

I locked the barn up, went to the house, got Duke some fresh food and water, and then headed to the truck.

Maybe a drive to town would help.

Chapter 14

Rae

I had a basket looped around my arm and was fitting each item into the basket like it was a piece to a puzzle. The last time I was here, I felt so exposed and like a spotlight had been focused right on me. I kept looking around as people came close, checking to make sure none of them got too close or that they weren't Ethan.

I was looking at the frozen French fry bags when I remembered I needed onion for another recipe. Selecting a bag of fries, I placed it in my basket and went back to the produce section.

As I was looking for the perfect onion, I heard a familiar and happy voice from the other side of the produce table, "Okay, we have got to stop meeting here and just decide to go to dinner or something."

I didn't even have to look up to know that was Caleb's voice, but when I did, I couldn't help but smile. I was very aware that my face was quite red but didn't bother to hide it this time. I let out a little laugh and rounded the table to join him on the other side.

"Caleb Walker, if I didn't know any better, I'd think you're stalking me, especially since you can see when I leave now."

Caleb's laugh was warm, and it caused me to blush again, "Oh gosh, I promise I was already on my way here when I got the notification that you were leaving your house. Plus, I didn't know you would be *here*. Promise."

He put his hand over his heart. "There's always a chance you could have had dinner plans with a friend—or maybe a date." He flashed me a silly grin.

My face twisted a bit, but I couldn't blame him for saying that since he didn't know anything. I quickly smiled. "Nope. Just by myself!"

He gave me a knowing look. Who was I kidding? He was not only my best friend for years, but also now a cop. He was trained to spot lies.

Caleb opened his mouth, probably to apologize, but I started talking first. "So what are you up to tonight?"

"Well, I came to get treats for the horses, and I always feel guilty, so I typically get something for Duke, my dog, too."

"Oh, fun! I was just trying to figure out what I wanted to eat this week." I motioned towards my puzzle of a basket.

"Hey, what are you doing for dinner tonight?" Did he seem nervous? Was he about to ask me to go to dinner with him? I didn't want to assume. "Oh, dang." I tapped my palm to my forehead. "That's what I forgot. I was thinking of getting a frozen pizza. Ha! Super glamorous, right?"

Caleb smiled as I laughed. "Would you…umm... Would you want to come over for dinner? Your basket looks like it can't fit a frozen pizza. Plus, I was thinking of doing a campfire dinner like my family used to do. It would at least be a bit more 'glamorous' than a frozen pizza, if you wanted."

60

"Oh umm—" I smiled, blushed again, and looked down at my basket.

"If you don't—"

"I'd love to, Ranger." I flashed him the biggest smile. I knew I was being too obvious about how excited I was to spend time with him, but I didn't care. I was nervous, but excited. I knew in my heart that Caleb was safe. I just had to keep reminding my brain of that.

"But can I make one request?"

"Anything." He gave me a look and I could tell he was curious about what I would say.

I shot him a cheesy grin. "Can I bring the wine?"

Chapter 15

Rae

"Oh, dang it," I grumbled as I dropped my bag while walking out the front door. When I left here earlier, I had thought I would be eating pizza alone tonight. The last thing I expected was to be invited to come over and hang out by the firepit while Caleb cooked dinner. I remembered how his family made campfire food for dinner one night a week on the farm, and I felt like I was intruding on a special tradition of his. When we were at coffee the other day, he'd seemed sad and said that since his parents passed away and his brother had moved, he kept the tradition alive, but it was typically just him by the fire. Today he told me having company would be nice if I wanted to join him. He'd made sure to tell me I shouldn't feel pressured to join him.

I agreed to join him and laughed when he told me not to bring anything. His parents would tell me the same thing when I used to come to campfire night. I picked up my bag and the two bottles of wine I had decided to bring, then turned around to lock the door.

Hearing the clink the bottles made in my bag made me giggle. I remembered one night I'd snuck wine out of my parents' house and brought it with me. Caleb and I opened the bottle when his parents took the leftovers to the house and tried it. We both hated the taste of the wine, spit it out, and hid the bottle to dispose of later.

I figured it was fitting that I brought a bottle or two tonight. Plus, a glass might help calm my nerves.

My stomach did flip-flops when I thought of joining him for dinner. Was I making a mistake by going? Just a couple of old friends catching up, right? So what if he was wildly attractive with those piercing blue eyes and that smile that made the butterflies in my stomach go crazy my first day back in town...and every day since? There was no way he liked me back then, and no way that he would like me now, right? Either way, I felt comfortable around him, and it would be nice to be around a friend for once.

I stopped in my tracks at the thought of the word "friend." This was the first friend I had hung out with without supervision of some kind in years.

I shook off the thought and continued towards my car. I was determined to have fun tonight.

The fire crackled in front of us as Caleb wrapped up the last of the food he had cooked. "Dinner was really good, Caleb. Thank you for inviting me," I said as I shifted back into the truck bed. He had brought a couple of couch cushions, pillows, and multiple blankets for us to sit on or use if it got cold. He even brought a couple of flannels.

"Thank you for coming," Caleb said with a smile.

My chest tightened slightly when he smiled at me. I remembered how sweet he was when we were in high school together. How much I trusted him. I also remembered coming out to his parents' farm on occasion for dinner by the campfire, and how I had wished we would confess to each other about our feelings for one another. Feelings that I had but had no idea if he'd felt the same. However, we never became more than friends, and then I moved away for college. Then I met...

"Rae?" He said my name with a curious and somewhat concerned tone in his voice, then passed me my glass that he'd refilled.

"Sorry, I must have zoned out for a bit there! I was just...Never mind," I said with a half-hearted chuckle.

"What were you thinking about? You looked far away. Focused." His voice was always so kind and warm when he spoke to me. He'd been that way back then, too.

"I—I was thinking about when I used to come out here in high school. How close we were. Then I lost touch—no, I just stopped reaching out when I moved away for college. Then when I met...Never mind. I'm sorry I stopped reaching out". I tried to keep the frustration sound out of my voice, but instead, the words just tumbled out.

My eyes stayed focused on the fire as I spoke, and I did not look away until he reached out his hand and put it on mine. I flinched when our hands touched and he pulled away, afraid he'd spooked me. *Dang it.*

"I'm sorry if I startled you. I just wanted to say that you have nothing to apologize for. I could have been better at reaching out as well, but we were kids. We both were trying to start our lives at college. Do I regret losing touch with someone I really cared about? Yes. You were my best friend in high school, and I cared about you. I was sad we lost touch. However, I am glad that life brought you back here—for whatever reason that may be."

I looked at him briefly, and whispered, "thank you" before tears started to well up in my eyes and I quickly looked back at the fire. *Darn emotions. This wine probably isn't helping.*

Shifting a bit closer, Caleb quietly asked, "Hey, are you okay? I mean it. You have nothing to..."

I tensed briefly but forced myself to calm down. I hoped he hadn't noticed because I didn't want him to think he was the reason. I looked back at Caleb and attempted to blink away the tears, but one fell. *I can't lie to him. He knows me too well.*

"No. I mean, yes. I'm okay. What you just said was probably the nicest thing that a guy has said to me in a long time," I said, just above a whisper, as I tried to hide the tears that were falling now. I quickly wiped at the tears with my hand and then smiled, hoping he would forget the words I had just said. "Sorry..."

Duke stood and walked over to me, placing his head in my lap. I gently petted his soft ears, wishing it would bring me some comfort.

Caleb sat quietly for a moment that felt like an eternity, until he said, "Rae, did someone hurt you?" His voice was so calm and comforting.

I sat there, looking at my hands twisting around the stem of my wine glass.

"Rae, you don't have to tell me anything, or you can tell me everything, just know that I'll be here for you if you want to talk," Caleb said in the most gentle tone I had ever heard as he put his hand out towards me, palm up. I really looked at him for the first time since the conversation had started. His brows knitted together out of worry, but his eyes were so kind.

Seeing him care so much broke the barrier the words were hidden behind. I took a shaky breath and let it out slowly. "My ex," I said with a voice flooded by tears. I couldn't help it. "It wasn't...He didn't..." I didn't know where to start, or even how to start.

His hand was still extended out towards me, palm up, steady, strong. I put my hand in his, feeling his warmth and saw the concern in his eyes. Thoughts about if I could trust him with this raced through my head. I was so scared to lose my friend if I told him.

Caleb noticed my hesitation, his expression only looking more concerned. His thumb moved slowly back and forth on my hand.

With a wavering voice, I continued to tell him, "My ex..."

Chapter 16

Caleb

I had been overjoyed when one of my closest friends had returned to town and looked to be staying for a while, but it seemed that there was a sad reason as to why she came back home, one that I had only guessed until now. I was hoping what she was about to tell me was not what I had imagined.

Rage pulsed through my veins at the thought of someone possibly hurting her. I was trying to stay calm so I could focus if she wanted to talk.

She had taken my hand, and it felt like she was holding on for dear life. Like if she didn't hold it tight, something bad may happen. When Duke saw her take my hand, he moved his head away but stayed right next to us, almost like he thought *Dad's got this.*

"My ex, Ethan, and I met in my final year of college. We were both studying at a cafe and went to sit at the only table available. We ended up sharing it and chatting with each other while working on our assignments. We saw each other there a few more times, and each time agreed to share a table while doing homework. Eventually..." She had a death grip on my hand and her wine glass. "...he asked me out and we went on a date. He seemed kind, charming, I thought..."

She took a sip of wine and cleared her throat. "Fast forward—" She paused again, took a shaky breath, and looked at me for a moment. "Sorry I'm taking forever," she said in a tiny voice.

"It's okay, Sunshine. You take as long as you need. I'm not going anywhere."

She took a deep, shaky breath, and continued. "We moved in together after a bit. I don't remember how long we'd been dating, but it was a little over a year after we'd met. Everything seemed okay and normal for the first year of us living together. Things were good for the most part. We would disagree on things, but nothing major. Just normal disagreements couples have. But then something changed in him. He had been getting a bit 'nit-picky' at things I would do, but then it got worse."

Her voice broke as she said those last words, and it broke my heart to hear it.

She stopped talking for a couple minutes and hadn't looked at me either. I, however, hadn't stopped watching her. She shivered despite the fire still being warm enough, and her hand felt so cold. I knew the shaking was probably mostly due to what she was telling me, but with my free hand, I grabbed a blanket from the corner of the truck.

"Rae, you don't have to tell me anything if you don't want to, or if you're not ready to," I reassured her as I wrapped the blanket around her. I picked the other one up and placed it over her lap.

She shook her head and wiped a tear off her cheek. "Thanks for the blanket, but no, I need to tell someone, and I trust you."

My chest tightened at those three words "I trust you" considering it sounded like she had no one she could trust right now. I offered my hand again, and she held it just as tight as before.

"He changed. He became angry at times for no reason. He would talk sternly to me, as if I was a child, and eventually he started to yell when he was angry. He would occasionally call me stupid." She let out a huge breath. "I was constantly told that my body was fat and that I needed to lose weight. He really disliked my stomach, hips, and thighs. I know I'm curvy, but...I..."

She blinked back tears.

"Anyway...He also was aggressive when he'd touch me. He—he would grab at my chest and be really rough with me instead of being gentle. He liked to grab me on one side, using his other hand to do other things, or restrain me. It wasn't just my chest he was rough with either. The things he did, they hurt." Her voice was barely above a whisper, and she was just letting the tears fall now.

I winced when she said that. "No one deserves to be called stupid or anything of the sort, and I'm so sorry—" I ran my free hand over my face. "I don't know why he would think grabbing at you or hurting you in any way was fun, or would make you feel in the mood, if that was even his intention. Those parts of you...All of you...You deserve to be treated gently, with love. You, your body, are also beautiful, and he was crazy for telling you otherwise."

I could feel my blood boiling but had to stay calm or it might scare her off. I needed to know as much as possible about this guy, but if she saw my anger, she might shut down.

She whispered her thanks and then started to talk again but paused and said something like "sorry for ruining the evening" and she'd stop there. I rubbed the back of her hand with my thumb. "You are not ruining anything. Nothing at all. You can continue if you want, Sunshine," I said with an encouraging tone, squeezing her hand a little.

Rae nodded and took a deep breath. "I had started to stand up for myself. Trying to make him realize he was being a jerk. One day, we were in the car and he'd been in a bad mood most of the day, so I asked him what the hell caused his bad mood. He said he was just stressed about a project at work that he had been assigned. He was frustrated that I'd gone out with a friend the night before instead of hanging out with him while he was stressed. My best friend out there had taken me out for my twenty-fifth birthday. Something that he had forgotten about." She said those last words with a bitter tone, and I could hear the fight in her voice. "When I told him I'd had that dinner with my friend planned for a while, he said I should have canceled it. I told him that would not be happening in the future and started to get out of the car."

Her breath shuddered when she inhaled. She breathed a bit faster for a moment, and I covered the hand I was already holding with my free hand, her breathing settled.

"He...he reached up to my head and grabbed my hair right here." She touched her roots. "He pulled me back into the car. It happened so fast that I hadn't been able to get the door open much yet. I guess he realized what he

70

was doing, so he let my head go, but I ended up hitting my head on the window of my door." More tears fell and her voice cracked.

My mouth fell open. I was in shock that someone could treat her like that.

"Sorry. I know you didn't ask for this."

"Yes, I did. When I befriended you all those years ago, I signed up for the good and bad. When I told you the other day that I would be there for you, anytime, I meant it. Anytime about anything."

She nodded and opened her mouth but then closed it immediately.

"Is that when you left?" I asked, hoping that had been the only thing that had happened. I also hoped that she was okay with me prying.

She sniffled and shook her head. "No. Sadly, it isn't. I went inside the house, thinking he would leave. He followed me, though, and said he wanted to apologize. I told him I needed space and he needed to go. He said—He said he would make it up to me, and he tried to kiss me." She pulled her hand away when she said that, and my stomach felt like it was in my throat.

She was quiet and didn't move for what felt like an eternity. When she spoke, it was the worst thing I could have imagined. "He...forced me to have sex with him. I told him I didn't want to. I told him to stop. He said he needed to make it up to me. He told me he was sorry." Anger laced with hurt and fear coated her voice.

"Rae, are you saying he raped you?" I was trying to stay calm. She needed me to be calm.

She sniffled and shrugged, "I mean, we'd been intimate before, but I asked him to stop..."

"Honey..." I said as sweetly as I could as I offered
my hand again. She didn't pull away or flinch this time.
Instead, she slid her hand into mine without hesitation.
For a moment, we sat like that, silence stretching between
us. I was about to continue talking when she shifted
closer, pressing her thigh against mine. I froze. This move
was so brave of her, considering what she just told me. I
slowly and carefully lifted my arm and draped it around
her shoulders, leaving the weight of it loose, ready to fall
away if she moved—but she didn't. She leaned into me,
resting her head on my shoulder.

We stayed like that for several minutes before I dared
to speak again.

"Rae, he raped you. Regardless of what you'd done
before, you told him to stop and he didn't." I could tell
she was processing the words I had just said. They were
not easy to say, and I could only imagine how heavy it
was to hear the reality of it.

"I was so stupid for not leaving right away. I should
have run right after that. I tried a couple months later, but
he caught me." My chest hurt hearing her say that. "Then
I tried a few months after that, then again, after my
twenty-sixth birthday. He had made me break off all
friendships and I only got to call my parents when he was
there so they wouldn't be suspicious about anything."

My shirt was soaked from where her tears fell. I
would gladly take the pain and fear she was feeling if I
could.

A chill shook her entire body, and I saw that the fire had died down. I hadn't realized that it felt a bit chilly. "Hold on just a minute." I moved away from her body and immediately wanted to be back with her, but I also didn't want her to be cold. I quickly added a couple of logs to the fire, waited for the flames to come alive again, then hopped back up in the bed of the truck. I knelt beside her before sitting back down in my spot, and I grabbed one of the flannels I had forgotten about. Removing the blanket from her shoulders, I held the flannel open for her so she could slip her arms into it, then replaced the blanket over her shoulders.

"This okay?" I asked as I sat down in the space I had been in. I didn't put my arm around her right away because I didn't know if she would be ready for that again.

She looked at me for a few seconds. I felt like she was staring into my soul. The flames danced in her eyes as she stared at me, and I was so in awe of her beauty.

Rae looked down at my hand and picked it up, moving it so my arm was around her again, then leaned her head on my shoulder. My heart felt like it would explode because of every emotion I was fighting off. She had just been so vulnerable with me, reliving something traumatic, yet she initiated putting my arm around her shoulder.

We were quiet for a bit. Just her hip against mine, my arm around her, and her head resting on her shoulder. I didn't know if she wanted to talk more, didn't know what to say besides the fact that I was sorry she had to go through that.

She reached for my hand, and this time she laced her fingers in mine.

"I gave up for about a year and just lived with it." Her voice sounded a bit stronger than it had before but it was still so quiet. "I was hoping he would change, or something. Every time I tried to leave, I did something different and he always caught me. If I came home late from work, even if it wasn't my fault, I would get in trouble. If I did not answer a text within a certain amount of time at work, he would appear at my work and make sure I was still there. I was so afraid to go to anyone who could help, even law enforcement. I tried once, and he made me seem like I was crazy. He never left physical marks on me, so I could never prove anything. It was mostly just emotional and mental pain he caused.

"He physically hurt me when he pulled my hair and occasionally when he wanted to be intimate. You know...being aggressive like I said or occasionally he would smack me if I couldn't get in the mood or...finish...I was finally able to sneak a call in one day when I got home before him, and that night was when I ran."

My brain was going a million miles a minute as I was trying to think of what to say. What do you say in a moment like this? I gently rubbed circles on her shoulder with my thumb.

The fire had died down again so there was only a soft glow illuminating our faces. "Rae. Sunshine. Look at me, please." The glow of the flames was bright enough to see the look in her eyes. The fear. The pain. But I could also see how strong she was.

74

As she looked at me, a single tear rolled down her face. I moved to wipe it away and she flinched before I could touch her cheek. Dang it.

"Sorry, I..." Her eyes fell.

"Hey, I won't hurt you. I won't ever hurt you," I said gently, getting choked up by my own tears as my palm touched her cheek and my thumb brushed away the tear. "You're safe here. You're safe with me. I am so sorry that happened to you. You deserve so much better than what he gave."

She hesitated for a brief moment and then gave me a hug. I froze in surprise, my one arm still around her. I let her decide how long to hold on for. She pulled back quickly and then looked embarrassed. I gave her a smile to let her know she was okay and that I understood.

She leaned against my shoulder again, with my arm around her, and whispered, "Thank you."

Chapter 17

Rae

We sat in the bed of the truck, holding hands, with one of his arms around my shoulder as I leaned my head on him until long after the fire died down. We didn't say anything for a bit until I yawned. I was exhausted.

I hadn't planned on telling Caleb my entire story tonight. I didn't know if I ever planned on telling him or anyone, but I did, and I actually felt better after. He didn't run away either.

Another yawn betrayed me.

"Would you like to hang out a bit more or would you like me to take you home? I know your car is here, but I don't want you driving when you are this tired. You could even stay in the guest room overnight if you wanted. I have extra clothes you can change into if you decide to stay."

I thought about his offer for a moment. It wasn't that I didn't feel safe with him, because I knew I would be, but I really didn't know if I could stay here. "I appreciate the offer, and for listening to me tonight, but I'm really tired. Would you mind driving me home?"

Caleb nodded and we moved away from each other so we could get out of the truck bed. It was noticeably colder away from him, and I hated it. Not that I hated the cold, but I hated how it felt away from him.

Caleb hopped out of the truck bed. He reached out his hand to help me down, and I took it. As soon as my feet touched the ground, one foot hit uneven dirt and I stumbled. I started to fall, but Caleb caught me and our faces were inches apart.

"I got you," Caleb said as his arms wrapped around me.

"Thank you." I gave him a small smile. "For everything tonight. Dinner, and listening to my horrible story. I'm sorry I couldn't keep my emotions—"

"Hey, no," Caleb said firmly but with a sweet tone. "Please don't ever apologize for telling your story. Don't apologize to me for telling me anything about yourself. Emotions or not, you're not a burden or an inconvenience, and I will always be here for you. Always." He rubbed little circles on my arm with his thumb. It was the smallest comforting action, but it meant so much to me.

I looked up at him, tears of gratitude in my eyes. I was afraid to speak for fear of crying again, so I nodded my thanks to him with a small smile. Caleb walked me to the passenger side of the truck, opened the door, and helped me inside.

The drive to my home was quiet—just the sounds of the truck on the road leading to my house. As he pulled into my driveway, we noticed the porch light was off, so he made sure his headlights were angled at the front door.

"Wait here," he requested as he jumped out of the truck. He walked to my side and opened up the door for me, extending a hand in my direction.

"Thank you. You didn't have to do that," I said as I took his hand and hopped out.

"Sunshine, you will never be shown disrespect by myself or any other man again if I have any say about it."

Without thinking, I leaned in and pressed a quick kiss to his cheek. The second I pulled back, my hands trembled. I hadn't planned it, hadn't thought it through—it just happened. My heart hammered as I glanced up at him, afraid of what I'd see. But his smile was wide and easy, his bright blue eyes glistening as he looked down at me.

"Thank you for trusting me, Rae," he said softly.

A shaky breath escaped me, one I hadn't realized I was holding, and for the first time in a long time, the relief felt real.

He walked me to the door and waited as I unlocked it. I reached inside to flip the switch for the porch light, but it didn't turn on. "Oh well. My parents probably have bulbs in the garage. I'll check in the morning. Thank you so much for... everything." Another yawn betrayed me.

"Do you want me to check the lights before I leave?"

"Nah, it's okay. I have the cameras and that light by my bedroom window. Thanks, though. You've helped me a lot tonight. Plus, it's really late."

He seemed hesitant but agreed, "Okay, have a good night, Rae." He turned as I closed the door, but did not walk away until the lock clicked in place.

Once I was safely locked inside, I peeked through the side of the blinds and watched as he walked to his truck. It was as if he could feel me watching him. When he got to his truck he looked back, with a smile already on his face, and he waved at me.

I didn't know how to feel when he saw me watching. I wanted to pull back and hide, but I didn't. Instead, I smiled and gave a small wave back in his direction. His smile grew and he turned back to his truck.

I saw him pull out his phone, illuminating his face in the dark cab of his truck. He looked focused but then looked up at me and waved again before turning his screen off and pulling out of the driveway, leaving me silently wishing he didn't have to go.

❤

The next morning, I woke up to the sound of a truck pulling into my driveway. I looked at my alarm clock and it said it was 8 a.m. My phone buzzed and I retrieved it and my glasses from the nightstand. I couldn't help but smile as soon as I saw who the text was from—Caleb.

Caleb: Good morning, Sunshine. I'm outside with some bulbs for your front porch light, in case you didn't have any. Take your time waking up, I'm in no rush. No need to change or do anything special to your hair, you look beautiful already.

I felt my face warm as soon as I read the words "you look beautiful already." Without asking, he brought lightbulbs over so I didn't have to worry about the porch being dark another night. *And he's calling me beautiful before he's even seen me.*

I replied briefly to the text to let him know I saw it. Then I ran to the closet to grab something to throw on and saw myself in the mirror. I didn't know how he could see any of this as beautiful. My hair was in a lop-sided top knot, and my shorter layers were falling out of the bun. I had absolutely no makeup on and was wearing a giant T-shirt and some leggings with mismatched tube socks on. My eyes were also extremely puffy after crying last night.

I was a sight to be seen, but I didn't want him waiting for too long, so I threw on some slippers and a large sweatshirt, then fixed my hair so it looked less crazy.

I ran to the door and then stopped suddenly, not wanting to seem too excited. "Good morning! I'm so sorry to keep you waiting, you could have called me, I wouldn't have mind," I said as I walked onto the porch.

Caleb stepped out of his truck. I couldn't help but notice the way his shirt fit, his muscles filling out the sleeves perfectly. "No worries. Like I said in my text, 'no rush.' I meant it. Plus, you're worth waiting for." Caleb reached up to rub the back of his neck and gave me a grin that made my heart race. To make me blush more, he looked at my outfit and said, "You look *really* cute by the way."

"You're just saying that to try and get a reaction out of me!" I laughed, covering half my face with a hand as we walked to the back of the truck.

Caleb grabbed the box of bulbs and gave me that same playful grin but then changed it to a sweet smile. He stepped towards me and was so close I could feel the warmth of his body. He knew I trusted him. His sweet smile widened, and I felt my whole body warm. "Yes, to get a reaction, but only because I love it when you blush." His voice deepened as he continued to speak. "But no, I'm

80

being serious. You look beautiful. I like this 'just woke up' look on you. You look comfy. At peace."

I blushed and got distracted by his sweet words and the chaos it caused in my brain that I didn't even realize he'd moved to the passenger side of the truck and was retrieving something from the passenger seat.

"I brought you something. You in the mood for coffee? Vanilla latte with cinnamon, honey, and oat milk, right? I remembered you can't eat dairy, so I hope oat milk was okay to choose."

I stood at the back of the truck, still trying to wrap my mind around what he'd just said, and then he went and said he not only remembered my food allergies, but he remembered my favorite coffee as well.

"Rae? Did I get the coffee wrong?"

I snapped out of it and refocused myself. *He is just being really nice and has a great memory. This means nothing besides that. Right?* "No! Oh my gosh, you remembered! Thank you, but you didn't have to do that! And the lights? Can I make you breakfast as thanks?"

"No thanks necessary, but I won't say no to breakfast," he replied as he set the bulbs down.

With a nod and smile, we went into the house and I started breakfast.

♥

After checking all the lights around the perimeter of the house, Caleb said he went back around and checked all points of entry to make sure the house was secure. He walked inside just as I was setting the food on the table.

He set the box of bulbs down and smiled at me. "I'll check the smoke detectors before I leave."

"Caleb, I really appreciate that, but you don't have to do all that for me. You have done so much already!"

Caleb moved to the sink to wash his hands and only replied after he was finished. "Rae, making sure my—you're safe and comfortable is high priority. It's never too much."

My mind started racing after he changed his wording. I wondered if he was about to say "my girl" again. Instead of asking though, I agreed, said thank you, and sat at the table.

The silence between us wasn't the easy kind that comes with comfort, nor was it heavy with danger. It was the kind that followed when too many words had already been spoken and the weight of them still hung heavy. Caleb looked like he wanted to break the silence but he didn't know how.

"One of your neighbors drives a really old and noisy van. It was making a strange sputtering sound for a long time. If you know who it is, I could introduce myself and offer to take a look at it."

"That's really nice of you. I'm not sure who it is though since the people closest to us have trucks."

"Oh, okay." Caleb nodded.

Silence lingered again.

"So, what do you have planned for today?"

"Honestly, looking for a job. Other than that, nothing," I confessed between bites.

"So, you're staying in town?" he asked, sounding excited.

I tried to hide the smile that his excitement brought and nodded. "I feel safe here. I just don't know where to start looking since the town is small. I left in such a hurry, I don't have interview clothes or an updated resume. I should probably add that to my schedule today, too." I let out a halfhearted laugh.

"Hold that thought," Caleb said, rising from his chair at the table. I stared at him as he exited the house to stand on the porch. He was on the phone with someone, but I couldn't hear a word of the conversation. While I waited, I cleaned up the kitchen.

Caleb came back in through the front door and stood in the kitchen smiling ear to ear. "You can't be mad at me," he began, which made me shoot him a very confused look. "I just made a call to someone at work. The sheriff's office is hiring a records clerk. The lady I called, Sage, has worked there for about six years, and she would be your boss. She's really cool and was excited when I told her about you. If you want the job, you can start in a week— or when you're ready. If you don't, no hard feelings."

I froze. Caleb just did the sweetest thing for me, without hesitation. I had planned on asking about the "HELP WANTED" sign outside of the corner store, but this would probably mean a full-time job.

"Rae? I'm sorry if I overstepped, I…"

"No. Thank you! I am just shocked. Truly, thank you." Tears started to well up again. Caleb pulled a tissue from the box on the counter and walked towards me. He must have noticed my slight hesitation because he paused before stepping forward slowly. I didn't step back. I could trust him. He had shown me that back in high school and every day since I came home.

He took one last step and stopped in front of me. "Are these happy tears or...?" He gently wiped at the tears on my cheeks.

"Happy tears. I'm just so grateful."

I stared up at his blue eyes as he tucked a few stray hairs behind my ear, his hand staying where my ear met my neck. My breath stilled at the touch of his hand, but not out of fear, although my pulse was racing. Every nerve in my body screamed at me to close the distance between us besides my brain. It told me not to do it. My brain was lying to me, I knew it, but I suddenly got nervous and broke the silence.

"Did you get enough to eat?" I questioned as I backed up out of his space and went to put the leftovers in the fridge. I realized I had been holding my breath the majority of the time we were close.

"Yes, thank you. I'll finish up what I was going to do." He smiled at me before he turned to walk away.

"Caleb." He looked at me with a half grin on his face. "Never mind. Thank you again."

Caleb smiled as if I told him what I was thinking, even though I hadn't said a word. He nodded and then went to check the smoke detectors.

Chapter 18

Rae

A few days passed, and Caleb had just finished another rotation at work. I had gone shopping for clothes for the job Caleb helped me get, and I sent him photos of each outfit. I let out a giggle at the memory of the replies he sent me after each photo. He had been honest with me about if he liked an outfit or not, and each compliment he sent had made me blush. He had been so sweet, and I didn't deserve it.

I even met him for lunch at the department while I was in town. He helped me fill out my paperwork and introduced me to my new coworkers. My new boss seemed awesome. I was really excited to start working again and making new friends. Caleb came over both nights before going home to say hi and check in on me as if we hadn't been texting all day. He also set up the camera app on my phone so I could watch it. However, I asked him to keep watching it, too. I just felt safer with him.

I checked my phone and smiled at the fact that there was only one text, and it was from Caleb. The texts from Ethan had been minimal, but I could tell he was angry.

However, it had been a good few days. I was happier than I had been in a while.

I was in the bathroom, singing and brushing my teeth with a plan to go to Caleb's farm later when I heard the doorbell ring.

Checking the cameras, I saw it was a delivery person and after they left, I went outside to get the packages.

I came back in and locked the door before setting the packages on the kitchen table.

I opened up the first package and inside was a top I'd ordered for work. It was a deep emerald green color and I had been looking forward to it coming in the mail. I excitedly unfolded the shirt and tried it on. It fit, and I walked to the bathroom to look in the mirror. I snapped a picture and sent it to Caleb.

Me: This is the top I was telling you about! It's one of my favorite colors.

Three little bubbles popped up and I felt butterflies instantly. I knew that was silly since he is just a friend, but I couldn't stop this feeling. His text popped up on the screen, and I got instant butterflies again.

Caleb: Dang, Rae. You look beautiful. That color makes your eyes shine.

Before I could even wrap my brain around that first text, three more bubbles appeared.

Caleb: I can't wait to see you.

These texts seemed more than friendly, and the heat I felt was unreal. I quickly texted him back.

Me: Thank you, Ranger. You are too sweet. I can't wait to see you too.

I didn't know if I was reading into his text too much, but I sent my reply anyway.

As I opened up the second package, I smelled something so familiar. I picked up the box and sniffed it but couldn't figure out what the smell reminded me of. As I lifted the lid of the box, the sudden realization as to why the smell was familiar hit me.

I began shaking.

I picked up a small picture frame with a photo in it. A photo of Ethan and me. He must have sprayed the inside of the box with his cologne because now the house smelled just like him. Under the picture frame was a small piece of paper that read "I miss you, Rae. I'll see you soon." written in his handwriting.

I dropped the frame and the glass shattered. I threw the note back in the box like it was on fire and backed away while staring at it, all the way to the couch. I pulled my knees up and hugged them, still not taking my eyes off the box.

He knew where I lived.

Chapter 19

Caleb

"Hey, buddy, she should be here any minute," I told Duke as we sat on the front porch. Duke had taken to Rae immediately when she was here the other night.

I checked my phone and realized there were no camera notifications saying she'd left her house yet, just the ones from her bringing packages in before she sent me the photo. I opened the camera and saw her car still in the driveway. Weird.

I called her, but it went straight to voicemail, so I texted her.

> *Caleb: Hey Sunshine, just checking in to see if you're okay. Duke and I are really looking forward to spending the day with you.*

Minutes passed. Nothing. No little text bubbles. She hadn't even opened the text.

"Hey Duke, you want to go for a ride?"

Duke's ears immediately perked up and he bolted towards the truck.

I grabbed my keys and locked the house up, then got in and drove to Rae's house. *I have to make sure my girl is okay.*

❤

"Rae? Hey, Rae! It's Caleb. Are you home, Sunshine?" I knocked twice while calling out for her.

No answer. The only sounds I heard were the birds in the tree in her front yard and the wind chime on the neighbor's porch.

"Come on, honey, are you home? I'm worried. I just want to know you're safe." My voice sounded more pan-icked than I meant it to sound. Duke stood at my feet, panting because he was feeding off my stress. I felt bad, but he would be better with me than at home.

Just as I was about to text her again, the blinds moved and, a few seconds later, the door cracked open. Through the slit of the open door, I saw her puffy eyes and her skin looked extremely pale.

"Hey, can I come in?"

"I...really don't feel like having company today." She sniffled and her voice cracked as she spoke, like she'd been crying for hours.

"Okay, what can I do? Can I just sit with you for a bit?"

Even though the door was still cracked open, she'd turned away so I couldn't see her. I could hear her snif-fling. A moment later, the door opened more and I stepped into her house. Duke followed close behind me. Every single light in the house was on, which was not normal.

She walked away from the door without verifying that I was inside or locking it, and I could tell it wasn't because she trusted me this time. Something made me think she didn't care at the moment. The soft sounds of her slippers shuffling on the hardwood floor echoed down the hall and into the front room. Her pace was much slower than normal. I turned to lock the front door and then followed her back to her room where she crawled into bed. She threw the blanket over her head and started to sniffle again.

"Umm...Hey, Rae. Can I come in?" I stood at her door, not wanting to enter yet in case it made her feel uncomfortable. Silence.

Duke ran in and hopped up on the foot of the bed, facing the doorway, like he knew she needed protection from something.

"Okay, honey, if you don't want me in here, now is the time to say so, cause I'm coming in." I paused again, waiting for an answer that never came.

I walked over to the side of the bed she was lying on and knelt next to the bed. "Hey. I'm here. What can I do to help?" I kept my voice gentle. I could see the blanket shaking so either she was shaking from fear or silently crying.

She sniffled and breathed shakily. "He found me." Her voice came out so tiny, I almost didn't hear it.

"Wait, what?" I thought I must not have heard her correctly.

"I don't know how. I never t-told him where my parents lived. Just the state." She took a long and very shaky breath. "I mean, sure, he could have looked it up online, but—" She was sobbing now, and I wanted so badly to take away the pain and fear she felt. "I don't even have the same last name as my mom and step-dad..."

"I mean, it's still possible to find it online, but why now? Rae, did he show up here? I didn't see any guys on the cameras." I reached out and touched her shoulder, still covered by the blankets. She jumped at my touch, and I quickly apologized for scaring her. *I'm an idiot. Of course she would be jumpy when she couldn't see me, especially after this.*

She pulled the covers off her head and looked at me. Her tear-streaked face broke my heart. She looked so scared. "No...He sent something...Kitchen table."

I walked into the kitchen and found the box addressed to Rae, the frame on the floor, surrounded by broken glass. I lifted the lid of the box, and the note inside, with a dish towel in case fingerprints could be pulled from them. I didn't care if there was a slim chance of getting a good print, but I was not about to take any chances. I looked at the note and then the bedroom door. I ran my hand over my face and pinched the bridge of my nose to calm myself. *No wonder she's shut down.*

I looked at the frame and realized that I had stepped on a couple pieces of broken glass. I bent over to pick up the frame from the ground and turned it over, being careful to not cut myself. As soon as I turned it, I saw a familiar face—shaggy blonde hair and a thin scar across his lip. My vision narrowed to the photo I was holding. I felt my world spinning. I had seen this man before but did not know he was her ex. The delivery driver. That was her ex. If I had known, I would not have let him get this close to her.

A wave of nausea hit me, and I forced the feeling aside. She needed me. He had been so close, scoping out the place and my awareness of the situation. He had been watching for so long. I wanted to hit the ground running so I could find this guy, but she needed me right now. I didn't know what to do at this exact moment, but I knew one thing for certain: she was not staying here anymore.

I walked back into her room and sat on the edge of the bed, pulling the covers off her face with care. She didn't look at me.

"Hey. Look at me." I touched her shoulder. "I'm right here." I made sure to be gentle with her. I couldn't handle it if I scared her again. "You are safe. He can't get to you when I'm here. I won't let him."

"Caleb—" She looked at me and then at the ceiling. "Can I stay with you?" Her voice was barely a whisper. "I don't feel safe. Not here."

Chapter 20

Rae

"Of course you can stay with me," Caleb replied without sounding like he was saying "I told you so." No judgmental tone present. *What did I do to deserve him in my life?*

"Caleb, I feel…" *How do I feel? I don't even know how to describe what I am feeling.*

"Hurt? Numb? Scared?"

I nodded, turning my face into the pillow. Those were the best words for the storm twisting inside me.

"Can I do something? And you promise you'll trust me?"

I nodded again. *I trust him.*

I turned at the sound of his boots hitting the floor, then the mattress dipping under his weight. Caleb slid under the covers beside me, careful to keep space. We were face-to-face in the dim light, not touching but close enough that I felt the heat radiating from him.

I held my breath. My mind was screaming at me to run, to pull away. I trusted him, but there was so much noise going on in my head that it started pounding. I closed my eyes, trying to focus, but the noise only grew louder. The last man I was in a bed with, the only man I had ever been in a bed with...He hurt me. In more ways than one. I couldn't think straight as I tried to tell my brain to stop. *Caleb won't hurt me.*

Slowly, Caleb reached for my hand. The second his hand touched mine, it's as if a switch was flipped. All the noise in my head stopped. I blinked at the absence of all the chaos screaming at me. His hand gently rested on mine, and his eyes locked on me.

"Hey," he said softly, "I know it's scary right now. But you've got me, and we're going to figure this out together, okay?" His thumb traced gentle circles against my palm.

Something inside me cracked. I inched closer and, without a word, Caleb shifted, wrapping his arms around me. He didn't hold tight, didn't trap—just a steady shelter waiting for me if I wanted it. This was the closest to being held by someone that I had felt in years, and I never wanted this feeling to end.

I didn't flinch or pull away. I focused on his breathing and matched mine to it. Instead of pulling away, I moved closer, and now was being hugged by the sweetest guy I knew. I felt truly safe for the first time in a long time. I let the warmth of his body seep into me, soaking up the comfort he offered until my trembling began to ease. For the first time since the package from Ethan arrived, I let myself believe I wasn't alone.

Chapter 21

Caleb

Duke lay at the end of the bed, and Rae stood next to him. For a few minutes the only sounds in the house were those of drawers and closet doors being opened and closed as Rae figured out what she wanted to bring with her. I told her we could come back here as often as she wanted, but she insisted on packing everything possible. I felt sorry for her. This was her childhood home, the place where she grew up feeling safe. Now, that was the opposite of how she felt.

I walked back into the bedroom after checking the doors and windows to prepare for when we left. "Okay, I have to call this in, to let them know what's going on," I told her while she was shoving clothes into her suitcase. I heard her unzipping her bag when it suddenly stopped.

Her back was to me, but I immediately knew she did not like that idea without her saying anything.

"No, please!" Duke's ears perked up, and he watched her intently. "I don't want anyone to know." Tears were in her eyes in an instant. I knew we needed a report taken, but I still felt bad for upsetting her. She covered her face with her hands, and she started to sniffle again.

"Hey, I'm so sorry I upset you." She took her hands off her face and looked at me. I opened my arms and she walked towards me without a second thought. She leaned her head on my shoulder and wrapped her arms around me. She seemed comfortable, so I slowly wrapped my arms around her as well, giving her time to pull away if she wanted to, but she only hugged me harder.

We stood there for a few minutes, just listening to each other breathe. I moved one hand up to the base of her head and ran my fingers through her hair. The fact that she didn't tense up or pull away made my heart ache in the best way. Her trust in me had grown since she'd returned to town. In some ways, our relationship felt like it had when we were in high school.

"Rae." What I was about to say wasn't going to be easy but she needed to hear it, and I was going to be there for her through it all. "This guy may have been the one at your window that morning. We can't confirm it, but he's obviously stalking you, because..." I didn't want to say it, but I knew I had to.

She leaned back and looked at me. Our faces were so close I could easily lean forward a couple inches and kiss her if I wanted to. Gosh, I wanted to. I wanted to make her forget, for even a moment, about how she felt at the hands of anyone else besides me.

"Rae, Ethan *has* been here before. I am so sorry. I didn't know it was him since I had never seen him before." She looked at me with shock, and her hands gripped my shirt on my back. "The delivery driver that dropped off the packages while I was putting up the cameras, it was him. I had a weird feeling about him, but figured I was just being protective over my girl, and...I'm sorry. I didn't know."

Shoot. I accidentally let "my girl" slip this time. I didn't want to seem possessive and controlling. I also didn't want her to feel awkward if the feelings weren't mutual.

As if she could hear the words I was thinking, she laid her head back on my shoulder and let out a sigh. I held her in my arms the same way as before.

"I don't want the cops to know about—" her voice trailed off. Her shaking hands still gripped the back of my shirt. I wished I could do something to help. "I feel so ashamed."

"About what he did to you? Sunshine, you fought as hard as you could. You went through something no one should ever have to, and you got away. That's nothing to be ashamed of." My voice stayed quiet because I knew I had to be careful with what I said. One thing I also knew, though was that she was strong. This situation was like walking on a tightrope.

"Rae, do you trust me?" I kissed the top of her head.

She nodded, pressing harder into me than she had before, like I was a lifeline.

"Let me tell my people. I trust them with my life, and I would trust them with yours. I'll tell them you don't want anyone to know, and you're not ready to press charges. But Rae, we need a report on this guy with at a minimum the information we have in case something else happens."

A long moment passed before Rae responded. She nodded against my shoulder before pulling away. "Gosh, I don't know how I even have any tears left to cry." She chuckled lightly as she wiped her cheeks. "I should probably continue packing, though." She looked at me with a shy grin. I wanted to tell her to please stay with me a little longer, but I also didn't want to push it with how fast she learned to trust again.

Reluctantly, I left the room to make the call.

❤

If there was one highlight to this happening at all, it was that the package came today while my crew was on duty. They left and took the frame with the note into evidence. I stayed by Rae's side the entire time. She was so strong when telling the needed parts of her story, regardless of my presence. The only reason I left Rae was to speak with my Sergeant separately, and I made sure she was comfortable with Santana and Duke before I left. I told my Sergeant I may need a few shifts off if the crew could swing it, but I'd let him know how things are going after the first rotation. With the knowledge of what was going on, he said he completely understood.

I then made a call to Rae's supervisor-to-be, explained the situation, without going into details, and bought Rae an extra week at minimum.

The front room of her house only had three people in it, other than her and me, but the way her eyes searched for me while I was not right next to her broke my heart and made me hurry back to her. I hated those years we were apart after she left for college. I didn't want to spend more time away from her than I had to.

❤

Now that we were alone together again, the house was quiet. Nervous energy buzzed between us as she

98

continued to pack. I could tell she was nervous about leaving, and more than likely, nervous about staying with me.

I needed to keep her mind off the reason for the nerves she felt, so I told her the only information I had that she didn't know. "Alright, I have time off for at least a rotation or two, maybe more if needed. I also bought you an extra week before you start work, at minimum. Sage was so understanding even though she knows nothing. She told me you could start tomorrow, in a month, or even part time if you wanted, but she wants you to be the one to fill the spot when you're ready." Rae rubbed the back of her neck and her face twisted as I spoke. *Shoot. She looks even more nervous than before.*

"Caleb, I don't want to inconvenience anybody with this. Also—" She looked at the floor.

"Also...?"

Her face turned red and she shifted nervously in her spot, not making eye contact with me. "I need money. Ethan and I split the bills, like our rent. I had my money in my own bank account, but I wasn't able to change my information fast enough for my online accounts before he got to it. I accidentally left my laptop there, so I'm guessing he was able to log in and transfer funds or something. I had been able to stash a bit of cash away before I ran, but since I've not been working, I only have a little bit left after buying clothes for work." The words spilled out of her rapid fire.

Memories of the beautiful woman standing in front of me as a teen started to flood my mind. Rae had always been about earning money and making every penny count. In high school she groomed people's pets, helped walk their dogs, and even got a job at the animal shelter for a few months after graduation before she left for college. Her parents had given her money when she needed it, but if there was something she wanted, she worked for it. Another thing that bastard took from her. I hated him even more now.

"You don't need any money, Sunshine. Whatever you need or want while you're with me, we'll get it. Whatever it is."

"Caleb, I don't want to mooch off of you."

"How about this? How about you help me around the farm? I need a chicken whisperer and someone to help ride the horses, too. Plus, this guy—" I pointed at Duke who was at Rae's feet "—I can only give him treats and ear scratches so often."

Rae giggled which was music to my ears. I reached out my hand and at first she hesitated, but then she gave me her hand. She'd been through so much, so the rollercoaster of whether she could trust someone or not made sense. I pulled her close, slowly, giving her a chance to pull away at any point, but she didn't.

"I've got you, Rae. No matter what," I told her as I looked deep into her eyes. "I've got you."

Chapter 22

Rae

Caleb was being so sweet, even though I've done nothing to deserve his kindness. Maybe I…

"Whatcha thinking about?" I was so deep in thought as I was zipping up my duffel bag, I didn't even hear him come up behind me. I jumped. He placed his hand on my lower back, grounding me, but also stirring up a fire inside of me.

"Oh. Nothing. Just packing." I gave him a small smile.

Caleb chuckled. "Rae, you realize we've known each other since high school, right? We may not have seen each other for a while, but that doesn't mean I don't know you still."

He was right. He knew me best back in high school, and he knows me so well still. Why was I hiding anything from him now?

"I was just thinking about everything," I admitted sheepishly.

"Well, that makes sense." Caleb paused and gave me a kind smile, then looked around the room. "Anything else you need that I can pack for you?" He took the duffel bag I'd finished packing a few moments ago to the hall.

"Ummm...No. No nothing else. I think I'm actually done." My eyes darted to the corner of my room, realizing he had returned faster than I thought he would.

"Is it personal? Do you want me to leave the room while you get it?" *Smooth, Rae. He knows you, so even if he'd not seen you looking around, he would still know.*

"It's silly. Stupid even," I said, frustrated. I knew my face was red, so I didn't look at him.

"I doubt it's stupid or silly, Sunshine. Try me."

I glanced up at him, over my glasses. Embarrassed, I walked over and pulled the night-light from the wall, then tossed it into my bag.

"Why is that silly?" He gave me a puzzled look.

"I'm a grown woman using a night-light. That's why." Why was he not laughing at me?

Caleb sat on the edge of the bed, looking at me, his face without a hint of humor on it. "Can I ask why you use it?"

"You promise—"

"That I won't make fun of you? Of course I promise that."

I stared at him for a moment and realized he was being sincere. I started to feel bad for not trusting him immediately.

"I'm not scared of the dark. I'm scared of what's in the dark. When I wake up from a nightmare, it helps me realize that I'm awake and nothing...and no one...who can hurt me is around. Ethan used the dark to hurt me at times." I let out a long sigh and his brows knitted together as soon as I said that last sentence. Talking to Caleb about everything was easier than I'd expected it would be—difficult still, but easier than I expected.

"I'm so sorry. That sounds like a good reason to me, though." He gave me a small smile. "Can I tell you a secret?"

I nodded and sat next to him, genuinely curious about what his secret could be.

"I have a small night-light in my bathroom, one in the guest bath, and one in the hallway. Reason is, I just flat out don't like the darkness. The farm is dark at night, so when my parents died, I put more lights up around the farm and a few night-lights around the house. I do still need to get cameras, but I have *plenty* of lights." He smiled at me in a way that took my breath away. That smile, paired with his confession, made my heart speed up.

"Really?" I tried to hide the fact that his confession ignited something inside me. I knew my cheeks were probably pink right now.

"Cross my heart, Sunshine."

His smile confirmed what he'd been telling me all along: that I wasn't alone in this. That thought both scared me and made me want more.

Chapter 23

Caleb

The front porch was quiet besides the occasional creaking of the porch swing and the crickets in the grass. The air was warm and still, and the stars were glowing so brightly tonight.

Rae sat with her legs crisscrossed with a glass of sweet white wine in her hands, her eyes focused on the sky. I sat next to her, a glass of whisky in my hand, watching her, and Duke lay at the porch steps, watching the yard. After we had come back to my house, she wanted to go change and ended up taking a nap as well. I made dinner for us while she slept. She'd woken up with a smile that I hadn't seen much of since she'd come home.

She seemed relaxed during dinner and happy when I suggested sitting outside for a bit afterwards. She was wearing leggings and an oversized hoodie and looked stunning, but there was now a storm in her eyes that made me realize she was not as calm and cozy as she looked.

"Feels like I lost you to your thoughts. Where'd you go?" I asked with a low and gentle voice. I wanted to pull her back from where her mind was, not scare her out of it.

"Y-yeah, I'm sorry. Just tired. It's been a long day." She stretched and rubbed at her shoulder, probably feeling all of the tension she'd been holding onto.

I nodded, understanding that. I twisted the whisky glass around in my hands, wanting to offer to rub her shoulders, to help her relax, but not wanting her to pull back from me. I didn't know if offering that would be too much for her, for us.

A minute of silence passed.

"Want me to rub your shoulders?" I decided to just ask. I would work every day to let her know she can trust me, so if she retreated a bit, I would work to regain her trust.

Rae stiffened almost immediately, and I noticed the change. Crap. Her body tensed the way it did when she told me her secrets the other night. However, her eyes were closed and she was breathing deeply. I watched her take a few deep breaths, and then she looked at me. She seemed nervous, like she didn't know how to answer without possibly disappointing me.

"It's just your shoulders, Sunshine, and no pressure at all. I promise."

After taking a couple more breaths, Rae nodded. "Okay," she said, her voice barely above a whisper as she turned towards me.

I smiled at her, took a pillow off the swing, and put it between my feet, motioning towards it when I looked at her. "Here, this should be more comfortable, and you can still change your mind if you want."

Rae hesitated but then slowly stood and moved to sit on the pillow.

"I'm going to move your hair off your shoulders first, is that okay?"

"Yes. Thank you for asking, Ranger." Her calling me by my nickname made me smile.

I started by slowly moving Rae's hair out of the way. When I put my hands on her shoulders, I started off with just a little pressure. Within a few minutes, I could feel her start to relax, as if she was melting under the warmth of my hands. The more she relaxed, the more pressure I added.

"You're carrying a lot of tension in your shoulders, Sunshine. You know, now you don't have to carry the weight of the world alone," I murmured as I gently worked to release the tension in her muscles.

"That's how it's felt all this time," she confessed as she closed her eyes.

"Well, you're not alone anymore. I've got you."

I continued to gently massage her shoulders and neck, and her breathing gradually changed. Deeper. Slower. The only sounds around us were those of the crickets in the yard. Soon she was so relaxed, she rested her head on my leg, and I moved my hands to her hair. I ran my fingers from the roots to the end of her hair without saying a word, and she continued to relax.

I smiled when I realized I'd not seen her this calm since she came back to town.

"Hey, can I ask a question?" I quietly asked.

"Mhm," she said sleepily, her head still resting on my leg.

"When was the last time somebody held you? I mean actually held you, and not like when I hugged you for a while."

She was silent for a bit, and hadn't moved, so I thought maybe she'd started to doze off. "It's been a long time," she whispered back.

I continued slowly raking my fingers through her hair, rubbing the pads of my fingers gently on her scalp. "Can I?" I asked, fully expecting her to tense up or say no, but she didn't. She nodded.

I helped her up, then sat back on the swing with one leg up and one hanging off and opened my arms for her. She looked at me for a moment, and I gave her a reassuring smile. To my surprise, she didn't hesitate. She sat and leaned her back against my chest. I gently kissed the top of her head and began playing with her hair again as I slowly swung the swing. Within a few minutes, her head became heavy on my chest and her breathing slowed. She was asleep.

I didn't dare move. She trusted me. At least enough to fall asleep in my arms, and I could not have been happier. We stayed like that for a while as I ran my fingers up and down her arms.

When the air cooled, I knew I should get her in her bed where it was warm. I moved as carefully as I could to avoid waking her and gently picked her up in my arms like she weighed nothing.

Her eyes fluttered open. *Dang it.*

"What's going on?" she asked, her voice heavy with exhaustion.

"Sshh...You're safe. I've got you," I whispered in her ear right before she put her head back on my chest.

I carried her inside and into her room, laying her on the bed. I pulled off her slippers and pulled the covers up around her.

I started to leave but turned back around to make sure the small night-light in the corner was on. I wanted her to feel safe while she slept. When I left the room, I kept the door open just a crack so she wouldn't feel trapped when she woke up. I checked the front door to make sure it was locked and then turned the light on in the living room, like I often did before bed when I thought my nightmares would keep me awake.

I headed to my own room and peeked through the crack in the door just to make sure she was okay still. She looked so peaceful. And for the first time in a long time, I hoped maybe we could both rest easy tonight.

Chapter 24

Rae

The next couple of days were so peaceful and exactly what my heart needed. We made plans for Luke and Jenny to come over on the weekend so I could catch up with them. I was excited to see them and felt no nerves about having them here for dinner. Every time Ethan had made plans for someone to come over, I always said something wrong that made him mad, and he would let me know how he felt later. With, Caleb though, I knew things would be different.

I had not heard anything from Ethan since the package arrived, and I was starting to hope that if he was watching, maybe he'd seen how Caleb reacted and decided to back off.

Caleb did anything and everything to make me smile or laugh, and when he could tell I was trying to process my emotions, he held me. There was something...almost intoxicating about being in his arms—more than just feeling safe and cared about. He never made me feel like a burden.

Having him hold me that first night was one of the best feelings I had ever experienced. I had been tired, but I hadn't realized how tired until I couldn't keep my eyes open any longer. Then I woke up in the guest room with the night-light on as well as the one in the living room. He remembered, and it meant the world to me.

Now, he was inside making lunch and wouldn't let me help. He said I could help with dinner if I wanted, but he wanted to surprise me with lunch.

"Hey, Ranger, are you sure I can't help?" I said loud enough that he could hear me from the porch. He had said this was where I should stay until he was done because "fresh air and sunshine were good for his Sunshine." He had winked at me when he said it, and my face only heated more. While I was still kind of feeling guilty about not helping, I was enjoying spending time outside, listening to the birds singing and watching Duke chase a butterfly.

Caleb appeared at the screen door with a big smile on his face. "Positive. Lunch is served." He carried two plates out and placed one in front of me. When I saw what he'd made, I didn't know if I should laugh or cry because this sweet man remembered something about me again. He made one of my secret snack obsessions from when we were teens: a peanut butter and jelly quesadilla with banana folded into it. He even remembered how I liked it, with half the tortilla cut down the center, banana on one side and jelly on the other.

Ethan had made fun of me prior to him even changing, so I had only made this once since leaving for college.

I stared at the plate in awe, then looked at him, then back at my plate. I had tears in my eyes and giggles flowed from my mouth.

I looked up at him again and saw a big smile on his face. Quickly placing the plate on the porch swing, I jumped up and wrapped my arms around his neck. "You remembered." I pulled back just enough so I could look at him. "Thank you."

He placed his hands on my hips and somehow pulled me closer than I already was, then leaned his forehead against mine. "You're not one I would ever want to forget, Sunshine."

I was suddenly very aware of his hands being on my hips and curves. I was feeling self-conscious and my pulse was starting to race, but I also didn't want this moment to end. I was fighting with myself and hating myself for not just being present.

"Where'd your mind go?" Caleb whispered, our foreheads still touching. His words brought me back to reality.

"Just thinking..."

Duke barked at the butterfly he was chasing, and it broke our focus on each other. We laughed as Duke happily jumped and spun when the butterfly landed on his head.

"Let's eat while you tell me what you were thinking about and while we watch that crazy pup make friends with a butterfly." He gave me a wink and a grin that made my heart melt.

I nodded and laughed but also didn't want to tell him what I had been thinking of. *What if he thinks it's stupid?*

We watched Duke run around in the yard for a bit. He eventually walked up on the porch and drank the water that Caleb had set out for him, then lay down to rest.

"Rae, you don't have to tell me anything, and I mean that, but it would mean a lot if you shared what was on your mind."

"It's...Nothing. Stupid, even." I took a bite of the snack he made me, loving the memories it brought back.

"I doubt that. Remember, I understood the night-light thing. Also, just so you know, even if I hadn't felt similarly about that, I still wouldn't have judged you. You're my favorite person."

I know I blushed at that comment, so I finished eating my snack until my heart rate slowed. He didn't pry.

"I was feeling self-conscious," I confessed, and he gave me a confused look. "Your hands were on my hips and your thumbs were rubbing back and forth on my waist."

"Did you not like that? I'm sorry if I made you uncomfortable."

"No. I mean, I thought I would have struggled with it since...but that wasn't it. I hate my hips and waist since they're...bigger."

"Oh. Rae, I'm sorry, not because of what I did, but because you don't see yourself how you really are. You are beautiful, curvy"—he scooted closer to me on the porch swing and looked at me with such intensity in his blue eyes— "and if you were mine, I would never let you forget it," he said with a low whisper, leaving me stunned.

He immediately stood up, took my plate from me, and walked to the door, leaving me with only my thoughts.

The screen door shut behind him, but the whisper he left me with lingered longer than I wanted to admit.

Chapter 25

Caleb

I woke to screaming and crying coming from the room next door. With Duke in tow, I ran to Rae's room and to where she lay thrashing around, having a nightmare. Tears were streaming down her face, but I could tell she had not woken up yet.

"Rae, Rae. Sunshine, honey, wake up. I'm here." I sat on the edge of the bed, leaning over her while brushing her hair back and rubbing her arm. I wanted to pull her into my arms, to hold her, but if she was dreaming that monster was grabbing her, then I didn't want it to be her reality as well.

At first, Rae continued crying but slowly, she started to open her eyes.

"Hey, Sunshine. Wake up. I'm here and you're safe. You have nothing to be afraid of." I spoke calmly but just firmly enough that maybe it would snap her out of her nightmare.

With a sense of panic, Rae threw herself into my arms, shaking. "You're here," she sobbed into my chest.

"Always, Sunshine. Always." I wrapped my arms around her and rubbed her back.

For a moment, she breathed erratically and shook. "It was so horrible, Caleb." Her voice still sounded like she was so frightened.

"Do you want to talk about it?"

"I'm not sure. It was scary."

I pulled her tighter into my chest, hoping the closeness calmed her and didn't scare her. Being this close to her was addictive. I loved every second she let me into her space, her heart, regardless of how much. "Well, I'm here if you need me."

She placed her warm hands on my chest, next to her head, and I kissed the top of her head while rubbing her back gently.

A few minutes passed and I could feel her breathing easier. "Do you feel better?"

"Only because you're here. I was so scared. I was back at the house with...He was hurting me like he used to. It was so real."

"Well, I promise you, it was just a nightmare. You're safe, with me."

She nodded against my chest, and it was like I could feel the tension melting off her body.

The room was silent for several minutes other than the air conditioner kicking on and Duke's tail swishing on the floor. She tried to hide a huge yawn, and I brushed her hair out of her face. "You ready to try and sleep again? I'll be right there, in my room, if you need me."

She shook her head, still nestled against my chest. "Can...no, never mind."

"No, what? What were you going to ask?" I tilted her chin to look up at me, keeping my voice low in case part of her mind was still being held by the nightmare.

"It was silly. I was going to ask if you could stay with me."

"Heck yes, I'll stay. If it makes you comfortable, I'll do it so you can sleep peacefully. Be right back." I left the room, realizing I probably sounded more excited than I meant to. *Dang it.* I grabbed the blanket from the couch and walked back into her room, leaving the door cracked so the living room light could still shine through.

I started to sit in the chair next to the bed when she gave me a perplexed look. "Wait, what are you doing?"

Before I could say anything, she continued as if she had read my mind. "I meant you could stay with me. Here. You can be on the bed so you're comfortable. I trust you, Ranger."

I didn't answer at first because I was in awe of how brave she was. I probably waited too long to answer because her face twisted in the cutest way, indicating she thought I would feel uncomfortable with her idea. She was so wrong. More time with her in my arms, sleeping next to her, it was all I have ever wanted. I immediately hated myself for thinking that. *She doesn't need that right now.*

Her voice interrupted my thoughts. "Unless—does that make you uncomfortable? I was just—"

I smiled at her, but then looked at the bed she was in. "One problem. Your bed is a twin. I won't fit."

She giggled which was music to my ears.

"We can always stay in my room, if you're comfortable with that."

She bit her lip and thought about it for a second. Timidly nodding, she got up and put on her slippers, then followed me to my room. She froze at the door of my room,

116

eyes darting around. "I'm so sorry, maybe this was a mistake."

"Rae, honey, I promise you, I will not do anything to make you feel uncomfortable. I can still sleep in the chair or on the floor of your room if you want."

She shook her head and went to the opposite side of the bed from me and got under the covers.

My heart melted at the sight of her in my bed. *She trusts me enough to be in the same bed with her, even if it's just us sleeping next to each other.*

"Oh, wait. I'll be right back," I said, then walked out of the room. I walked back in carrying the little night-light from her room, plugged it in, and crawled back into bed. *It wouldn't hurt to have an extra one in here.*

I was careful not to crowd her. It was a king-sized bed, but she had gotten comfortable closer to the middle than I expected. Suddenly, I felt her arms wrap around me, and she placed her head on my chest. I froze, not expecting this.

"Why are you so nice to me?" Emotion laced her voice.

I moved my arm so it wrapped around her, and I pulled her a bit closer. I thought about how to answer that question, instead of just blurting out how I really felt, as I ran my hand through her hair. With my other hand, I rubbed her arm that she'd wrapped around me, knowing this was a move she was comfortable with.

"You deserve to be taken care of, Sunshine. You deserve to feel—" I paused as soon as I heard her snoring. She was still snuggled up next to me with her head on my chest, and she was snoring. The thought of her being comfortable enough to sleep brought a smile to my face.

Emotions ran through me.

You deserve to feel loved, Sunshine, and I am going to make sure you know how worthy of love you truly are.

Chapter 26

Rae

The sun shined brightly through the spot in the curtains where Duke was watching the birds. I looked up without moving my head and realized I was still curled up next to Caleb in the exact same spot where I fell asleep. I felt kind of embarrassed I had fallen asleep curled up next to him like this, but I couldn't move my body and still felt sleepy. His heartbeat was such a calming sound. The comfort of that and the heat of his body made me start to fall asleep again.

I did not realize waking up next to someone could be this amazing.

"Good morning, beautiful," Caleb said with a sexy, gravelly voice. It snapped me out of a daydream state between being asleep and awake. I was suddenly aware of being wrapped in the heat of his body, and to make matters worse, I realized my leg was over his.

I sat up in a panic. "Oh my gosh, I'm so sorry. I must have fallen asleep while I was hugging you."

"No apologies necessary, Sunshine." He placed a hand on my back, and I could feel the warmth of it soaking through my shirt. "How did you sleep?"

"Really well, actually. If I had a dream, I don't remember it. Thank you for being there for me."

He rubbed my back a little and smiled at me. The instant heat I felt through my entire body was new to me. Why was I feeling like this? Caleb couldn't feel that way about me, could he? *He knows my story, that I'm broken because of it.*

"Are you hungry?" His gravelly voice pulled me from my darkening thoughts like it had since I returned home.

"Starving."

"Stay right here." He took Duke and left the room and I settled back into the warmth of his bed, thoughts swirling in my head.

Chapter 27

Caleb

I had been in the kitchen for about twenty minutes, cooking Rae breakfast.

I hope she's comfortable being in my bed while I'm gone.

It was so nice being able to cook for her, but all I wanted was to be back with her. The bacon took the longest, but I knew she would probably love it.

I had to do some work on the farm today since Jenny was working at the department, and Rae was going to help me. If today's weather is anything like yesterday's, it would be really warm later in the day, so I wanted to get out there soon. However, I also was not about to rush making Rae feel cared for.

The bacon was finally done, so I pulled the plates out of the oven where I had been keeping them warm and placed the bacon strips on the plates.

Duke came back to the front door after his morning adventure around the front yard and made a beeline for the bedroom to go see Rae. *This dog loves her more than he does me.*

I walked back to my room with breakfast and coffee. "Breakfast is served!" As soon as I said that, I looked up and stopped dead in my tracks. Rae was sitting up with the blanket pulled up under her arms, resting her back against the headboard, reading a book that I had on the nightstand. I was looking at the most beautiful woman I had ever seen, in my bed, looking completely at home. She'd pulled her hair back into a bun before bed, and strands of it were falling out of place. I couldn't help but notice that she hadn't fixed her hair after sitting up. She was stunning.

"Caleb?" she said quietly. I hadn't moved.

"Hey, um, sorry." I gave her a smile as I walked toward the bed with our plates.

"You okay? You stopped suddenly."

I set her plate on the nightstand before easing onto the edge of the bed. "Yeah, I'm fine," I said, giving her a smile. "Just wasn't expecting to walk in and see you like that."

Her head tilted, eyes narrowing a little. "Like what?"

I hesitated, running a hand over the back of my neck. "Like you fit here," I admitted, voice low. Then I picked up her plate from the nightstand and passed it to her with a grin. "Not that I'm complaining. Just caught me off guard, Sunshine. Go on, eat before it gets cold."

She looked at the food and her jaw dropped. "You made all of this for me?" She turned towards me and sat with her legs crisscrossed while I settled on the other side with my food.

"Mhm. Thick-cut applewood smoked bacon, eggs with a bit of spinach in it, hash browns and—oh. I didn't make the fruit." I gave her a smile and a wink.

Gosh, she was stunning with her messy hair and flushed cheeks she got when I made her blush.

She laughed and she took a bite of bacon, closing her eyes as she chewed the bite. "This is delicious. Thank you."

I reached across the small space between us, setting my hand on her knee. "Anything for you."

Rae immediately blushed and looked down at her food.

I hoped she knew I meant it.

We ate in silence, just enjoying each other's presence. The only sounds in the room were Duke's tail wagging as Rae snuck him the tiniest piece of bacon and the forks clinking on the plates.

I hadn't noticed the details of what she was wearing last night, but now I couldn't help myself. The loose tank she wore shifted with each breath, soft against her skin, the fabric not hiding much in the morning light. Her shorts brushed mid-thigh, her long legs crossed in front of her, curvy and beautiful, and her fuzzy socks because her feet are always cold. She looked beautiful. As I watched her, I noticed her shoulders moving a little bit.

Without being obvious, I watched as she took another bite of bacon and then a sip of coffee. Her shoulders moved slightly in a dancing type of motion. I let out a little chuckle.

"What?" She glanced at me over her glasses and took another bite of bacon.

"Did you know you were happy dancing when eating the bacon?" I chuckled again.

"Oh my gosh, did I? I'm so embarrassed!" She covered her face with her hands.

"Oh, hey, no." I reached out and took the plate from her lap and set it on the bed before gently pulling her closer to me, her legs now touching mine. Her breath stilled but she didn't pull away. "I thought it was really cute." I gave her a smile and brushed stray hair from her face that fell out of her top knot. The only space between us was made up of our crossed legs. My hands rested on the outside of her thighs, neither of us had broken eye contact.

After a few moments, she leaned in and pressed a gentle kiss to my lips. I gently returned her kiss, slow and following her lead.

She let out a nervous sigh. "Oh umm...Well, I'm going to, umm...Thank you for breakfast" She scrambled off the bed and left the room.

I stayed frozen where she left me, the warmth of her lips still lingering on mine. For half a second, my body screamed to follow her—catch her wrist, gently pull her back to me, and show her she had nothing to be embarrassed about. But I forced myself to stay. She did not need me crowding her. Not when she was still piecing herself back together.

I leaned back against the headboard, running a hand over my beard as I let out a breath. A smile tugged at the corner of my mouth despite the way she'd bolted. "Here I thought breakfast with her would be the best part of my morning," I muttered to the empty room.

My chest tightened. Not from doubt but from certainty. She'd kissed me. She wanted me. She just might not be ready to believe I wanted her just as much—hell, maybe more.

I stretched out on the bed, staring at the ceiling, letting the smile win. "Take your time, Sunshine." I whispered. "I'm not going anywhere."

Chapter 28

Rae

Caleb was outside cleaning the barn. I was supposed to help him, but after running away was too embarrassed to go outside. I had changed clothes and then paced back and forth in the spare room for thirty minutes until the guilt of him working out there alone won over.

I walked into the living room and headed toward the kitchen window to see if I could spot Caleb. I watched as he walked out of the barn and then back in, carrying bags of what I assumed was chicken feed. Now I felt worse because that was part of what I had asked to help with.

I walked onto the porch and right away felt the temperature difference from the cool house. It was really warm for a spring day. I noticed the humidity in the air and some small puddles on the ground. It must have rained last night. I needed to change shoes before I went out on the property, so I walked back inside and found some of Caleb's extra rain boots by the front door.

There was a small note on the toe of one of the boots. I picked it up and it felt as if my heart was melting the second I started reading.

I noticed it rained overnight. I would hate for your shoes to get muddy, so I left these for you to wear if you want. Sorry, I don't have any that fit you, but your new ones will be here tomorrow night.

Yours,
Ranger

I reread the note again and tears prickled the backs of my eyes. The constant kindness he had shown me since I got here—I didn't deserve it. And the words *"yours, Ranger"* made my heart race. I quickly walked to my room to put the note on the nightstand before walking back to the front door. I was definitely keeping it.

Since it was hot outside, I grabbed a couple of cold water bottles from the refrigerator and put on the rain boots he had left me. They were way too big for me, but I didn't care. I just wanted to be out there with him.

When I stepped out on the porch again, I saw him walk into the barn, Duke following close behind. Caleb's muscles were flexing under his shirt, and it sent heat through my body.

I was still beating myself up for kissing him, and even worse, running away. How stupid was I to kiss him? He was just being nice since I told him about my ex the other night. There was no way he would ever fall for someone as broken as me. Right?

As I rounded the corner of the barn, Caleb walked out and we collided. I stumbled due to the big boots and he caught me, pressed a warm hand against the small of my back and pulled me close so I didn't fall. I placed a hand on his chest as I steadied myself and immediately noticed he'd taken his shirt off. Feeling flustered, I pulled back and tried to hide my cheeks that I knew were bright red now.

"I'm sorry! I didn't hear you coming," he said as he glanced down at the boots and smiled.

"No worries, I, um... I brought you a water bottle since it's hot out here."

He gave me an appreciative grin and took a long drink of water. He motioned for me to follow him into the barn and offered me a stool at the workbench. Duke lay just inside the barn so he could lie in the sun but not get too hot.

I sat there watching Caleb for a moment before either of us spoke. He had pulled up a stool and positioned it closer to me than where he found it but still left me some space. He took a small towel from the workbench and wiped the sweat from his head and face, his muscles flexing with every movement. Suddenly, I realized I had been so focused on him, I didn't notice he was now watching me. I was so embarrassed but chanced looking at him anyway.

I figured he would make fun of me immediately. However, he smiled at me with that sweet smile that always met his kind blue eyes. Then he winked at me, which caused me to blush again.

I didn't know how to act. Ethan always humiliated me. At first, it had been him teasing me, which was fine cause it was just for fun. I can joke and have fun, but after he changed, he did anything and everything to humiliate me, sometimes publicly.

Caleb must have noticed I had been staring at him and hadn't said a word, so he broke the silence first. His voice was low and warm. "Enjoy the view, Sunshine?"

I realized that even though I had been lost in thought, I hadn't stopped staring at Caleb. Without a chance to

128

recover from blushing after he'd winked at me, I knew I had to be a brighter shade of red now. A nervous laugh escaped my lips, and it caused his smile to grow even bigger.

"Sorry, I—" I couldn't make the words come out.

"Don't apologize, Sunshine," he said as he flashed another genuine smile. The warmth in his voice made my heart feel a bit lighter, like I had been weighed down by bricks for years and they were now slowly being chipped away.

"Caleb, I want to apologize for this morning when I kissed you." I blurted the words out, almost too fast. Caleb's face twisted into a look I couldn't read. Confusion? Hurt? Disappointment?

"I... I'm sorry. I hope I didn't upset you." Again, I spoke too fast, hoping I hadn't upset him.

Caleb looked at me with a look I'll never forget—all warmth and quiet understanding, like he could see straight through the walls I'd built. "Rae, the only reason I'd be upset is because you think you can't be yourself around me. Because I want you to be comfortable around me and I don't want you to feel like you need to apologize for anything. What he did to you, I would never do. You have nothing to apologize for. That kiss..."

I stood up from the stool and walked toward the barn door but didn't leave. His kindness was almost too much, and I didn't know how to process it.

The warm breeze felt nice in the shade of the barn. The only noises were the rustling leaves in the trees and the chickens. I tried to focus on those quiet sounds instead of the storm brewing in my mind.

I hadn't heard him move but I could tell he was behind me. Even though he didn't touch me or say anything, the heat of his body radiated near mine.

"Sorry, I just needed air," I murmured, unsure if he would've heard me since I said it so low.

"Sunshine, that kiss showed me that you feel safe enough with me to let your guard down a bit. I hope...I can continue to show you just how special you are." He walked in front of me, cupped my chin, and looked into my eyes. "So...incredibly...special," he said slowly, as if each word were its own sentence.

He pressed a small kiss just next to my lips, and I knew it was so I could pull away if I wanted to and not feel forced into it. The fact that he thought about that meant the world to me. Before he had time to pull away, I turned my lips to his. As soon as our lips met, he pulled me gently to his chest. Everything went silent. All the chaos in my mind vanished the second our lips met and I was in his arms.

I leaned into him, one hand on his arm and one around the back of his neck. My heart was racing. Nothing about our movements was rushed. He was letting me lead, letting me set the pace. I had never felt so safe in my entire life.

Slowly, he moved one hand to the back of my neck, and with the back of his other hand gently rubbed my arm. My body somehow felt numb and every nerve felt alive at the same time. I started to smile while kissing him and he

130

pulled back slightly to look at me. His blue eyes almost had a glow to them.

"That was..." I didn't even know how to describe that kiss.

"I feel like any word would be an understatement." He chuckled. The sound of his laugh was music to my ears.

"Ye— mhm." I tried to form a word, but he gently touched my cheek with the back of his fingers, and I lost my train of thought. He leaned in, kissing my forehead, and I closed my eyes, hoping this moment would never end.

Chapter 29

Caleb

After that kiss, Rae asked if she could help with something. I showed her where the chicken feed was and then told her about the apples for the horses that I had in the house.

The kiss, the moment, had just ended, and I already wanted her back in my arms. She needed to know how special she was, and I wanted to show her just how much I cared.

I looked up from wiping down my tools after changing the oil on my truck. I saw her out in the coop talking to the chickens. I couldn't hear what she was saying, but I heard their clucking, and they all seemed rather happy. She leaned down and scooped up one of the chickens. It was the only black and white chicken, and it seemed to take to her immediately. She held it the entire time she was in the coop, even fed it by hand.

Seeing her like this brought back memories of us in high school, out here on the farm. She had always been an animal person—so tender with them—and I had always teased her that she used our friendship so she could come to see the animals. She swore that was the farthest from the truth, but she was always so content when she was out here, I knew it was a favorite thing of hers.

I walked to the sink in the barn so I could wash my hands and run cool water over my head and face. I should've changed the oil in my truck when it was cooler, but the clouds looked like they could dump buckets on us at any moment, and I didn't want to wait any longer.

I heard a small voice behind me and turned to see Rae was back in the barn, feeding apples to the horses and talking to them.

"Having fun?" I kept my distance, gripping the edge of the barn sink harder than necessary just to try and have some self-control. Gosh, all I wanted to do was walk over to her and wrap her in my arms—show her she was safe with me and how much I loved her.

Her smile could've lit up a dark room. It was the biggest and most genuine smile I had seen since she had come back to town.

"Yes, I am. That black and white chicken in the coop was so cute and seemed to like being held, and this big guy"—she rubbed the nose of one of the horses, my mom's horse— "he's loving this apple."

She must've noticed the change in my expression because there was no hiding it. I tried but failed.

"Hey, Caleb. Now I'm asking, are you okay?"

"Yeah, sorry. That chicken's name is Pepper, and this..." I shook off the memories running through my head and ran a hand across my face. I crossed the space between Rae and me, hoping she didn't mind, and petted the horse's nose. "This was my mom's horse. Bandit. She got him as a foal a few months before she passed. They bonded, and when she died, he got depressed. My brother and I did everything to help him, but he never acted the way he did with my mom, with anyone else—until now.

The way he noses you, the way he closes his eyes when you pet him—he was like that with her. Not even with any other woman."

Rae turned around to face me, and Bandit put his face over her shoulder, pulling her back towards his stall.

"Hi, baby. His momma was special. I liked her, too." She looked up at me and her eyes softened, like she understood everything I hadn't said out loud.

"Bandit hasn't done that with anyone besides my mom either. I think he's chosen you as his person." As soon as I said that, Bandit happily nickered and pushed Rae forward—right into my arms.

Both of us stood there laughing, the world around me narrowing to just her. I reached up to brush hair out of Rae's face and my hand lingered as I tucked the strands behind her ear. She stilled and, to my surprise, leaned slightly into my hand. I could feel her pulse racing and hoped it wasn't entirely nerves. My pulse matched the speed of hers, and for a second, I wondered if she could feel the same charge running between us that I did.

"I think Bandit has great taste," I whispered. Rae's cheeks flushed, and she dropped her gaze, but not before I caught the smallest smile tugging at her lips. I didn't say anything else. I didn't need to. The air between us had already said enough.

Chapter 30

Rae

I heard Caleb walking around his room, opening and closing drawers, to find clothes to wear after his shower. We both desperately needed to clean up after working outside.

Since the rain hadn't come, we'd hung out in the barn after finishing up the chores until the sun went down. I realized I hadn't thought of anything besides Caleb and being here with him while we were out there. It was nice.

I had showered, dressed, and was searching for my extra toothpaste in my bag on the counter. I had only found travel sizes of my toothpaste before coming to stay with Caleb and hadn't remembered to order it online yet.

I heard Caleb open his bedroom door and walk past the guest bathroom. Duke sniffed at the guest bathroom door and the sound made me laugh. I love that dog and his silly personality.

"Come on, boy. Give her time. She'll be out with us soon…Good boy, Duke." The way he spoke to Duke, praising him when he listened and speaking kindly even when he didn't, it made me smile. I always loved how sweet Caleb was with animals.

I froze, realizing something that made me happy and scared me at the same time. I also loved how he was with me. His gentle words and how patient he was with me—was I falling for Caleb? I mean, I'd always liked him, maybe even loved him, but was it too soon after everything that happened?

When I kissed him earlier, it was like nothing I had ever experienced.

I finished looking through my bag and still hadn't found my extra toothpaste. Frustrated, I left the bathroom and walked into my room. Maybe I threw it into the wrong bag while I was packing at my parents' house.

"Ugh I am such an idiot. Where did I put it?" I grumbled to myself as I shoved the bag back onto the bed and knelt to search under the bed.

"I can promise you, there are no monsters allowed under the beds in this house," I heard Caleb's voice at the door. I looked up at him and realized how silly I must look. I stood up quickly and felt dizzy. I started to stumble and Caleb crossed the room in a couple of steps, grabbing my elbow to support me. Duke ran to us and sat at our feet.

"Easy, Sunshine. You okay?"

The spinning feeling finally stopped. "Yeah, sorry. I must have just stood up too fast. Thank you for helping. I was trying to find my other toothpaste since I ran out of the one in the bathroom. I can't seem to find it, though."

"Why don't you use mine until we can get you some more?" he said as he let go of my elbow.

"You want to share toothpaste with me?" I asked, figuring I misunderstood what he meant.

The look on my face must have shown how confused I was because Caleb laughed. "I can run to the store, if you're opposed to that, and we can order more. However, in the meantime, yes. Just use mine."

"You...don't mind?" I waited for him to say he was just kidding, but he didn't.

"Nah. We've kissed a couple of times, and I would gladly kiss you again, if you let me. It wouldn't have bothered me before, and it bothers me even less now." He winked at me, knowing the mention of our kiss and the wink combined would cause me to blush. He wasn't wrong.

"I'll go get it for—" a deep roll of thunder cut Caleb off. "Hold on. I have to take Duke out before it starts raining really bad. You can get it if you want, or I can when I come back inside."

I smiled at him as he left the room, appreciating his kindness. I headed to his room and walked past the windows where lightning streaked across the sky. Thunder boomed loudly, shaking the entire house and causing me to jump.

"I'm okay," I kept telling myself as lightning flashed and booms of thunder made the walls shake. I hate storms. Ethan always...

No. I'm not thinking about that right now. I am safe with Caleb.

I forced myself to start looking for his toothpaste and not stand there, frozen. I heard the front door open, and Caleb laughed as Duke shook, probably trying to shake all the water off his fur.

I opened a drawer and saw it in a drawer organizer, right next to his toothbrush.

"Hey, Rae, did you find the toothpaste?" Caleb called from the front room. I could hear him laughing still, and it sounded like it was because Duke had the zoomies.

"Yup! I—"

Suddenly, lightning struck and all the lights in the house went off. I froze. *No. This can't be happening.* I dropped to the floor and scooted back until my back hit the wall. I tried to scream, to call for Caleb, but nothing came out. My chest felt tight, and it hurt to breathe.

I heard footsteps running down the hall and into the bedroom. They sounded just as loud as the thunder.

Oh no, Ethan is here. I was wedged into the corner of the bathroom wall and the cabinets. I was cornered and had nowhere to go, and nothing to protect myself with.

I heard a voice. It was a man's voice. *Oh my gosh, he's here. He found me.*

The footsteps stopped and the voice said something, but I couldn't make it out. It didn't really matter what he said to me. The actions always hurt more.

Lightning lit up the bathroom and the silhouette of the source of the footsteps was right in front of me. *He found me.*

I pushed harder against the wall and kicked my foot at him as he backed up and sat across from me. Was he taunting me? He spoke again and I felt like I was going to be sick. There was a weird tapping sound as he spoke. Then a moment later, I heard a thump, then he spoke again, right before a flash of lightning filled the room. I wished my eyes could adjust enough for me to see before the darkness swallowed me whole again.

Why was he not moving towards me? *I wish he would just get whatever he had planned over with.*

Thunder shook the wall my back was against and I tried to not react, to not show my fear, but he knew. He said something to me and a wave of nausea came over me again. I felt like I was going to throw up, but if I did, I would be vulnerable and he could use that to his advantage. I tried to calm myself, but it felt like my throat was closing up. I started to gasp for air and felt like I was choking.

He said something and moved towards me. I jumped. I was still cornered.

He touched my arm and the wave of anxiety only grew as I wondered what he was waiting for.

I had to fight. My arms felt like they were made of lead, but I had to try. He tried to speak to me again, but I couldn't focus on his words. I just had to fight. I felt his hands on my leg, then my arms, and I tried to scream again, but nothing came out. I pushed and hit, but he was too strong. I knew I had scratched him, but it hadn't stopped him.

"Rae! Sunshine! It's me!" I heard Caleb's voice.

"Caleb, help!" I cried.

"Rae, honey..." Suddenly, I felt arms wrap around me and hold me close. They didn't squeeze, but instead they just held me. "Sunshine, it's me. You're safe. I promise. It's me. I got you."

"Caleb?" My voice squeaked when I said his name.

"Yeah, honey. It's me, Ranger." He ran his fingers through my hair in an attempt to comfort me.

I grabbed his shirt and pulled him closer than he already was. I buried my face against his chest and tried to match my breathing to his. Caleb kept whispering things I couldn't quite make out, but the sound of his voice was enough to keep me anchored.

Little by little, the world stopped spinning. My hands were still trembling, but his warmth didn't leave. For the first time since the lights went out, I felt a flicker of safety.

Chapter 31

Caleb

Lightning struck, quickly followed by rolling thunder so loud I felt it in my bones.

"Come on Duke, we gotta go in before—"

As if the sky was taunting me, it immediately opened the floodgates. Duke had almost made it back to the porch before the rain began, too.

Duke jumped up on the porch and skidded to a stop at the door. "I'm sorry, buddy. I had no idea it would rain that hard, that fast." I opened the door to let us in and asked him to sit in the entryway while I grabbed a towel from the laundry room. Duke shook before we came in, but water spots still speckled the floor when he shook again. The look on his face made me laugh because I could tell he really hated the rain and was not too pleased with me right now for the last-minute bathroom break.

Duke sat at the door. He was such a good boy, but I needed to hurry before he couldn't handle sitting still any longer.

I grabbed a clean towel and walked back to Duke, still sitting like a perfect gentleman.

"Good boy, Duke." I dried him off as best as I could and then released him so he could let his zoomies out.

I smiled to myself as I looked down the hall and saw my bathroom light was on. Rae was getting the toothpaste by herself, so that means she trusts me enough to know I am not setting her up to using it and then getting mad—good.

I laughed as Duke spun around in the middle of the room before stopping, only to run, spin, and stop again. *Gosh, I wish Rae was out here to see this.*

"Hey, Rae, did you find the toothpaste?" I called to her while laughing at this crazy dog.

"Yup, I—"

Lightning struck, and we were in immediate darkness. *Crap.* I checked my pockets and didn't have my cell phone with me. *Where did I even leave it?* I walked to the couch and felt around but couldn't find my phone. Normally, I'd be fine since I knew this house like the back of my hand, but I also didn't have any candles or lanterns ready for Rae.

I started to walk swiftly down the hallway to the closet where I kept the lanterns when I heard a loud thud, followed by a groan sound. *Did she fall?* "Rae, honey! I'm coming now. I'm sorry I don't have my phone with me to give us light."

Lightning struck and it illuminated my path to the bathroom for half a second.

"Hey, Sunshine. I'm here." I really need to get solar night-lights for moments like this. I heard small thudding sounds near the ground like something was hitting the bathroom cabinets.

Lightning struck again behind me, and I saw her curled up in the corner of the bathroom, wedged in the corner of the cabinet and the wall. *Crap.*

"Hey, Sunshine, it's Caleb. I'm walking up to you."
I felt her foot make contact with mine and then it sounded
like she was flailing her arms and only making contact
with the cabinets. She was trying to protect herself—
good. The smallest sounds came from her direction, but
no words.

I needed to try and talk her down before making any
contact, so I sat a couple feet away from her.

Lightning blinded us every few minutes, and the
thunder shook the entire house. Duke seemed worried
about Rae but also scared of the thunder, so he tried to run
to her for comfort and to comfort her.

"Hey, not right now, Duke. Lie down, boy." I could
hear his claws tapping on the bathroom tiles, and then I
felt him press against my leg before lying down with a big
thud. "Good boy, Duke."

I spoke to Rae again, just letting her know I was here,
and she sounded like she was struggling to breathe—like
she was choking. Oh my gosh, my attempt at calming her
did nothing to help. I instantly felt horrible.

"Rae, it's Caleb. It's me, honey." I moved in front of
her.

"Caleb," she squeaked out, and my heart broke. She
was terrified.

I reached out and touched her leg to try and make
some gentle contact. She kicked me. I pulled back
quickly. I didn't know what to do besides try and wrap her
in my arms so she could feel it was me. She hit and kicked
me, but I didn't care. I needed her to know she was safe

because right now, she was terrified. Sharp pain hit my jaw, and I felt blood start to trickle down my neck.

"Rae! Sunshine! It's me!" I shouted. She stilled for a heartbeat and then started to fight again. "Caleb, help!" she cried. Her voice was so faint, so scared.

"Rae, honey, I've got you," I told her as I wrapped my arms around her. I didn't squeeze her so she didn't think I was trying to hurt her.

I just held her. "Sunshine, it's me. You're safe. I promise it's me. I got you," I whispered the promise to her.

I'm not sure if it was my words, me holding her, or both, but she said my name clearly this time.

"Yeah, honey. It's me, Ranger." I ran my fingers through her hair, hoping it would comfort her and bring her back to me.

She grabbed my shirt and pulled me closer than I already was. I continued to whisper to her that she was safe with me as I ran my fingers through her hair. She buried her face against my chest, and I felt her take a couple of deep breaths.

"I got you, Sunshine. I'm right here and I am not going to let you go."

A few moments passed before her breathing evened out, and her pulse slowed to a more normal rate.

I could tell she was nervous, but I didn't dare move—not until she was ready. When she finally loosened her grip, I knew she was starting to come back to me.

♥

She was still clinging to my shirt, but she seemed calmer than before. It was still dark in the house. Only the occasional flash of lightning lit up the room. I had offered to grab the candles, but she did not want me to leave her, so I waited until she said she was feeling a bit better.

"How are you doing, Sunshine?"

"Okay, I guess. I'm...really cold right now." A chill went through her, and I rubbed her back.

"Can I help you up?'

Rae nodded, so I held out my hand for her to hold as I wrapped my arm around her waist and lifted her up.

"It's so dark, Caleb." We held hands as I started to move us out of the bathroom, but she moved her arms to wrap around mine.

"I know. I'm really sorry, I couldn't find my phone or get any light before I ran to find you." Thunder shook the house and Rae jumped. "Sorry. That startled me." I could hear the fear in her voice.

While it was dark in my room, I could see the outline of my dresser and the open door next to it. If she was okay with it, I could quickly move through the house to get the lanterns. I stopped walking and turned towards her. Keeping my voice low, "Hey Rae, do you trust me? I won't be upset if you say no."

"Yes, of course."

I reached up to touch her cheek with the back of my fingers. "Why don't you sit on the bed with Duke and I'll go get the lights? It will be quick and you don't have to walk around in darkness."

"Duke can stay with me?"

"On one condition. When I am back with the lights, you let me be the one who makes you feel safe again. It's where I'm meant to be—right there with you." I kissed her forehead and for the first time since the power went out, she seemed to relax.

"I can try that."

"Okay. Duke, go to bed." I heard him hop up on the bed and lie down, so I led Rae to the bed. "I'll only be gone for a couple minutes, promise."

She acknowledged me with only a sound, and I left her side to find the lights and candles.

I left the room, but part of me stayed right there— with her and Duke—exactly where I belonged.

Chapter 32

Rae

I sat on the bed as I heard Caleb walk to the door of the room. He said he would only be gone a couple of minutes, and I believed him, but it didn't help my fear of the darkness.

My eyes had adjusted some, but it didn't help that lightning occasionally messed that up. Every noise seemed amplified. I heard Caleb's footsteps, the creaking of the house with the wind, and every noise seemed louder than normal.

I needed to focus on something else for the time he was gone, so I reached out to touch Duke. The sweet pup pushed his cold, wet nose against my hand before standing up and coming to where I sat. I felt him turn and face away from me, and I knew it was because he was watching out for me. He sensed I was scared and understood that Caleb wanted him to stay with me. I pet his head and back, feeling a bit calmer.

"Hey, Rae, I got the lanterns and flashlights, but I am trying to look for the extra batteries I thought I had in here. Are you doing okay?"

"I—think so." Duke nosed my hand before turning around to watch out for me again.

"Okay, Sunshine. I will only be a couple more minutes. I'm so sorry."

"No. It's okay." I tried to be brave or at least sound like I was. I felt so bad that he was doing all of this for me, that I was crippled by the fear. I was so embarrassed.

My thoughts were interrupted when I heard noise coming from the front room, like Caleb was ripping open cardboard packaging. Maybe he found the batteries.

A few moments passed before light illuminated the front room and I saw Caleb holding a little lantern. I breathed a sigh of relief as he picked up the box and walked towards the bedroom.

"Hey, sorry it took so long. I apparently forgot to put the batteries in the box after I bought them."

He walked over, set the little lantern on the nightstand, and began lighting the candles, filling the room with a soft glow.

♥

It had been a long time since the power had gone out, and while the storm had shifted to just rain, the power had not been restored. Caleb's and my phones had died about two hours after the power went out and it was kind of nice to be cut off from the world, since I was here and safe with him.

Duke was lying at the foot of the bed, and I sat across from Caleb, surprised at the calm feeling in me. If I had been in this situation without Caleb, it would have felt suffocating. I wouldn't have been able to come out of the panic attack. However, with him, I felt strong, maybe even brave.

He had brought us snacks from the kitchen since we couldn't cook dinner. We were having jerky, cashews, and crackers with peanut butter for dinner, and I enjoyed the simplicity of it.

"Want another cracker?" Caleb asked as he held out a sleeve of them.

I laughed at the idea because I was so full. "No, thank you, though."

He smiled at me, the flames of the candles on the nightstand flickering in his blue eyes. The warm light they gave off caused the red tint in his beard to stand out more. He was so handsome.

He placed the crackers and jar of peanut butter on the nightstand and then shifted closer to me. Our legs were crisscrossed in front of us, and that was the only thing preventing him from coming closer. He took my hands in his and looked at me, like really looked at me. I found myself thankful for the darkness the power outage brought because I knew I was blushing. I looked down at our hands, feeling nervous and shy but somehow safe at the same time.

"How are you feeling, Sunshine?" His voice was warm and comforting, like when he had pulled me out of my panic attack earlier. That voice, *his* voice, is what brought me back to reality.

If I was honest, I was embarrassed and ashamed, but I didn't want to admit it.

He reached up and pushed my hair behind my ear, leaving his hand at my jaw and gently moving it along my skin. "Honey, there is no reason to be embarrassed about having a panic attack."

My eyes immediately met his and locked in. "How—how did you know exactly what I was thinking?" *Did I say what I was thinking and not realize it?*

"Because I know my girl." His thumb traced back and forth along my jaw. That movement, the fact that he *did* know me so well, and the smile he gave me caused warmth to bloom through me, melting the fear I didn't realize I was still holding, reminding me what safety was supposed to feel like.

"I scratched you, though, bad enough that you bled, I kicked at you...I let my fear take over. I only snapped out of it because you made me feel safe, even after I hurt you."

Caleb shook his head and leaned in. "And I would gladly do anything for you if it meant that you felt safe and cared for."

I wanted to kiss him. I was nervous about what would happen next, but I so badly wanted to kiss him. I leaned forward, and he did the same just as the lantern flickered and went out.

"Dang it. That lantern was one I didn't think I needed to change the batteries in yet. Just a minute."

Caleb straightened his legs as he started to get up, but I put my hand on his arm, stopping him. "Wait." Nerves and excitement made my pulse race as I scooted closer to him, placing one leg on either side of him, scooting as close as I could. The light in the room was dimmer than before, with the glow of a few candles.

"Hey," he said with a smile on his face as he placed one hand on my thigh and the other on my hip. I instantly grew nervous at how intimate this was. *I shouldn't have done this because, what if he is now expecting something and I'm too scared to do it?*

I was frozen and couldn't move to kiss him, and I couldn't move away. I felt his arms around me, and he pulled me into a hug.

"I love hugging you," he said in my ear. I wrapped my arms around him. I loved hugging him, too. I felt so safe with him, so why could I not move past this and kiss him in a moment like this? I buried my head in the curve where his neck meets his shoulder, breathing in the warm scent of his soap and the oil he used on his beard, and he wrapped his arms tighter around me.

Several silent minutes passed, with only the sounds of our breathing and his pulse in my ear.

"What's on your mind?"

He knew me too well. I couldn't lie to him, even if I wanted to.

"I don't want to tell you because I'm afraid it will disappoint you."

"Disappoint me? Rae, I think that would be impossible for you to do. Look at me." I lifted my head so I could look at him, and he moved one of his hands to my cheek. "Tell me, please?"

I took a deep breath. "After you said you would do anything for me…and then when you started to get up because the lantern battery died, I saw how sweet you were being because you didn't want me to be scared. I asked you to wait because I really wanted to kiss you, but then…"

He rubbed my cheek with his thumb, like he understood.

"But then I sat like this and it felt so...intimate. I got nervous because, what if you expected more and I got your hopes up?"

Caleb shook his head, his thumb tracing slow circles along my cheek. "Rae," he said softly, "you never have to worry about disappointing me. You don't owe me anything—not a kiss, not a single thing you're not ready for." He leaned in a little closer, his voice steady. "I don't want *more*, I just want *you*—whatever that means. You being here, letting me hold you—that's enough for me. Always will be."

His words sank into me, quiet and sure, and something inside me eased. The tension in my chest that I hadn't even realized I was holding started to fade with every slow brush of his thumb against my skin.

He didn't look at me like I was fragile. He looked at me like I was *his*—not in a way that claimed me, but in a way that promised I was safe here. Safe with him.

My throat tightened. Caleb saw the real me. Before I could stop myself, I leaned in just a little closer. Our lips met with a lingering kiss that felt like a promise. My fingers curled into his shirt, and I pulled him with me as I lay against the pillows. We continued to kiss slowly until I couldn't keep from smiling. Caleb smiled back at me before pulling me close, so I rested against his chest. I realized how tired I felt as I lay in his arms.

He started to pull the covers up when he stopped and started to sit up. "I almost forgot, we have to change the batteries in the big lantern and blow out the candles."

"Caleb, wait. Did you change the batteries in the little lantern on my nightstand?"

"Yes, but that's a rechargeable one, and thankfully I had recharged the battery and not had to use it yet. I don't know how long it will last."

"Just blow out the candles. Don't get out of bed. Please." I looked at him, realizing what I was asking for, but knowing I would be safe with him.

He looked at me, searching for any hesitation I may have, but he wasn't going to find any.

I turned and blew out the candles on my nightstand before turning back to him. He kissed my forehead before turning to blow out the candles on his side.

Darkness surrounded us, but Caleb pulled me close. "You still okay? You can change your mind at any point."

While I didn't like the darkness, I didn't need the light with him. "Better than okay," I murmured while burying my face in his chest.

For the first time in a long time, I didn't need the light to feel safe—and I fell asleep with that truth wrapped around me.

Chapter 33

Caleb

I turned from the pantry and looked at Rae who I had placed on the kitchen island. She sat there, with her feet swinging slightly, as she munched on cereal she pulled out of the box piece by piece.

The power had come back on, but since it had been off for almost twelve hours, the food in the refrigerator was spoiled.

The red in her auburn hair shone in the light from the kitchen window. She pushed her glasses up with the back of her hand and popped another bite of cereal into her mouth, her messy bun moving each time she swung her feet.

She looked at me and smiled. *Gosh, I would do anything to make her smile like that every day.*

"So, what's the plan today?" she asked between bites of cereal.

I walked to the counter and leaned on it, just barely brushing her leg. "I have to go check on the horses and make sure the fence didn't get damaged in the storm. Then I figured we would prepare food for tomorrow night, so I have to go to the store, too."

"Can I come?" She sounded excited.

"Grocery shopping with my girl? My best friend? I wouldn't have it any other way." I reached into the cereal box and popped a couple pieces in my mouth.

154

She had been smiling but the look on her face changed. She looked far away for a moment but then resumed munching on cereal, piece by piece.

"Where did your mind go, Sunshine?"

"You said 'best friend.' It just had me thinking about something for a moment."

She closed the cereal box and slid off the counter, walking to the pantry to put it away.

"I was thinking about my best friend I left. I wasn't as close to her as you and I are, or how close we had been with Jenny and Luke, but she was the closest I had had to a best friend before..."

She looked at me and knew she didn't have to say anything. I already knew.

"How long has it been since you spoke with her?"

"A couple years. We could only hang out or talk when Ethan was around, near the end of the friendship. Then, he cut the friendship off entirely. She was the last relationship he cut off because he knew she lived close by. I have not tried reaching out. I honestly don't know if she would want me to call. It's fine. Just a silly thought I had."

I could tell she didn't want to talk about it anymore, so I walked to where she stood and offered my hand to her. "It's not a silly thought, and if you ever want to try and contact her again, I will be right there with you, if you want me to be. She would be lucky to have you back in her life."

She smiled that million-dollar smile at me again, and it confirmed what I already knew. Anyone would be lucky to have her in their life. I knew I was.

♥

I was making dinner for tonight and tomorrow, when Jenny and Luke were coming over. Rae was at the kitchen island working on a batch of cookies. She seemed so happy still, like facing her fear of the dark last night was like a reset her heart and mind needed.

I put the food in the oven and set the timer before walking to the sink to wash my hands.

As I passed by her, I gave her a small smile and then kept looking at her from across the kitchen. I couldn't get enough of her. Just being around her felt like...Home. She caught me staring. "Do I have something on my face?"

"Actually, yeah. Here, I'll get it for you." I crossed the small space and in one swift motion dipped a finger in the flour and brushed it on her cheek.

She began laughing. Gosh, I would never tire of hearing her laugh.

"Caleb, I'm gonna get you for that!" she shouted as she swiped flour across my chin. We both stood there laughing, and I threw my hands up as if I was surrendering.

"Okay, okay. We should probably be mature adults." She giggled.

As soon as she started to turn back to the counter, I flicked flour at her, laughing the entire time.

"Oh, now you're asking for it," she said as she tossed flour at me again.

We began to have a flour fight. We ducked behind the counter and held up cookie sheets to block ourselves from getting hit. Duke watched from the couch, and laughter filled the kitchen.

The battle only ended when I caught her around the waist, pulling her away from grabbing another handful of flour. "Nope, I gotcha this time!" I lifted her off the ground as she laughed uncontrollably. I spun her away from the flour and sat her on the counter. Standing between her legs, I stared at her, getting lost in her green eyes. Even covered in flour, she looked beautiful. Her smile was so bright.

My thumb rubbed the inside of her wrist. Heat coiled low in my stomach, but I forced myself to breathe steadily. This wasn't about me. It was about her.

I picked up the towel next to us and began wiping flour off her face. I gently wiped the towel across her forehead and cheek, then went to the sink to get a bit of warm water on it. I felt her eyes on me the entire time.

I stood in front of her again and began wiping at the remaining traces of flour on her face.

Much to my surprise, she leaned in and kissed me so lightly. I slowly returned the kiss as I put my hands around her hips and pulled her closer to me. Her kisses were timid, and I followed her lead. Her arms were resting on my shoulders and one hand traced circles on the back of my head.

I moved my hands from her hips to her lower back, and my finger traced the small space where her shirt had lifted. I moved slow enough that if she wanted to pull back, she could.

When I touched her skin, I felt her smile through her kiss. After a moment, I put my hand under the back of her shirt, tracing her curves with my fingers. She stilled for a brief moment, and I pulled my hands back from her body.

"Do you want me to stop?"

"No, sorry, I just needed a second." Her eyes were closed and she took a deep breath. Then another.

"Sunshine, you just say the word and I'll stop at any point."

She smiled and then leaned in and kissed me again.

I kissed her back and then trailed kisses down her jaw and then throat. I saw a smile cross her face before her head fell back. I stopped at her collarbone and pulled her tank strap down so I could kiss her shoulder. Her breath stilled for a brief moment, and I watched her out of the corner of my eye.

When I felt her relax, I continued and let my hands wander again, taking my time but remembering how her ex had hurt her. She moved her arms off my shoulders to touch my arms and I smiled at her before putting her arms back on my shoulders.

"Not yet, Sunshine, it's my time to take care of you. I promise I will not do anything to hurt you. That okay?" I whispered in her ear as I ran my fingers up and down her arms. She breathlessly nodded, and I continued kissing from her ear down her neck again.

Each of my movements was slow and careful. I wanted her to know what it's like to be loved, cared for. The bastard that hurt her didn't know what he would be losing.

158

I moved my hand under the back of her shirt, tracing the lines of her bra straps while my other cupped her cheek while I kissed her.

I began to lift her shirt up over her head, but she stopped me—not deliberately. It's as if it was a reflex.

"Hey, Sunshine, talk to me."

"I'm so sorry, I'm just nervous. What if you don't like what I look like or—"

I lovingly shushed her. "Not like what you look like? Rae, you're perfection. Beautiful."

"I don't know. I just hate my body. My thighs and my stomach—"

"Are amazing. Curvy. Perfect. I want to show you how amazing I think you are. I want to see and kiss every curve. Treat you how you deserve." I brushed a few strands of her hair behind her ear. "But if you're not ready, we can stop."

She had tears in her eyes and I immediately noticed. "Hey, did I say something wrong?" I reached up and wiped at the tear that fell.

While shaking her head, she put my hands on the hem of her shirt and kissed me deeply.

I didn't rush her. I moved her shirt up a couple inches at a time, tracing her spine with my fingers as I went. I could feel her shaking slightly, but she didn't stop me.

When her shirt was off, she started to move her arms to cover her stomach, but I stopped her. I placed her arms over my shoulders again and looked into her eyes. I wanted her to have time to readjust, and she noticed the gesture.

"You are beautiful, Rae."

She smiled at me, nervousness still behind her eyes.

"Hold on. I'm going to move you off this counter so you're more comfortable."

She giggled as I picked her up and carried her to the couch. The sound of her laugh melted my heart. I laid her down, propping her head up with a pillow.

Just then, the timer on the stove went off. Dinner was done. "Don't move, Sunshine. I'll be right back."

She lay there on the couch, and when I glanced over at her, I saw her watching me. I gave her a smile and finished up what I had to do.

When I returned, I joined her on the couch and stared at her for a few seconds. "Gosh, Rae, you're stunning." She blushed.

I held her close, tracing my fingers along her shoulder and then around her back to her bra clasp, pausing for a few seconds.

"Can I?"

She swallowed and gave a soft "yeah."

I unhooked it and dropped one strap from her shoulder, pausing between each movement, giving her time to breathe. I kissed her bare shoulder and paused when she tensed slightly. When she didn't say anything, I continued to kiss my way down her chest, stopping right above her heart. "Your heart is safe with me," I whispered.

Slowly, I slid the straps down her arms and let the fabric fall.

My heart was already beating out of my chest, but now, it was beating so hard I was sure she could hear it.

160

I took a moment to look at her—not just her body, but really see her. The way her breathing quickened and her skin flushed. "Gosh, Rae, you're so damn beautiful." I brushed my fingers along her arm.

A small smile curled her lips as she looked at me.

I kissed just above her heart again and my fingers skimmed her waist, just below her ribs. I watched how her body reacted to my touch.

I leaned down and my lips grazed the slope of her right breast. Slow. Gentle. Her cheeks were stained pink. My hands moved slowly to her sides, near her ribcage.

That's when it happened. Her whole body stiffened and she turned away from me, shutting her eyes.

"Rae? Hey...talk to me."

"I'm so sorry. I need a minute."

I quickly moved back onto the couch and passed her the blanket behind me. She grabbed it and pulled it around her.

"Here you go. There's nothing to be..."

"I-I'm so—"

"There is nothing to be sorry for, Sunshine. You don't owe me anything." I reached out with an open hand but she pulled back and covered her face with her hands.

"I really wanted—I'm sor—" She got up and ran to her room. She shut the door behind her slowly, and then I heard her sob.

My heart dropped and I felt helpless. I hated that she still felt like she had to apologize to me. I wanted to go to her, to fix it, but I knew the only way to love her right now was to let her have the space she needed.

Chapter 34

Rae

The second I got into my room, I crumpled to the floor and started sobbing. He probably hates me because I ran from him. No one would ever forgive someone after that.

I cried until my eyes hurt and it felt like there were no tears left. I picked myself up off the floor and walked to the bed. The bed I didn't sleep in last night because I was with him, feeling safe. The man who had never hurt me. For two nights now, he let me sleep next to him, with no strings attached. But yet, I ran from him just now. I wanted to be with him, but my stupid brain got in the way.

I reached for my phone I had left on the nightstand and saw a text notification.

Caleb: No pressure to come out at all. I put your bra and shirt right outside the door for you. If you want, I can put dinner on a plate for you and leave it there too. Or you can join me if you want. I waited for you, just in case.

He waited for me. I looked at the time on the phone which read 7:30 p.m. I remembered the timer on the stove went off at about 6:45. *He must be really hungry since he waited for me to eat.* I stood up from the bed and walked to the door, the blanket still wrapped around me. I reached out and picked up my clothes he'd set outside the door. They were folded so neatly.

I glanced towards the couch where I had left him. He was sitting on the couch reading a book. He turned the page and glanced up at me with a small smile, just long enough that our eyes met before looking back at the book. I walked back in the room and closed the door behind me while I got dressed. *This man, this sweet man. He cares so much, and is being so patient with me, but I bet he won't try anything again for fear of me rejecting him.*

As soon as I was dressed again, I took a deep breath and opened the bedroom door.

Chapter 35

Caleb

I heard the spare bedroom door click as she turned the knob. She walked into the hallway as I looked up from my book and smiled at her. "Hey, Sunshine."

She was holding the blanket in front of her, shoulders sagging, one side of her mouth turned up in a strained smile. I could tell she was embarrassed and beating herself up.

"Come here." I patted the couch with my hand. She sat on the cushion next to me but not touching me, her face turned down. I heard her stomach growl and knew she had to be hungry. I knew I was, but I wanted to wait for her. "Hungry?"

"So-so." She shrugged.

I got up off the couch and went to the kitchen, pulling out plates and Tupperware.

I felt her eyes on me as I plated and reheated the food.

I poured a glass of sweet red wine for her and carried it and the food to her, setting it on the coffee table. When I was coming back with my food and wine, I saw her wipe a tear off her cheek.

I set my dinner down and sat next to her, facing her, only my leg touching hers. "Hey, what's wrong?"

She refused to look at me and her voice sounded gravelly when she spoke. "Why are you being so nice to me after—" She started to cry. Her entire body shook as tears fell, and my heart broke. I reached out a hand and touched her arm, gently moving my thumb along it. When she didn't pull back, I pulled her into a hug, hoping she wouldn't pull away. She didn't, so I gave her a gentle squeeze.

I tipped her chin so she was looking at me. "After you were brave? After you stood up for yourself and told me you needed a break? Rae, I'm not mad at you, or even disappointed. I'm proud of you. You told me what you needed."

"But I know you won't hurt me. I know you're not him." Her body shook as she tried to calm her breathing.

"Okay, but Sunshine, he hurt you—badly. No one should ever have to deal with anything you went through, or be kept from the world and people they love. I wouldn't be any better than him if I was mad at you."

She started to say something but stopped, just leaned her head on my shoulder.

"What are you thinking?" I asked, rubbing her arm, knowing it was a motion she was comfortable with.

"I feel broken. I think I'm broken. I feel like I'm always crying, and…What if I can never—" Her voice trailed off.

"You're not broken. Far from it. You're strong and brave. When you first came back to town, you were flinching when I touched you—but look at you now. You went through something traumatic, but now you are letting me hold you. You slept next to me twice now, you've even kissed me. You are learning to trust again. You're healing."

"I trust *you*."

"I'm honored you do. I won't ever do anything to betray that trust you have in me." I paused, letting those words sink in before continuing.

"Also, if you can't, then that's okay. If you want to try again, at your pace, then that's okay, too. No matter what, I'm not going anywhere." I wanted to say more, to tell her I loved her, but I didn't want her to feel obligated to say it back, or to think I was just saying it to make her feel better.

"Wait, what?" She blinked as if she heard me wrong.

I pulled her legs over mine, and when she didn't move away, I pulled her even closer in a gentle but firm hug.

"I'm not going anywhere, even if you decide you're never ready. You're strong and you will come back from this, but if you still decide you only want to go so far, I'll still be right here. Yours. If you want me to be."

Her eyes filled with tears and she nodded quickly, then buried her face in my chest as I hugged her. She clung to my shirt as if she was scared to let go.

I've loved you since high school, Rae, and I'm sorry I never said anything to you back then. But now I will do everything in my power to keep you safe and let you know how special you are.

Chapter 36

Rae

This morning had been a blur. Caleb and I had baked the cookies we forgot to finish last night and cleaned the rest of the way before Jenny and Luke came over for dinner. Caleb had been so kind last night and all day today. He made me laugh, flirted with me, kissed me, and kept his promise about not going anywhere. He didn't push the conversation. He made me feel normal.

He seemed excited that Jenny and Luke were coming over. I had seen them around the farm on the days they were here but I never did more than wave.

They would be here in just a few minutes, and I was excited and feeling kind of nervous—but why?

"Where's your head at, beautiful?" Caleb startled me, and I dropped the plate I was holding. He caught it before it hit the floor.

"I'm so sorry! I must have zoned out."

"It's okay." He smiled at me, and it felt like butterflies were flying around in my stomach. He set the plate on the table before turning to take the others from me that I'd pulled from the cabinet.

"I was just thinking...I don't actually know. I kind of feel nervous about Jenny and Luke coming over, but I'm not sure why."

Caleb's face turned thoughtful. "Do you think you're nervous about it since you've not had time with people alone, besides me?"

"Maybe? Ethan always controlled conversations. But what if we don't reconnect easily, or what if they say something and I get uncomfortable and make it awkward?"

Caleb chuckled as he wrapped an arm around me. "Rae, do not worry. If I see that you're feeling uncomfortable, I will change the subject or something. I'm not going to throw my girl to the wolves." I held him close, loving how he called me his girl.

"Don't hate me but I told them we won't be talking about college and where you lived. They know nothing and didn't even question why. If you want to tell them, that is your choice. Plus, if you need an out, just tap my shoulder or say you're going to use the restroom and then ask if I can help you with something. We'll figure it out."

We looked at each other, still wrapped in each other's arms. "What did I do to deserve you, Ranger?"

He kissed my forehead. "You existed" he said, his breath on my skin.

♥

"Dinner was great, you guys. And Rae, these cookies you made are so good. Thank you for having us over," Luke said before he took another bite.

"Agreed. This has been fun!" Jenny chimed in.

They were not wrong. The conversations flowed easily, and I was having fun. Caleb reached for my hand under the table and gave it a squeeze. I smiled at him in return.

Jenny and Luke exchanged a look and I looked down at my hand, fingers linked with Caleb's. His thumb moved

168

lazily along my thumb, sending a tingling feeling through my entire body.

"So, when is the horseback riding date?" Luke said as he picked up his sweet tea and grinned at me before taking a sip.

"Date? I was thinking more like a lesson." Caleb chuckled.

"Sure." Luke laughed. "Next thing you know, he'll be teaching you to 'hold on tight,'" he said with a wink as he sipped his sweet tea again.

"Luke!" I laughed and covered my face with my hand.

"Can't say I'd mind that." Caleb smirked and squeezed my hand.

Jenny laughed. "Oh my gosh! You two are ridiculous."

"Terrible. Absolutely terrible," I chimed in. My cheeks were warm but I couldn't stop smiling.

Caleb's thumb brushed along my thumb again and he smiled at me. "You love it."

He wasn't wrong.

Chapter 37

Caleb

The next morning, I reluctantly crawled out of bed. After dinner, Rae and I had stayed up late, talking about old memories with Luke and Jenny, and once they left, Rae and I stayed up even longer. When we decided to go to sleep, Rae stood at the doorway of the guest room, not wanting to assume she could just join me in my room. If she thought for one second that I wouldn't want her sleeping next to me, she couldn't be more wrong. Having her close to me made this house feel like home.

"Where are you going?" she asked sleepily, with a touch of sadness in her voice.

"I'm so sorry I woke you, baby." I had planned on leaving Duke with her and writing her a note to let her know where I was.

"Baby?" She blushed, a smile crossing her face.

I crawled back to her and rubbed her cheek with my hand. "Yeah, you okay if I call you that?"

"Mhm," she hummed while I gave her a gentle kiss.

"I have to get an early start today. I'm going to feed the animals and then maybe clean the barn before it gets too hot."

"Can I help? I told you I don't want to mooch off of you."

I chuckled. "I mean, you can, but if you don't want to, that's fine as well. It's going to be a long morning. Plus, it's not 'mooching off me' if you're going to be my girl-friend," I said with a wink.

"Your girlfriend?" The look on her face was a mix of happiness and shock. She looked so cute.

"Yeah, my girlfriend. I don't go around kissing just anyone. That's saved for one special person." I kissed her again and felt her smiling.

"I love the sound of that. Let me get dressed. Did you make coffee?" She sounded excited as she threw back the covers.

"Thankfully I remembered to prep the coffee pot last night. I'll bring you some. Be right back."

I walked out into the kitchen while she went through her clothes, trying to find something that would work for working in the barn. We had done laundry before Jenny and Luke came over for dinner so our clothes were mixed in the basket, in my room. If I had my way, she would move everything into my room and it would be our room.

I let Duke outside before walking back into the room just as she was pulling her pajama shorts down, trying to get dressed.

"Oh I'm sorry." I turned around to give her privacy. "I don't know why I didn't think you'd still be getting dressed."

Her voice was laced with confusion. "Why are you sorry?"

Without turning around I answered her, "Because I want to be respectful and I walked in on you changing."

Silence fell between us for a brief moment before I felt a hand rest on my back. I glanced behind me but didn't turn around.

"Caleb, thank you. I appreciate that, but I do want to be comfortable, in every way, one day. With you."

A smile tugged at the corner of my mouth.

"Plus, you've seen me with my top off already," she added playfully. "You don't have to turn around unless I ask you to." Her hand moved to my shoulder, and she made a slight pulling motion, as if to ask me to turn back around.

When I turned, I looked into her eyes, searching for any signs of hesitation, but I found none.

I passed her the cup of coffee. She thanked me and walked back to get dressed. I had only looked at her face until she walked away and I realized she hadn't put her shorts or pants back on before walking up to me.

I walked to the side of the bed I slept on and sat down, not completely facing her but still able to see her.

The soft morning light showed through the spot where the curtains met, and it made her ivory skin glow. Her long curvy legs, her hips, she had the most beautiful body I'd ever seen. I stared at her lustfully and reverently. She was everything I ever wanted but someone worth waiting for.

She started to talk to me as she lifted the shirt she wore to bed up over her head, turning to grab her bra and shirt. I could hear nerves in her voice as she only became more vulnerable, but she was trying so hard to be brave with me, something I would never take for granted.

Her shirt had been long enough to brush her thighs, and now that it was gone, I forgot how to breathe. The graceful line of her back, the curve of her hips—it all hit me at once, a rush of desire I fought to keep steady.

The nerves in her voice made her voice crack, which snapped me out of the trance I was in.

"Ranger?"

"I'm so sorry, Sunshine. I didn't hear what you said."

"Oh. You said 'yes' to one of my questions. What was the last thing you heard?"

I chuckled out of embarrassment. "Honestly, I don't even remember you asking me a question. I'm so sorry, I got lost in...Well—" I motioned my hands to her. All of her.

Sounding a bit shyer, Rae asked, "In what?"

Hoping my confession hadn't made her uncomfortable, I replied with another one, figuring I was already in deep. "My mind got lost while watching you. Gosh, you're beautiful, Rae."

Thirty seconds passed. Thirty seconds that felt like an eternity. "I'm sorry, I hope I didn't make you uncomfortable."

Turning a deep shade of red, Rae stared back at me. She opened her mouth and then closed it, not knowing what to say. She picked up her regular bra and changed into it instead of the sports bra.

"Rae, I..."

"I'm not uncomfortable. I'm sorry. I..." She let out a nervous, breathy giggle.

"Can I come over there?"

She nodded with a small smile on her face.

I walked over to her, desire tight in my chest, where she was still standing just in a bra, socks, and panties. What mattered more than my feelings was making sure she saw it wasn't just that—it was her.

I tipped her chin up so she could look at me. "Can I hold you?"

She answered by stepping towards me and wrapping her arms around me.

I wrapped my arms around her, feeling her soft skin as I touched her. "Can I try something? You can tell me to stop and I will. Promise."

She nodded without even asking what I was thinking.

With just the tips of my fingers, I began to slowly trace the curves of her body.

I ran gentle fingers along her shoulder blade and spine, her waist and up to her rib cage. She tensed and started to pull away. I reached for her hand, and she let me hold it. Our eyes never strayed from each other. She trusted me, but I could tell she was still nervous, hesitant. Her brain was lying to her, telling her not to trust me.

She didn't pull farther away, so I pulled her close again, wrapping my arm around her and putting a gentle and firm hand on her back. I made sure my voice was calm and gentle when I spoke to her. "Hey baby. Stay. Look at my face."

Her breathing was a bit more erratic, but not at the level it was the other night.

"Do you trust me?"

She swallowed hard and nodded. "I do. I promise."

"Please try this. Trust that I won't hurt you. I won't do anything I *know* you won't like. If you don't like this or if you are uncomfortable, stop me, at any point. Okay?"

Her green eyes were locked on mine. "I trust you," she whispered before she rested her head against me.

Gosh. Her saying those three words meant so much more than she would ever know. Rae trusting me after what she went through was the greatest honor.

I placed her hand that I had been holding around me. My fingertips grazed her curves as soft as a whisper. My touch never lingered in one spot. I traced the curve of her back and her hips, gently running my fingers along her rib cage, right under her chest. She tensed, and her breath hitched, but she didn't pull away. When my hand moved away from her ribs, I felt her body relax. It was like her brain was starting to rewire itself.

Her heart knew I wouldn't hurt her, but her brain still had walls up—walls that were slowly crumbling. After what that sick bastard did to her, I couldn't blame her for being hesitant or even terrified of letting anyone close.

Rae timidly put her shaky hands on my chest and then pressed her body closer to mine. My hand was still on the small of her back, and I could now feel her shaking more than before.

"I will never hurt you, baby," I whispered to her before I kissed her temple. She smelled like peaches and flowers, and it drove me wild.

Every part of me wanted to scoop her up and take care of her in every way, but I didn't want to scare her. My fingertips trailed, feather light, up and down her back.

When I finally moved past that, I was sure the lies in her brain would scream at her, making her move away, but she didn't.

Please be comfortable with me, baby, I silently pleaded.

My touch was unhurried as my hands moved over her hips and down the length of her thighs before gliding back up, warm and steady. I wasn't pushing for more; I was reminding her of the truth she was still learning to believe.

She was safe here. Safe with me.

"You okay, Sunshine?" I kissed the top of her head still resting against me.

She nodded and was still shaking some but didn't move.

"You sure? Did I push it too far?"

She shook her head.

"Hey...what are you thinking?" I ran my fingers through her hair.

She tilted her head back to look at me. It was like she was staring into my soul, searching for something. After a moment, she buried her head against me again. "I'm thinking...that I want to...try again, with you. I liked that." A giggle bubbled out of her. "Gosh—I really liked that. My heart knows I'm safe with you, Ranger. My brain..."

She looked up at me, and I touched her cheek. She leaned into my hand.

"Is lying to you?"

She nodded.

176

"Then I'll just have to keep telling it what the truth is, and hopefully soon, it will know what your heart knows." I kissed her forehead. She closed her eyes, leaning into me more.

We stayed like this for a few minutes until Duke barked at the door, upset he was outside alone.

Rae let out a breathy laugh. "Something my heart knows at the moment is that if we don't go outside to feed the animals, I may never want to leave your arms."

"I wouldn't mind that." I kept my voice playful. "How about I go pull out the food for the animals and then you meet me out there when you're ready?"

She nodded, and I left her with a smile.

Chapter 38

Caleb

I was glad I asked for a few days off because this time with her, it was good for both of us—absolutely necessary. We'd gotten closer emotionally and reconnected more than we already had before she moved in. Physically, I could tell she was feeling more comfortable with me, especially after what I just did—her allowing me to touch her skin more. I could feel the shift coming, the one I wanted for her more than anything. But if I was being honest, I wanted it for us, too.

She seemed happier now since facing another fear with me, and I could see the sunshine coming back into her eyes. While I wanted normalcy for her, for us, a part of me also wished we didn't have to go back to work in a few days. Not hearing from Ethan at all worried me, but I had hoped he decided to move on.

"Where's Duke?" she asked while looking around.

"I took him inside because...I have an idea," I said to her as she walked towards the barn after feeding the chickens. I'd been watching her, admiring how she was with the animals. She was so sweet and loving with every single one of them, I knew she'd love what I was about to say.

She brushed her stray hairs out of her face and gave me a curious look.

I reached out a hand and when she took it, I pulled her close. I wrapped my arm around her waist and leaned into her, a motion that she'd grown comfortable with quickly. She blushed, giggling under her breath, and something in my chest pulled tight. That sound—*gosh*—it nearly undid me.

"How do you feel about taking a ride with me?"

"Wait, like...on the horses?" she asked with such excitement, her voice echoed in the barn.

The look on her face when I nodded was one that would stick in my brain for the rest of my life. She was ecstatic. She loved the horses and going riding with me when we were teens.

I'd already prepped the horse's saddles and led her to the horse she'd be riding, Bandit.

Rae looked at me with wide eyes and she wrapped her arms around one of mine "But Caleb, this is your mom's horse. Are you sure you want me riding him?"

"Yeah. He's not been the same since my mom died, until the other day, with you. He's not let anyone ride him or even put a saddle on him. However, I tried it this morning after you walked in the barn to grab the chicken feed, and he let me." I smiled at her before turning to pet Bandit's nose. "Huh, boy, you love her, too, don't you?"

Rae looked at me when I said that, but I interrupted any thoughts she had when I asked if she wanted a hand getting into the saddle. I helped her get in the saddle before I got on my horse, and then we left the barn, followed by the other horses.

♥

The ride out to the pasture was good for Rae. I could see happiness not just in her smile, but in her eyes, too. There was almost a sparkle in them.

We spoke here and there, but I'd let her start the conversations. I could tell she was deep in thought. Happy, but thoughtful.

"How about here as a stopping point? We can sit over there and watch the horses run."

Rae blinked like she'd been far away for a few seconds and then focused again. Her hair almost had a glow to it, and it was blowing in the cool breeze. She sat confidently in Bandit's saddle and looked stunning.

Gosh I love her. Had for years, but I still didn't know if admitting it would be too much for her at the moment. I couldn't forgive myself if I pushed her before she was ready.

"Yeah," she said with a smile. "That looks good to me."

We swung down from the horses and removed the saddles, setting them aside. I pulled out a blanket from one of the bags and Rae helped me spread it over the grass. She sat and took the water bottle I passed to her.

"Did you enjoy the ride?" I asked.

Rae tilted her face towards the sky, soaking in the warmth of the sunlight. "More than you know. It's been way too long since I've ridden. Thank you for doing this for me."

I didn't watch the horses; I watched her, the way her eyes followed them, something soft and unguarded about her expression. Like a window that had been opened for the first time in a long time.

The quiet settled around us, warm and easy.

"You know," I said softly, breaking the silence. She looked at me with a curious expression. I reached out my hand, and she laced her fingers through mine without hesitation.

"When my parents died..." I paused to breathe, to steady myself. "I sank into a deep depression. My parents were two of my favorite people, ripped away from our family and friends. I came out here a lot after their services. It was where they came when things got stressful and they needed a break from the chaos." I could feel Rae watching me. Her hand tightened slightly around mine. "Watching the horses run, the fresh air and the open field...It brought a feeling of freedom and peace. My parents had taught me to come out here to breathe and clear my mind when life got to be too much. So, after they passed, I was out here multiple times a week. Somedays, just for the horses, but at first, it was mostly for me so I could breathe."

I looked over at Rae as she gently squeezed my hand again. She looked at me, her brows knit gently, listening intently. I hadn't talked too much about my parents with her, or really anyone, for that matter. It had been the most difficult thing I had ever gone through, and no one really knows the pain unless they go through it. I wouldn't wish the heartbreak of losing a parent on my worst enemy.

"The horses," I said as I nodded towards them. "They didn't care who was watching. Just moved like the whole world belonged to them. Wild, free...unbothered by all the things that tore me up inside. And for a long time, I hated that. It felt like the world had the nerve to keep going when mine had stopped."

I paused, my eyes following the horses as they galloped by, manes flying like fire.

"But then I started seeing it differently. Like...maybe they weren't ignoring the pain. Maybe they were showing me what comes after it. That even when life kicks the breath out of you, you can still find a way to run again. To live again. It took a long time for me to learn that, and I still struggle with it, but coming out here helps."

I leaned towards Rae, voice softer now, tilting her chin up so I could look into her eyes.

"And watching you today? The way you smiled up in that saddle...that light in your eyes?" I smiled at her. "Reminded me of that. You're getting there, Sunshine. Bit by bit. Doesn't matter if you gallop or take it slow. What matters is, you're moving. And you're not carrying it all alone anymore."

She continued staring into my eyes, the sunlight catching the softness in her expression, and my heart swelled.

Rae let go of my hand and scooted closer to me, facing the opposite way I was, so she could still look at me.

My eyes were on her—only her. A soft breeze blew her auburn hair around her face. The faint scent of her shampoo was intoxicating.

"Caleb." Her voice was barely over a whisper. She reached for my hand again and laced her fingers with

182

mine. "You make me feel so safe, and like you see the real me. I still feel..." She looked down at our hands, still linked together, which I gave a gentle squeeze. She let out a long breath and continued, "Somewhat broken and scared, but honestly, when I'm with you, I feel like I can breathe again."

She looked at the horses and took a deep breath before looking at me again. The sun had started to dip lower in the sky, causing her eyes to have a glow to them. "Will you be patient with me...again? I want to feel close to you. I want to feel *us*. If you still want that, too."

Chapter 39

Rae

Caleb didn't answer with words. He lifted my hand to his lips and kissed it, then leaned in and found my lips. It was a kiss that felt like a promise. The kiss began soft and searching, then deepened until the rest of the world fell away.

Caleb spoke first when we stopped kissing. "I need you to know, if you decide to stop, then we stop. I won't care—I just want to be with you no matter what we're doing. Okay, Sunshine?"

"I want this," I whispered. "I want you." I really did want to be with him. Forever.

He drew back just far enough to look at me, his thumb brushing my cheek. "I'm already yours, Rae."

My mind was spinning. From kissing him like that, to thinking about the possibility of forever with him, to him saying "I'm yours," I felt...Breathless. I loved the idea of being with him forever, and I know he said he wouldn't be going anywhere, and that he was already mine. Did he mean forever, though?

There was so much kindness in his blue eyes. Caleb truly cared about me, and I loved him for that.

"One thing, if I can make a request. Let me take care of you. No pressure, no expectations. Just us."

I nodded. A cool breeze lifted around us, smelling faintly like spring flowers. The sun was slowly sinking in the sky behind us, but all I saw was him. I tried to hold on to that thought—*just us*—as he guided me down to the blanket. Every movement was deliberate, as if he were giving me time to decide with each touch.

He eased my shirt upward, fingers grazing the small of my back, his palms steady and warm. When the fabric was gone, he traced the lines of my shoulders. The slow rhythm of his touch was intoxicating. I felt tension leaving my body a little more with every breath.

His hands traced along my back, fingers brushing over the line of my bra. When he went to unhook it, he paused, brows pulling together. "There's… no clasp?"

A breathy laugh slipped out of me. "Front clasp," I said, fingers trembling just a little as I reached between us. "Here. I've got it."

I took a slow breath and unhooked it. The cups fell away, the straps sliding down my shoulders. Caleb didn't rush. He eased the straps the rest of the way down my arms and helped me out of my bra, gentle like always.

He'd seen me before—but this was different. This time, I was letting him have me. All of me.

Nerves fluttered in my stomach, but I didn't hide, didn't cover myself or look away. I met his gaze and let him see what I couldn't seem to say out loud: *I trust you. I choose you.*

He looked at me for a long moment, and instead of shrinking from it, I let him see me. The tenderness and heat in his eyes steadied me more than words ever could. Caleb always saw the real me—the messy, healing, imperfect me—and loved me as I was, not as who I thought I needed to be.

He eased me back onto the soft blanket and kissed a path down my neck, to the peak of my breast. Tongue tracing over it, my body responding to his gentle touch. When he moved to show the other side the same attention, I didn't have time to react because of the memories it brought up. Caleb kissed and touched me with such featherlight movements, like he was trying to show me how gentleness could rewrite what pain once taught me.

An involuntary sound escaped my lips, and Caleb paused to look at me—the setting sun causing his blue eyes to look like they were glowing. "I could stay here for hours, just learning you—listening to every sound you make," he said with a smile that made me giggle.

He worshipped me with his mouth—slow, patient—taking his time as if he wanted to learn me. Each slow pass of his tongue pulled quiet sounds from me I didn't know I could make, and when my hips lifted toward him, he kissed lower, down my stomach, his hands warm where they held my sides. His lips teased over my skin, sending heat through me I couldn't ignore. It had been so long since anyone touched me with this kind of care, and every unhurried slide of his hands drew a deep, aching response from me, like my body was finally remembering what safety felt like.

His mouth brushed along my hip, pausing as he breathed against my skin. "You're beautiful," he murmured, voice rough. His hands continued their slow exploration, skimming over the curve of my hip and the faint

186

tremor of my stomach. His touch wasn't a demand; it was a language all its own, a conversation that my heart understood.

When he reached the waistband of my jeans, he paused and looked up. "Still good?"

"Yes," I said, breath catching a little.

He unbuttoned and eased them down my legs, slow and careful. His fingertips brushed my skin on the way, and a small shiver moved through me. When I tensed, just an old reflex, I couldn't hide it fast enough.

Caleb noticed immediately.

He didn't ask what was wrong. He didn't make it a big deal. He just came back to me, bracing one hand beside my head as he leaned in and pressed a gentle kiss to my lips.

"I've got you," he murmured. "Always."

A cool breeze blew across the field and something loosened inside me—like the breeze was blowing away the tension I held onto. I hadn't even realized I'd been holding my breath until I finally let it out. I reached up and kissed him, needing that closeness for just a second more before letting him continue.

He slid my jeans the rest of the way down, taking the lacy fabric underneath with them, until there was nothing left between us. My thighs pressed together briefly, nerves flickering under my skin. Caleb didn't push or rush—he simply lowered himself again and pressed a slow kiss to the inside of my knee, his hands warm where they rested on my legs. Another kiss, higher on my leg this time, and my breath stuttered.

"So damn beautiful," he said, voice low and laced with heat. "All of you."

His fingertips traced the inside of my thigh, slow enough to make my breath catch. His gaze followed the path of his hand, and when it settled, his eyes darkened, like he was already lost in me.

His hand trailed slowly up my thigh, giving me time to feel every inch of his touch before he reached me. When his fingers finally brushed over me, the first stroke pulled a gasp from me; the second stole my breath entirely. He watched me fall apart under his touch, his rhythm shifting to match every change in my breathing, every restless shift of my body. He explored me carefully, like he was learning what I liked, what made my body react, and every slow stroke made my hips lift, asking for more.

The sounds leaving me were raw, honest, and uncontrollable. My composure slipped, along with any hope of hiding how much I needed him. I was getting close—my body tightening, breath catching—as his name fell from my lips. And when it hit, I went over the edge fast, shaking, lost in him.

My breathing was still uneven, a small laugh escaping before I could stop it. I felt flushed, dizzy, and a little shy, but happy in a way I hadn't felt in a long time.

Caleb smiled that sweet smile that always melted me. He brushed a strand of hair from my cheek, his eyes warm. For a second, it seemed like he thought that might be the end—that we'd stop here.

But I didn't want to stop. I propped myself up on the blanket that was now slightly rumpled and looked at him—the man I knew cared about me more than anyone else.

"I need you," I whispered, still breathless.

He froze—not tense, just surprised. His eyes searched mine, and emotion flickered in them. I reached for his shirt and pulled him to me. "Please, Ranger," I whispered, voice barely there.

He shifted closer, his hands still patient. Then he reached toward the saddlebag beside us. The sound of leather and a small metallic rustle made me laugh through my nerves.

"You came prepared?" I teased.

He grinned, voice low. "Didn't want to ruin the moment by not being ready for you."

That flicker of humor eased what little tension was left inside me. I was nervous, yes, but not scared. Not with him.

Caleb leaned back in, his forehead resting against mine, and everything else blurred—the grass beneath us, the faint whinnying from the horses, the warmth of his breath on my lips.

I pulled him in to kiss me, the kind of kiss that left me a little dizzy and smiling against his lips. My hands found his belt, trembling as I worked the buckle, and he helped. When his clothes were gone, the air between us felt heavier, charged.

I looked at him, eyes wide, a breath catching in my throat. "Wow…" The word came out soft, almost a laugh. "You're…wow."

His mouth curved into that half-smile that always undid me. "Yeah?" His voice was low, playful in a way that melted me. "You're pretty wow yourself."

I met his gaze and saw a tenderness in his eyes that I'd not seen before. At that moment I knew I loved him.

He slid into me slowly, watching my face the whole time. A small sound left me, and he paused to press a kiss to my forehead.

"You okay?" he whispered.

I nodded, pulling him closer. "Better than okay."

He let out a quiet laugh, breathless. "You're gonna kill me," he whispered.

He moved again, slower this time, burying himself in me inch by inch until he was fully there. A low groan escaped him as he kissed along my jaw and down my neck, his breath warm against my skin.

He began to move, slow at first, finding a rhythm that made my breath catch. Each deep roll of his hips drew a quiet sound from me, my body meeting his like it already knew the pace. His hand slid along my side, tracing up until his palm rested over my breast. His touch was feather-light, exactly how I liked it, fingers brushing over my skin in soft, coaxing circles.

A quiet sound left me, part groan, part sigh. "I love making you feel good," he whispered against my neck. "You have no idea what you do to me when you fall apart like this."

He explored me with quiet patience, each slow movement in perfect rhythm with the way we moved. Every soft sound that escaped me pulled another breath from him, another tremor through his body.

"You're perfect," he murmured, voice rough but tender. "Everything about you."

Pleasure built fast, sharp and consuming, and when it broke, I clutched at him, his name escaping my lips. He followed with a low, broken groan, both of us trembling through the aftershocks.

He eased down beside me, pulling me close until I was tucked against his chest. His lips brushed over my shoulder, my temple, soft, lingering kisses that said everything words couldn't.

"That was...You were…" he said softly.

I smiled into his chest, my breath still uneven. "Same."

He brushed his lips across my hair and held me close.

The wind moved through the tall grass, tugging gently at the edge of the blanket. For a moment, there was nothing but the two of us—quiet, safe, and whole.

He stayed close for a while, both of us still catching our breath. The air was warm, the sunlight low and golden across the field. Soft orange and pale blue still streaked the sky. Everything felt slower, quieter, different in the best way.

When he finally pulled away, it was slow, careful, like he didn't want to break the stillness that had settled around us.

"Don't move," he requested.

He reached for the saddlebag and pulled out a couple of small towels. I watched as he poured a bit of water onto one, the fabric darkening as it soaked in.

My brow furrowed. "What are you doing?"

He looked up, a small grin tugging at the corner of his mouth. "Helping," he said quietly.

"Caleb," I whispered, my voice catching, "you don't have to…"

"I want to."

He cleaned me up with a tenderness that made my chest ache, his touch slow and careful, like this, too, mattered. Taking care of me was as natural as breathing for him. I tried to blink back the sting in my eyes, but the tears still came. He noticed, of course he did, and brushed his thumb under my eye before I could look away.

His voice was soft and a little rough. "You have no idea what it does to me, being the one you trust like this."

I nodded, my throat too tight for words. He just kept moving, gentle as ever.

When he finished, he used the other towel for himself just as quietly, setting them both aside before coming back to me.

He pulled me into his arms again, the warmth of his skin against mine, sunlight still glinting off his shoulders as the sun hung lower in the sky. Everything around us glowed in this moment, caught somewhere between day and dusk, and for the first time in a long time, I didn't want to be anywhere else.

192

Chapter 40

Caleb

Back in the barn, we were feeding and brushing the horses when Rae's phone rang. She looked at the screen and then placed the phone on the hay bale next to her. Her face did not show any fear or frustration, so I was not concerned. We hadn't heard from Ethan in several days, so I expected every call or text to be one from him at this point.

I watched her with Bandit. He trusted me enough to let me take care of him, but he trusted her like he had trusted my mom. My mom and Bandit had been inseparable, even for the short time they were together after she brought him home. Bandit's personality came to life again with Rae here, and she let her guard down more when she was around him, too.

I was about to turn back and continue feeding the last of the other horses when I saw Rae step towards Bandit's chest to brush him. Bandit lowered his head towards Rae's shoulder, wrapping his neck around her gently. I heard a giggle spill out of Rae as she leaned into Bandit, wrapping her arms around him, before whispering something to him I couldn't hear.

While watching her move around the barn, I couldn't help but let my mind wander. I had been trying to hold back everything I felt for her. Every thought I had that would pull me in her direction, I tried to hold back because she needed time to heal, and I wanted to give her that time and space. I tried. No matter what, no matter how many times I tried to tell myself to stop thinking about her like that, I couldn't. Having her back in town, within reach, changed everything.

I never felt bad about loving her. I had loved her since I met her. What I felt guilty for was when my thoughts had drifted too far, imagining things I shouldn't have. They were thoughts that went beyond protecting her. She had been through enough, and the last thing I had wanted was to make her feel like I was pushing too hard, or at all.

Now, as I watched her drift through the barn, a faint glow clinging to her skin, I saw something different in her. Everything changed tonight. She felt safe, at ease. For the first time, I let myself watch her and my mind wandered.

I watched as she moved to say goodnight to Bandit and lock up his stall. Her curves were everything. Every part of her body that Ethan had made her hate, I found addicting. I couldn't get enough of her, not just every beautiful inch of her, but the way she was finally starting to see herself the way I always had.

I finished up what I was doing and moved towards her. The sun had disappeared for the day and storm clouds were moving in, leaving the barn dimly lit by the moon-light and the lanterns we had near us. Rae briefly turned towards me, smiling, and the happiness on her face made my knees weak. I walked up next to her to put the brush I had been using in its place and wrapped my arms around her. She leaned her head back onto my shoulder to look at me, and I kissed her cheek. My arms were around her waist, and I gave her a small squeeze which caused her to

194

giggle. Gosh, that sound would be my undoing. I would do anything just to hear her laugh and see her smile.

Still wrapped in my arms, she turned enough to kiss me and lifted her hand to my face, her fingers tracing the line of my beard. With her arm raised, her shirt lifted a bit, and I ran the tips of my fingers along her skin. She didn't pull away or even tug her shirt back down.

Gosh, I love her. The desire to tell her how I felt was strong, but would it be too soon? Would she think it was because of what we'd just done and nothing else?

"Rae, Sunshine, I want to tell..." I decided to take a chance and tell her how I felt. If she didn't feel the same way yet, I would be okay with that, because my feelings had never changed. I tried, but her phone ringing again interrupted my words.

Rae glanced at the screen and looked confused. "My parents landline." She showed me the screen and the look of confusion on her face echoed how I felt. They were not due home for another few weeks.

"Maybe they came home early since you're home?" I shrugged, hoping I could hide my nerves about her possibly leaving if her parents came home. I never wanted her to leave.

Her eyes widened and a look of excitement crossed her face at the thought of possibly seeing her parents. It had been a while since she'd seen them since Ethan had not let her visit. She put the phone on speakerphone so I could say hi with her.

"Mom? Dad?"

A voice that sent chills throughout my entire body echoed throughout the barn. "Wouldn't that be nice if it was them? Where are you, Rae? I miss you."

I had only heard his voice once before but based on the fact that Rae's normally ivory skin was now ghostly, I knew who the voice belonged to.

I glanced down at my phone and saw no camera notifications from anywhere outside her parents' house. I tried switching to the live camera feed, but all I got in return was an error message. That bastard. I didn't know how he managed to disconnect the cameras, but I had to get the cops en route.

Rae hadn't moved yet, hadn't said a word. The barn was eerily quiet. I had only removed one of my arms from her waist to grab my phone, and she was digging her fingers into my other arm. I could feel her body shaking. I had to take over and snap her out of this. I couldn't let him get to her again.

"Hey, asshole, what are you wanting from her? She doesn't want to be with you anymore."

I put her phone on mute and let go of her only so I could look at her eyes. She was so scared, and my heart broke for her. I touched her cheek gently so I could try and bring her back to me.

She blinked and somewhat focused on me. "Caleb..."

Ethan was talking in the background, saying something about this all being her fault, like he always did. I was listening as much as I could, but I had to get Rae to help.

196

"You think anyone is going to believe anything you say, bitch?" Rae flinched at Ethan's words.

"I know, baby. Take my phone and go call 911. Tell them everything—and to rush to your parents' address." She immediately came back to me, her gaze locked on mine. She took the phone and walked just outside the barn before dialing.

She was obviously shaken, but so strong. It made me love her even more.

"He doesn't love you like I do, Rae. I mean, you're not perfect. We can fix that if you come home." Ethan continued spouting lies I was glad Rae couldn't hear.

I waited to see that she was talking to a dispatcher before turning her phone off mute so I could resume talking to Ethan. "Why don't you leave her alone?"

"She's mine. Not yours. You stole her from me."

Knowing I had to keep him talking, I switched to cop mode just as Rae walked back in with my phone. I put a finger to my lips, a silent shush to let her know I had it under control. She nodded and walked over to me. To my surprise, she wrapped her arms around me and buried her head in my chest. She clung to me like she was going to fall over if she let go.

I started recording the call with my phone. "Why do you think that I stole her from you?"

Not caring about listening to his answer, especially since I was recording the call, I muted the phone and turned to Rae.

"They said they are on the way. I told them to go in and get him when they got there." Her voice was so strong despite how I knew she felt.

"…I was good to you, Rae. He may have stolen you from me, but you'll always be mine." I caught the tail end of what Ethan was saying, enough information that I could reply.

"No. You hurt her and she ran. Rae is her own person. She doesn't belong to anyone, so she's not something that can be stolen."

He laughed an evil sounding laugh, and tears started to form in Rae's eyes. I pulled her closer, even though our bodies were already as close as possible, and I kissed her temple.

"I'm going to find her just like I found her parents' address, which was basically dropped in my lap."

"How did you find it? Online? Those records are not always accurate." I knew you could find out pretty much anything online nowadays, but I had hoped her parents' last name being different than hers would have thrown him off.

"No. Even better. Her mom sent her a postcard, from their vacation, to our address. Probably didn't know the little bitch ran away. She put the return address on it— their address."

Rae whimpered and started to pull away from me as tears fell fast. I tightened my grip around her only enough so she wouldn't pull away. "I've got you," I whispered in her ear.

"Listen, Ethan. You need to stop while you're ahead. You think she's yours, but she's not. You've assaulted and abused her, and now stalked her. Those things, separately, are not things you can come back from. If you think I would let you anywhere near her, even after doing just *one* of those things, think again."

His voice turned calm. A little *too* calm. "I gotta go before your buddies come inside, Deputy Walker."

The line didn't go dead. We heard the clatter of the phone being dropped and within the next minute, my squad announced themselves as they rushed into the house. They called out as they cleared the rooms. Ethan had vanished.

My Sergeant called me, and I answered after the first ring. "Let me guess, he got away."

My Sergeant spoke to me, stating facts about how they think he got inside the house and that Ethan damaged the cameras somehow. I saw the fear in Rae's eyes and turned the phone off speaker so only I could hear it. She buried her head in my chest more, and I wished I could take away all the pain she must be feeling right now.

My Sergeant told me that they were calling the crime scene unit out to take photos, try and pull prints, and take anything into evidence if they found anything else. Before we hung up, I made sure to thank him for allowing me to take the time off, especially without any warning time. He reminded me of something he'd told anyone who had requested time off for family matters, and that was that if you cannot take care of yourself and your family, you can't be fully present to take care of the community we serve. I thanked him once again, and we ended the call.

Rae pushed hard to get out of my arms, and even though I didn't want to, I let her go. If she needed a bit of breathing room, I would give it to her.

I set down the phone and held out my hand to her. "Come here, honey."

She shook her head, looking at the ground, her arms wrapped around her waist. I walked over to her and pressed a kiss to the top of her head. She was shaking violently, and she felt cold.

"Hey, you're safe. I'm going to call your parents and let them know not to come home right away if they don't have to. I'll let them know you're safe and what's going on."

"I don't want them to know about—"

Rolling thunder sounded, low and angry.

"Don't worry, if you want to tell them, you can. I'm only telling them what's necessary. But let's get inside the house first before the rain starts."

She nodded, and I went to lock up the last of the horse stalls before ushering her out of the barn. The thunder cracked again and lightning lit up the sky.

I locked up the barn, only letting go of Rae for as long as I had to, and then we quickly ran towards the house as the moon disappeared behind the clouds. The lightning streaked across the sky again, seeming angrier, as if the weather knew of the shift in our moods.

Chapter 41

Rae

We got inside the house just as the floodgates opened and the rain began to pour. I stood at the window, watching the storm. It felt like the storm in my mind was rushing with the same intensity as the one outside.

Caleb kicked off his boots and came to stand by my side. I didn't move, didn't speak, I couldn't. What should I say to the man who just gave me the feeling of freedom and love, only for him to deal with my ex right after? I hated myself for bringing him into this mess, thinking I could just start over with him without burdening him with my past.

"Hey, Sunshine, when you're ready to talk, I'm here. You're covered in half the barn and the field." He let out a breathy chuckle, trying to lighten the mood for me. I wanted to respond, but it was like I was physically incapable of doing so. Caleb continued, "I'm going to go get you some comfy clothes to change into, okay?"

I nodded and whispered my thanks to him. It was all I could manage at the moment. He kissed my temple and went into the bedroom.

The rain on the roof was deafening. I heard the soft footsteps of Duke behind me. As if he knew I wasn't ready to speak or play, he curled up at my feet, just being there.

I heard Caleb in our room, opening and closing drawers as he spoke to someone on the phone, I could only assume was my dad. The rain made it almost impossible to hear him, or really anything.

Thunder rolled and shook the walls of the house. I stood at the window, still staring out at the rain and my chest felt tighter. Lightning struck. My breathing started to accelerate, and I felt like the walls were closing in on me like that night the power had gone out. I needed air. I needed space, so I stepped out on the porch and, without thinking, walked out into the storm.

Chapter 42

Caleb

"Hey, Babe. I got you one of my hoodies..." I heard the door open as I exited our room with her clothes and one of my hoodies in hand. "Rae?" My heart sank. Ethan was too close now. What if he found out where I lived and came to get her? I threw the clothes on the couch I'd left her by and rushed to the still open front door.

I let out a sigh of relief as I looked out the front door and saw she was okay physically, being watched by Duke, who sat on the dry porch. My heart hurt, though, when I saw she was anything but okay mentally. She was standing in the mud out front, arms wrapped around herself, sobbing and breathing hard. *Dang it, I shouldn't have left her alone.*

I rushed to throw my boots back on and then ran to her. "Rae, baby, what are you doing out here?" The storm was so loud, I had to raise my voice so she could hear me.

"I couldn't... breathe." She choked back a sob, still not looking at me. I put my hand on her arm, and she was freezing.

"You were probably having a panic attack, Rae. I'm sorry, I shouldn't have left you alone. I should have encouraged you to go with me to get your clothes."

She finally looked at me. Her hair was soaked, her tears mixed with raindrops on her cheeks, and her lips had a tinge of purple because of how cold the rain was. I wrapped my arms around her and held her close. She clung to my shirt, and the tension in her shoulders eased a little.

"I'm so sorry—" she cried. "Sorry I ruined today. Sorry I brought this mess into your life."

I had to tell her. I didn't care if this was the wrong timing. I just knew I had to tell her how I felt.

"No, Rae. Don't you dare apologize to me, for anything. Please." I spoke more intensely than I meant to. "You coming back into my life has been the single greatest thing to ever happen to me." I kept my voice as sweet as possible but needed her to know how serious I was.

"Rae, baby, I have loved you since I met you all those years ago, in high school. I was an idiot for not telling you back then, but I was a teen and I was scared. Scared I'd lose my best friend if I told her how I felt." My voice cracked. "So, I let you go to college, hoping things wouldn't change for us. Again, I was an idiot."

Rae looked up at me, and I shielded her eyes from the rain.

"When we lost connection and then I lost my parents, all I wanted was to talk to you, to get some Sunshine in my life. Then we bumped into each other at the store, it was like the light had returned in my life." Her eyes grew wider and her tears continued to flow, but her body had stopped shaking.

"That bastard kept you from everything and everyone—from me. He's the one that will be apologizing when we catch up to him, not you. Never you, baby. I *love* you, Rae. Until my dying breath, I will love you." My voice

204

broke with those last words, and I realized I'd started crying.

Rae's lip was quivering, "You...love me?"

I nodded, lowering my head until our foreheads touched. "Yeah, Sunshine. With everything I am. I've loved you for years, and I will love you until my dying breath."

She wrapped her arms around my neck and kissed me so fast it took my breath away. "I love you, too, Ranger."

I walked to the bathroom door with arms full of items I thought would help my girl relax. I had started a warm bath for her, but told her to rinse off before getting in the tub, so she wasn't sitting in all the mud that was on her. She said she was okay, so I left Duke guarding the door while I found what I needed. I went through the checklist in my head as I looked at the items in my arms: *wine, wine glass, plastic cup, candle, lighter and bath bomb. Got it all.*

I knocked on the bathroom door. "Hey, Sunshine. Can I come in?"

"Yeah, you can come in." Her voice sounded a little brighter and that put a smile on my face.

I told Duke to stay, and he positioned himself so he could watch out for us. When I opened the bathroom door, I was relieved to see the outline of her perfect body still behind the frosted glass. I turned off the water that filled the tub, seeing that it was at the perfect height, and then stole a peek in her direction. I was getting distracted and needed to focus, but all I wanted to do was join her in the shower.

I couldn't help but glance at the outline of her body behind the glass as I set everything up. I lit the candle, poured the wine for her, and put the bath bomb in the water just in time for the shower water to shut off.

Rae opened the door and looked out at me. I couldn't control my smile when I saw she wasn't hiding her body from me. Steam curled around her, the light catching every little droplet of water that slid down her skin. My gaze traced the curve of her thighs and her hips, up to the rise of her chest. Every inch of her pulled me in until I forgot to breathe. She was strong, beautiful, and completely mine to love.

"What? Do I still have mud on me?" She let out a tiny laugh, pulling me out of my thoughts.

"No." I ran my hand over my head, embarrassed that I was caught staring. "You are just amazing. That's all. The most beautiful woman I've ever seen," I admitted, which caused a blush that started at her cheeks and gave a pink tinge to other parts of her ivory skin. I was struggling to keep my composure and make this moment about her.

I reached for her hand as the blush only deepened. I walked her to the tub and she stopped and stared at the tub at first, and then at me.

The bath bomb I had used made the bathroom smell like flowers and peaches, her favorite scent. "Did you...use a bath bomb?"

"When we were packing your things to bring here, I grabbed a few from your bathroom. I hope this scent is okay."

"It's...perfect. Thank you." Her voice cracked as she spoke.

"There's more, but get in and get warm first." I held her hand as she stepped into the tub. As soon as she was settled, I put the candle on the windowsill next to the tub and brought her the wine.

"Wait, all this? Really? For me?"

I knelt down and kissed her gently. "Anything for you, Sunshine." She returned my kiss as a thank you.

I grabbed the shampoo and conditioner bottles from the shower, and the cup I brought with me. "Can you scoot forward real quick?"

"What are you—"

"Taking care of my girl." I kept my voice soft, leaving no room for doubt in her mind about whether I loved her. As she opened her mouth to protest, I held up my hand. "Nope. None of that. Lean forward please," I said with a teasing tone.

She leaned forward and I filled up the cup with warm water from the spout, then gently tilted her head back as I poured the warm water over her hair slowly, so it didn't splash too much.

Rae let out a soft sigh, her shoulders relaxing under the stream. I ran my fingers through her hair, spreading the warmth through each strand before reaching for the shampoo.

I worked the shampoo into a lather between my palms, then gently massaged it into her scalp. My fingertips moved in little circles, not rushing a thing, wanting her to know I would take all the time in the world to care for her.

Rae's lips parted slightly, her eyes still closed. "Mmm...that actually feels amazing."

I smiled, more to myself than anything. "Good. That's the goal."

I took my time rinsing the soap out, pouring cup after cup of water, shielding her face with one hand and letting the other smooth the water down the back of her head. When I added conditioner, my fingers moved, working it through to the ends. I gently untangled her soft waves and then rinsed out the conditioner.

I saw her wipe her cheek. "Did some of the shampoo get in your eye?" She shook her head and let out a shaky breath.

"Hey, what's wrong?"

"I'm so sorry. Nothing is wrong. It's stupid." She laughed as she cried.

"What's stupid?" I continued to gently rinse the conditioner out of her hair.

"Don't worry. These aren't tears from fear or me being sad." She let out a choked laugh. "You're just so sweet, taking care of me like you've been doing since I got here. I've never had someone care for me the way you do." She looked at me, tears making her eyes glisten.

"Well, get used to it." I kissed her temple as I grabbed her hair wrap and wrapped her hair up in it. Then I placed

208

a rolled up towel behind her neck and encouraged her to lean back on it. "Cause I plan on taking care of you, if you'll let me, for the rest of my days, Sunshine."

Rae smiled and thanked me as I stood. I passed her the glass of wine, and she took a sip.

"If you need anything, I'll be right out there in the living room. You just lie here and relax."

"Wait, you're leaving? Can you stay?" She paused and a blush appeared on her cheeks. "There's room in here for two," she said quietly, like she was afraid I may say no.

"You want me to join you?"

"You deserve to relax, too. We could relax together if you want." She gave me the sweetest smile.

I nodded and turned to the counter. I'd been holding it together decently, from her stepping out of the shower without hiding from me to her trusting me as I washed her hair. Just being around her drove me wild. That smile, though, added onto everything else, did me in. I was trying to control my mind before I went back over to her. Every muscle in my body tightened, desire stirring low and sharp. The ache was impossible to hide, and when I stripped down to my boxers, there was no hiding what she did to me.

I heard her start to refill the tub with warm water as I turned towards the shower, needing to rinse off before getting in the tub. She giggled. "You struggling, Ranger?"

"Only every time I think about you. So, constantly."

Her cheeks flushed again as I stepped into the shower.

I washed off the remaining dirt, making sure I didn't take it and sweat into the tub. I had still not been able to calm the fire that she'd started in me.

I walked over and settled into the warm water, pulling her into my arms, leaning her back against my chest. "I wanted you to relax," I murmured.

"I relax better when I'm in your arms." She leaned her head back onto my shoulder, and I kissed her jaw.

My arms were wrapped around her, and I gave her a gentle squeeze. Just as she said, she immediately relaxed.

"I love you, Rae," I whispered to her as her breathing changed.

She didn't say the words back, but the way she melted into my arms, feeling safe enough to fall asleep against my chest, said everything for her.

Chapter 43

Rae

I turned over and reached out for Caleb, but he wasn't lying next to me. I abruptly sat up and let my eyes adjust to the dim lighting in the room. Caleb wasn't in the room with me, but Duke was at the door of the room, lying in the door frame.

Checking my phone, I saw a text message notification and opened it. When I saw it was from Caleb, I breathed a sigh of relief. The message had only been sent five minutes ago.

Caleb: Hey baby. I'm so sorry, I couldn't sleep and was getting restless. I didn't want to be selfish and wake you, so I went to the living room, until I felt tired enough. I love you.

The bedroom door was open slightly and the light of the TV flickered on the hallway walls. I walked out of the room and to the end of the hallway. The volume of the TV was on but low, sounding like whispers.

"Caleb?" My voice was no higher than a whisper in case he had fallen asleep on the couch.

"Oh gosh Rae, I'm so sorry I woke you up."

There were worry lines on his face and dark circles under his eyes. Something was really bothering him.

"You didn't. I did get nervous when you weren't in bed, though. Couldn't sleep?"

He ran a hand over his face. "Pretty much."

I sat on the couch next to Caleb and placed my hand on his arm. "What's on your mind?"

"Ah, it's nothing. I'm sorry if I worried you."

I gave him a look and he immediately knew I didn't believe him.

He leaned forward, resting his elbows on his legs, head in his hands. "I had a nightmare. Partially about my parents." He sounded exhausted.

"Oh my gosh, Caleb. I'm so sorry." I reached for his arm and gave it a gentle nudge. Then I motioned for him to come to me. I guided him to rest his head on my chest, and when he did, I wrapped my arms around him. "If you want to talk, I'm here." I gently started to trace circles on his head, feeling the slight prick of the stubble. He had done this for me multiple times, and it helped, so I figured I would try it. Thankfully, it did.

"Thanks, Rae. Dreams don't normally mess with me, especially after all these years, but this one was different."

"How so?"

"It started like every other dream I have like this. My parents were driving and my brother and I were in the back. The crash happens, but this time...you were there, too."

My breath stilled for a moment, but then I relaxed again. I wrapped my arms around him, holding him close. "Don't worry, I'm right here. I'm safe."

"I know, I just didn't want to see my parents' accident again and then possibly one with you in it. I couldn't stop it, couldn't help you...like I couldn't help them."

"Caleb..." My voice was soft but sure, the kind of calm he always gave me when the panic crept in. "You were in the car. You lived through it, too. You couldn't have stopped it." My fingers moved slowly over his shoulder, grounding him. "You were in that crash, too, and didn't walk away untouched. You survived something that should've broken you. That's not failure, that's strength."

He didn't speak, but the way his hand curled tighter around my arm said everything.

"And as for the dream...I know how real they can feel. But I'm not gone. I'm right here. You didn't lose me." I tilted my head and kissed his cheek, my hand moving gently on his arm. "You couldn't stop the crash, no. But you've been protecting people ever since, protecting me. You never stop trying."

He swallowed hard, his voice rough. "I don't know what I did to deserve you." He shifted slightly, his hand resting over mine. "But I swear, Rae…I'm not letting anything happen to you."

"I know."

After a few minutes, his breathing started to change. "Hey...come back to bed with me." He gave me a smile as I tugged him to his feet. We walked to our room and climbed into bed, with Duke at our feet.

Under the covers, together again, I pressed my forehead close to his and whispered, "You're not alone in this, Ranger. You don't always have to be the strong one."

His eyes were heavy and he tried to keep them open so he could look at me. "As long as you don't feel like the broken one." He placed a gentle kiss on the tip of my nose.

My throat tightened but I smiled anyway, leaning forward and brushing my lips over his. "Deal."

Finally, Caleb's breathing eased and sleep finally came.

Chapter 44

Caleb

Despite being up late, Rae and I were both up early, cleaning the barn. Jenny had to work a few extra hours this week at the office, so since I was home, I told her I would do what needed to be done.

I couldn't help but watch Rae from across the barn while she was sweeping up old hay. Doing daily tasks with her made the normal things more fun. When she looked in my direction, I smiled at her and tipped my hat. "Just admiring the scenery."

Rae blushed and giggled "You're not so bad to look at either."

Duke was lying in the sunshine at the edge of the barn, and he let out a huge sigh. It seemed almost too perfectly timed, like he was tired of our flirting, so it made Rae and me laugh.

I grabbed my water bottle and took a long drink of water. Rae watched me for a moment while finishing sweeping, her eyes not leaving me as I moved throughout the barn. I needed to stack the hay bales before it got too hot, so I decided now was probably the best time. Plus, if I wanted to flirt with Rae some more, I should probably get this done first, so I wouldn't have to take a break later.

When I was out of sight, I heard her start talking to one of the horses while sweeping. I loved listening to her talk to them, like they were her best friends. Several minutes passed by, and I had finished moving around the stacks of hay. It was really hot, so I took my shirt off and walked to get my water bottle. I heard Rae sweeping in one of the last stalls, the last two horses still in the middle of the barn. She was humming a song, and the sound made me smile. I began walking toward where she was working. When I got just outside the stall door, the humming and sweeping sounds stopped. I leaned against the door frame as she turned to look at me, a wild look behind her stunning green eyes.

"You know, I've been watching you all afternoon, but now that I'm this close, I don't know if I'll be able to keep my hands to myself," I said as I gave her a small smile.

"What ever could you mean, Ranger?" she teased, her voice probably a little breathier than she meant it to be.

I didn't answer with words, but instead I stepped into the stall slowly, pulling the door closed behind me. Rae bit her lip as she smiled and looked down at her feet. I didn't move yet, but just took in the sight of her. Her hair was slightly tussled after working around the barn, and there was a bit of hay sticking out of the bun. It had been cooler today than the last few days, so we sat outside, and small traces of the dirt from the ground were still on her jeans.

I'd seen Rae in pretty much every setting now—dressed up with makeup on, just waking up, standing in the rain soaking wet, even with nothing on, as she let her guard down and trusted me. Every single moment, she always looked beautiful, but there was something about this

216

look that did me in. She was effortlessly beautiful, and she wasn't even trying to be.

"I mean," I said, stepping closer until she had to look up at me, "that watching you all flirty and gorgeous all morning…it's been driving me crazy." Somehow, even after working most of the day, she still smelled like peaches and flowers.

Rae stepped back until her back met the wooden wall behind her, her breath catching as I moved in. She looked at my chest and then down towards my boots before giving me a small, flirty smile. I returned the smile with a wink. "And what are you gonna do about it?" she asked, trying to sound sassy, but a tremble in her voice betrayed her.

I smirked, one hand bracing the wall beside her head while the other trailed gently down her arm. "Depends," I murmured. "You gonna tell me to stop?"

She shook her head slowly, eyes locked on mine. "No."

That was all I needed.

I cupped her cheek, brushing my thumb along her skin, then leaned down and kissed her, slow at first, deepening after just a moment. The kiss turned hungry fast, all heat and years of tension crashing into that one breath.

My hands found her waist. I started to pull back when she stilled, but her hand came up, fingers wrapping around my wrist, keeping me there. "What are you thinking, baby?" I asked softly.

She took a slow, steady breath. "I'm reminding myself that I'm not broken. You're a safe place. My safe place."

Something in my chest tightened. I smiled, brushing my thumb along her jaw. "Always and forever, baby."

"Sorry, I'm still…"

I stopped her with a gentle kiss, barely a whisper of one. "Don't apologize for anything. Just let me love you."

She guided my hand beneath her shirt, letting me feel her skin. The warmth of her made my pulse stumble. "Just not…"

"Don't worry, baby." My voice came out rougher than I meant it to. "You lead the way, I'll follow."

That was all she needed. She kissed me again, deeper this time, her nails lightly digging into my skin. She gasped softly against my mouth, her body arching instinctively into mine.

"You always smell like peaches," I murmured against her throat, "but right now you also smell like hay, and it shouldn't drive me as wild as it does."

Her hands slid across my chest, fingers tracing along the edge of my muscles. "You're one to talk," she said, breathless. "You walk around here all shirtless and sweaty like it's not a problem."

I laughed quietly, the sound low against her skin. "Guess I'll have to start wearing a shirt then."

She laughed, then wrapped her arms around my shoulders, pulling me closer until there wasn't an inch of space left between us. "Don't you even think about it."

218

Our lips met again, messier this time, more desperate, and when my hand slid under her shirt again, she didn't stop me. She trusted me, and being trusted by her was an honor I didn't take lightly. I moved slowly, tracing her skin like I was learning her all over again, every inch of her soft and warm beneath my hand. She reached down and lifted her shirt over her head, tossing it aside, then reached behind her to unhook her bra. When it came loose, I just stared at her face first, then all of her.

"Gosh, Rae." The words came out rough, barely a whisper. "You have no idea what you do to me."

I gathered her against me, wrapping my arms around her and feeling the warmth of her skin against mine. For a moment, everything slowed—the air, our breathing, the space between heartbeats. She was soft and real in my arms, and it stole the breath right out of me.

Her breath caught when my thumb brushed over the soft peak of her breast, teasing until her quiet gasp filled the space between us. I kissed a slow trail from her lips down her neck, across her shoulder while my hands moved again, gentle, steady, giving her time to breathe, to feel.

Her hands gripped my back, nails digging lightly into my skin as her body reacted to every touch. Heat built low in my stomach, steady and insistent, and when my hand slid to the button of her jeans, she didn't hesitate. She helped me, her fingers moving with mine, wanting it as much as I did.

I slipped my hand beneath the waistband of her jeans and beneath the soft fabric below, touching her, slow, careful, deliberate. Her moan came fast, her hips moving to meet my touch, and when my fingers circled her again, she gasped, pushing into my hand like she needed more. I found the pace that made her breath hitch, the sound that left her lips somewhere between a sigh and a moan. I kept it slow, steady, giving her time to climb higher with every touch. My mouth stayed near her neck, my breath warm against her skin as she trembled against the wall.

Her breathing grew uneven, a quiet sound leaving her throat before she gasped my name. Her whole body tightened, then shook as she came apart, her face pressed to my shoulder, her hands gripping at me like she needed something to hold on to. I held her through it, whispering quiet words she probably didn't even hear.

"I got you," I murmured against her skin, my arms still wrapped around her. "Always."

"What do you want for dinner?" I asked as I looked in the refrigerator for something to make.

Rae stared at me from across the room while rubbing her shoulder and wincing at the tightness in her muscles. "If I wasn't so sore, I'd say something flirty like 'how about you,' but this tension—" She groaned and laughed. "The hot water from the shower didn't do anything for this either."

I chuckled at the face she made as she stretched. "Let's eat dinner and get some painkillers in you. Then I'll work on those tense muscles if you want."

"Deal." Rae chuckled as she stood and stretched. "How can I help?" she asked, joining me at the refrigerator.

"By going and lying down on the couch." I kissed her cheek as I passed by her with my hands full of items from the refrigerator.

"No, Cal—" I held up my hand with a playful look on my face. "But I want—" I shook my head.

I set the skillet I had pulled from the cabinet on the counter and then walked to her, pulling her into a hug. "Rae, baby. When will you understand that I love to spoil you, and take care of you? I didn't even get to see you for several years, and now you're here and I get to love you, and you love me back...This is all I've wanted. Spoiling you and taking care of you, in every way, is all I want to do." She looked at me, our faces so close to each other's. "So will you please go sit down on the couch and snuggle our pup so I can spoil you, like you deserve?" I had kept my voice sweet but serious, but I changed it to a silly tone to continue what I was saying, and it got her to belly laugh.

I gave her a gentle squeeze before pointing at the couch with a big smile on my face. She rolled her eyes and laughed before turning and walking towards the couch, grabbing a blanket on the way. Duke jumped up next to her, and she covered both of them with the blanket. I chuckled at the sight. *Duke's got her under his spell.*

"Can I ask you something?" I asked as I started to brown the meat. I decided to make pasta since it was simple and Rae could get painkillers in her system faster.

She nodded.

"I don't want to bring up bad memories, so please don't hate me, but I was curious about something. Is there anything you wanted to do, while you were...at college that you didn't get to do?" I looked at her for a moment, hoping to not see the shadows covering the sunshine I'd seen in her eyes all day. She smiled at me and then turned thoughtful.

I continued cooking as she thought for a few moments.

"So, there's only a couple of things I can think of, right this second. One of which isn't necessarily something I wanted to do while...at college, but just in general. The other is something I thought I would get the chance to do, but never did, surprisingly."

"Alright, let's go with the first one."

She pulled her legs up under her and got a bit more relaxed, which I took as a good sign.

"I wanted to travel some. Nowhere specific, not really out of the country, just...going somewhere. I would have even loved to go camping, but I would have needed a working toilet and a shower..." The face she made at the thought of going camping without those things was one that would live in my head for the rest of my life. A genuine moment. "...or go on a road trip somewhere. Anywhere."

"With someone, or a solo trip?" I asked, hoping her answer would be with someone so I could take her somewhere. I turned to dump the pasta water out and heard her laughing behind me.

"Ranger, can you imagine me on a solo trip? I would get so lost or be bored by myself!" She giggled before turning thoughtful again, not serious, just like she was thinking of something before saying it. "I would want to go with...with you, if you'd want to go somewhere with me, at some point."

I turned back towards the island just in time for her to see my smile as she said that. "I will take you anywhere you want to go, Sunshine." A look of pure joy was on her face. *Gosh, I love her.* "Dinner is ready. Do you want to eat there or here?"

She groaned as she stood up and pointed at the table as she winced and laughed at the tension in her muscles. She covered Duke with the part of the blanket she'd been using and then walked over to where I was plating the food.

She pulled a couple of glasses from the cabinet and filled them with water. I loved that she felt at home here.

"Before I answer the next question, can I ask you something, but you promise you won't hate me?" she asked timidly.

I nodded as I grabbed the last of what we needed for dinner.

"What's your favorite memory with your parents after I left for college? I know that's a sad question, and I'm sorry. I loved your parents, though, and being here makes me miss them. I'm really sad I never got to say goodbye, so I was hoping maybe a funny memory of yours, that I didn't know about, would help. Plus, you really have not spoken about them..."

"Sunshine, breathe." I wrapped my arms around her. She was talking so fast as she realized that the question she wanted to ask would possibly make me sad. "You're not upsetting me, so get that out of your beautiful head. I miss my parents, yes. Talking about them helps and sometimes makes me sad, too, but it helps keep their memory alive. Thank you for asking me about them." I looked down at her with a smile.

She smiled back up at me, and I wrapped her in my arms again.

"You can ask me about them anytime and it won't upset me. Promise. To answer your question, though...my favorite memory would have to be from when my parents got stuck in a rainstorm together while on a ride. They had taken the horses out, and nothing had gone right. A strap on my dad's saddle broke, and from how my mom described it, my dad spun around and hung upside-down for a moment. The horse thankfully didn't get spooked.

"My mom tripped and fell in a mud puddle during that same trip—face-first in the mud. Bandit was scared of the rain at the time, so they had to try and coax him back to the barn. Sugar cubes were melting in the rain, and the boy would not budge." Rae giggled against my chest at the thought. "When they came back from their ride, they were soaked and covered in mud, but they were laughing uncontrollably and enjoying every moment."

Rae continued giggling. "That is so funny. Thank you for sharing that with me. Oh, to have a love like that."

I pulled away only enough to look at her. "We do, Sunshine. I would get caught in a rainstorm or fall in a mud puddle with you any day."

She giggled again and hugged me tighter.

"Come sit down and eat." We walked to the table, and I set the food in front of her before kissing her forehead. Then I sat next to her. We ate in silence for several minutes, our feet tangled with each other's under the table.

"What's the second thing, the one you thought you would get the chance to do?"

"This seems silly, but I thought I would have gone out late with friends. You know, like at a bar or restaurant, or even a movie. The latest I remember staying out was until about midnight when we went to see a movie. We were back in our dorms by midnight."

"Really? You didn't get to go see a movie premiere or go out drinking with friends?"

She shook her head as she took another bite of pasta, closing her eyes for a moment as she did. "Okay, first, this is delicious."

I smiled my thanks at her because I had just taken a bite. She was right, the pasta had turned out really good.

"So, no, I never got the chance to do any of that. Our late nights were always spent studying. Classes were so insane my first two years, and I had friends, but none I really clicked with like that. I was really homesick those first two years, so I came home when I could. While I was still homesick the third and fourth year as well, I had made a friend by that point. She was my roommate those last two years. The movie I mentioned going to, but being back by midnight, that was her that I went with." Her face looked a bit sad at the last part of that statement.

I reached across the small space between us and held out my hand. She put her hand in mine and continued eating for a bit.

"Remember me talking about my best friend at college? Her name is Cierra. We were roommates for a while." She sighed. "I moved in with Ethan around the same time she eloped and moved in with her husband. They had a baby pretty soon after. She loved Ethan at first because she always got to see the side of him he wanted everyone to see. I tried hinting at how things were, and she started to change her mind about him, but that's when he cut me off from everyone. She had a second little one about a year before I wasn't allowed to see her anymore. Both her kiddos learned to walk in my living room. I've not seen her in a long time, and I always wondered if she hated me after I stopped answering calls. I've wondered if she questioned things since I had hinted about stuff, or if she thought I just didn't want to be friends anymore."

My heart broke for her. I knew how that felt, to a certain extent, since I had been cut off from her. However, being the one who lost basically everyone, and wondering what they thought and if they hated her for it, I couldn't wrap my brain around that.

"You said her name was Cierra?" She nodded. "Have you tried to contact her since leaving?"

"No. Honestly, at first it was because I was scared Ethan may somehow find out. I'm not saying she would have put me in danger on purpose, but she came home

226

with me one summer. It was the last year I came home, that week you were on a camping trip and I didn't get to see you. I didn't know I wouldn't be coming back." She said that last part like she was trying to convince me she hadn't known Ethan wouldn't let her come back. Her voice sounded so small. While I knew she had overcome so much since moving back, I wished she didn't feel like she still owed anyone an explanation, especially me.

Rae cleared her throat before continuing. "She knows where my parents live, so since she didn't know the whole story, I'm just scared she'll hate me. It's been a long time since we spoke."

I squeezed her hand, letting the silence fall between us for a moment as we finished the last couple bites of dinner.

"Do you still have her number? We could call her together. I mean, we know Ethan knows where you are now."

She shook her head and thought about what I said for a moment. "He kept her number in my phone for a while so he would know who is calling, or in case he needed to see if I tried to contact anyone. One day, though, messages from her just stopped coming in, and her number was gone. I'm assuming he told her I didn't want to talk or something and then deleted her number. Or maybe she just got upset that I didn't answer, since Ethan told me I couldn't, and she got tired of waiting." A strained laugh escaped her. "I tried to change someone's name once, so their number came up as someone else. I was hoping he wouldn't know who I was really calling. He was prepared for that, so maybe that's why it was deleted." She stood to take her dishes to the sink. "As long as you're involved, though, I would like to try and contact her. But...only if you're involved. I'd be too nervous without you there."

I joined her at the sink, and she took my dishes and rinsed them off for me while I wrapped my arms around her and held her. I brushed the hair away from her neck and gently kissed her skin, causing her to giggle. She turned to face me, and I stepped forward, gently pinning her to the counter with my hips pressed against hers.

"We'll figure this out, Sunshine. You'll get to live again, the way you want."

Rae's eyes had a sparkle to them as she looked at me. She lifted her hands to my chin, her fingers tangling in my beard. "I have everything I want, right here, Ranger," she whispered before kissing me.

Just like her, I also had everything I wanted, right here.

Chapter 45

Rae

"How about I work on those sore muscles now? Would you like that?" We'd sat back down at the table and talked for a bit after cleaning up after dinner.

Gosh, would I ever, but he must be tired and sore, too. "Are you sure? I don't want to—"

Caleb put his hand up to stop me. "Nope. None of that. My girl will not be thinking my offer to give her a massage is an inconvenience for me."

His girl. I would never get tired of hearing that.

"Okay, okay...Point made." I laughed and rolled my eyes. Caleb stood and offered his hand to me before leading me to our room.

The light in the room was low, warm, and honey-soft from the lamp on the nightstand. I took off everything but my undergarments and turned to see Caleb staring at me with his eyes wide and mouth open some.

"Wha—? Should I not have..?" I reached for my pajama pants.

Caleb was next to me within half a second. "Rae, stop, honey." He turned me to look at him. His hold on my arms was firm but not controlling. I looked at his eyes and I knew one thing for sure. Caleb loved me.

I'd seen videos or photos of grooms seeing their brides on their wedding day. They would cry at the sight of them. I had wished that someone could love me like that, but I never got that from Ethan, not even in the early days of our relationship. But here I was, with Caleb holding me and looking at me the way I had longed for.

"I thought clothes would get in the way, but then I realized I should have asked. But..." I got lost in the look on his face and didn't finish my thought. As if he knew what I was thinking, Caleb finished it for me.

"They do get in the way." He flashed me a mischievous smile. "And you realized you don't have to ask with me, and don't have to be anything but yourself with me?" His voice was low and had a slight rasp to it.

Desire flared immediately, like a small fire doused in lighter fluid. It was like an immediate switch. While I had been so unbelievably attracted to him before and felt the pull to him that I felt right now, nothing had felt like this before. Even though we'd been together before, I had to force my brain to listen and not put walls up. Now, it was like my head finally caught up with my heart. I wanted him so badly, right now, forever, in every way. The heat inside me only grew more intense.

"Hey, where did you go?" I heard his voice, like it was far off in the distance, and it made me snap back to reality. His arms were wrapped around me, and our faces were inches from each other's.

I focused on his face again. "Sorry, I got lost in thought. Don't worry, though, they were good thoughts." I gave him a little wink and smiled.

"Okay, good. I was wondering." He returned the smile. "Let me help take away this tension," he said with that rasp that had started the thoughts I had. The tension he spoke about was not the one I was thinking of.

I removed the rest of my clothes, giving Caleb a mischievous smile as I did so. I could tell he was trying so hard to keep his composure. I lay face down on the bed, completely bare beneath one of the flannel blankets, the edge tucked under the curve of my hips. My hair had air-dried into soft waves after my shower, a few loose ringlets fell against my cheek.

The mattress moved as he climbed onto the bed behind me, carefully straddling my thighs. I could feel the weight of him, solid but gentle. He moved my hair off my neck and leaned down to kiss my skin before whispering that he loved me. He smelled like the warm scent of whisky and coffee, the smell that had become familiar and safe.

I closed my eyes as Caleb picked something up off the nightstand. The sound of his hands rubbing together filled the quiet, and then the first touch of warmth spread across my back as he pressed his palms to my skin.

He didn't rush. His hands started at my neck and moved to my shoulders. Each movement was slow and steady, working out the knots I'd earned from hours of lifting, sweeping, and bending, the kind of soreness that ached with movement. His touch was firm and warm, and I felt like I was melting with every touch. A low breath escaped me before I could stop it. The tension I hadn't realized I was still carrying started to unravel beneath his hands.

"You're all knotted up, baby," he murmured, his voice quiet and low, like he was talking more to himself than to me.

His hands moved lower, along the slope of my back, his thumbs brushing along the sides of my ribs before sliding down again. He didn't pull at the blanket or uncover more than what I'd already given him. But his touch…it was everything. Careful. Intentional. Devoted.

My lashes fluttered closed as I sank deeper into the feeling of it. Every pass of his hands seemed to reach something beyond muscle, like he was untangling more than just the knots in my body.

When he reached the middle of my back, his hands paused, heat radiating through his palms. His voice was quiet. "Can I go lower?"

My answer came out soft but certain. "Yes."

The blanket shifted slightly as he tugged it down just a few inches, exposing the top of my hips. His thumbs kneaded slowly along my waist, then my hips. Every time his hands glided over my skin, my breath grew a little shakier. He adjusted, working down my legs. He massaged my calves first, then back up my thighs. His thumbs traced my thighs with measured pressure, skimming close enough to make my pulse quicken. He didn't intentionally do it, and that only made me want him more. A small moan slipped out of me, quiet and unguarded.

He froze, hands still. "Too much?"

My fingers curled into the sheets. "No," I whispered, breathless. "Not enough."

Caleb's breath stilled just slightly, the air between us shifting. "Yeah?"

I nodded into the pillow, then turned my head just enough to see him. "I want more. I need you."

232

He stared at me for a moment, like he was looking into my soul. He leaned down, his lips brushing the top of my thigh. "Whatever you need."

I rolled onto my back slowly, the blanket still draped across my waist. He reached out as if to help but didn't pull, just waited. I let the blanket fall on my own. I didn't feel the urge to hide.

"I want you to touch me," I said quietly.

His eyes darkened, but his hands stayed gentle. He bent forward, his lips pressing to my stomach, then lower, tracing soft paths across my skin. Every touch, every brush of his breath, sent warmth spilling through me until I couldn't tell where his touch ended and mine began.

Caleb shifted to the edge of the bed before quickly tugging me towards him. His hands moved on my thighs as he smiled up at me. "You are so beautiful, Rae," he whispered just before his mouth was on me in a way that made the world blur. The first brush of his mouth drew a sound from deep inside me, quiet but desperate.

He took his time, learning what made me gasp, what made my fingers clutch at the sheets. Every motion was patient, each one meant to pull me closer to that breaking point. He didn't stop when my body started to tremble, didn't stop when I whispered his name. He stayed with me through every shiver, every breath, coaxing me higher until I finally let go, the room spinning and quiet except for the sound of us breathing.

When I opened my eyes again, he was watching me, his expression soft in the dim light.

"Come here," I whispered, needing him closer than he already was.

He moved up the bed, his hand finding mine as he kissed me. The taste of him, the warmth of his body against mine, it all blurred together. I pulled back just enough to look at him, to let him see me.

"I want you, Ranger," I confessed as my hands slipped under his shirt. "All of you. Right now." As soon as his shirt was gone, I reached for his pants. He had changed into soft flannel pants after his shower, and I couldn't get the knot undone. My hands were shaking a bit because of how badly I wanted him. Caleb helped undo the knot and soon there was nothing between us. I felt the heat of his body against mine immediately, as well as how badly he wanted me.

"Lie back," I said. My voice shook, not from nerves, but from wanting him in a way my brain had never let me before.

He blinked once, maybe surprised, but then he gave me that soft smile. "Yeah, baby," he murmured as his thumb brushed over my cheek.

He eased back, lying on his back, relaxed. I straddled his hips carefully, my thighs trembling slightly. I felt exposed, but not unsafe. Never unsafe with him.

"Oh, wait. I need to grab a..." He started to reach for the nightstand, but I placed my hand on his arm to stop him. "Caleb, wait. You don't need to do that. I was in my head the first time and forgot to say anything. I'm on birth control. I was forced to take it, and it became routine, so I just continued."

234

His eyes searched mine for a moment before I leaned down and kissed him. As I sat back up, he followed, continuing our kiss. I playfully pushed him back before I placed my hands on his chest to steady myself, feeling the steady rise and fall beneath my palms. My breath came slow, uneven, my eyes moved down his body before finding his again. "I've never been on top before," I said quietly. There wasn't shame in what I had admitted, just truth. "It wasn't really something I ever got to do."

His warm hands slid to my hips, grounding me in a way words never could. His gaze held mine. He gently squeezed my hips slightly before moving them over my thighs. "You're in charge now," he said quietly. "Take what you need, Sunshine."

Something inside me loosened. I leaned down, kissed him, and everything that followed was slow, steady, and real. Not about proving anything, not about forgetting, but about remembering what it felt like to want and to be wanted without fear.

My lips parted on a soft breath as I steadied myself over him, my hands resting lightly on his chest. For a moment I just breathed, letting myself feel the warmth of him beneath my palms. Caleb made a low sound the second I touched him, deep and quiet, and it gave me enough courage to keep going. I moved slowly, guiding us closer, letting my body adjust. The first bit of pressure pulled a gasp from me, my breath catching before I could stop it. Everything about this felt intense and overwhelming in the best way.

I placed my hand more firmly on his chest, using the steady beat under my palm to anchor myself.

Caleb's hands settled at my hips. "Nice and slow, baby." His voice was soft in a way that settled something deep inside me.

I nodded and kept moving, taking my time. Each shift sent warmth curling through me, my breath uneven as I found a pace that felt right. He stayed relaxed beneath me, letting me lead without pushing me in any direction.

When I finally settled against him, my head dipped forward and a quiet sound slipped from my lips. "Gosh, you feel so good," I whispered, my voice shaking just enough to give me away.

Caleb let out a strained breath and a smile. "You feel like heaven, baby. And you look so beautiful."

I began to move slowly, learning the rhythm as I went. Everything about it felt intense, and it only made me want him more. His hands stayed at my hips, grounding me without steering me. When I shifted a certain way and a gasp slipped out, I did it again. My pace stayed slow and careful, but I grew more confident with each small roll of my hips, especially when he reacted as I moved. My palms slid across his chest, clinging to him as I found what felt good.

"Sunshine, I love seeing you like this." His voice was a bit raspy. "Taking what you want."

Heat moved through me as his words caused my body to react before I could even think about it. I rocked harder, deeper, my thighs trembling with the effort, but the pleasure pushed everything else aside.

236

Caleb lifted his hips in soft, controlled movements that met mine perfectly, each sound he made pulling another wave of desire through me. We moved together slowly, finding a rhythm that felt right between us. Warmth built inside me with every movement, my breath growing unsteady. Caleb let out a low groan, trying to hold himself back for me, but I knew he was close.

When it finally washed over me, it took my breath away. My whole body drew tight in a way that felt so overwhelming, a quiet cry slipping out as I fell apart with his name on my lips. That was all it took for him. His body tensed beneath my hands as he followed, a rough sound leaving him as he buried his face in my neck.

We stayed there, breathing against each other. Our racing hearts slowly settled. I melted against his chest, warm and weightless, and he pressed a gentle kiss to my temple, brushing my hair back with his fingers. We stayed tangled together, holding on to the quiet, letting the moment soften around us.

Caleb's hand moved along my back, soft and unhurried. "You didn't just take control tonight," he whispered. "You owned it."

I smiled against his skin. "Gosh, I liked that."

He laughed softly, the sound low and warm. "So did I."

Chapter 46

Rae

A gentle, satisfied feeling, like a fog, settled over my thoughts. It almost blurred the edges of the world, as I lay there with Caleb's arm wrapped around my waist. Neither of us moved from the bed after we finished. We just lay there, tangled in each other's arms. My back was pressed against Caleb's warm chest, and I knew I would never get tired of this feeling.

This is love. This is what it's supposed to be like.

Despite Ethan harassing me, with Caleb, it seemed like all the extra chaos was drowned out when he was around. Caleb kissed the top of my head, and I leaned my head back into his neck in an attempt to get closer than I already was. One of his arms was under me, stretched out with my hand resting on his. His other arm was wrapped around my waist, his fingers moving in little circles around my ribs. I was sensitive about certain touches, but not this. Not with him. He paid attention, he learned me, and he never judged me for things I didn't like.

"I could stay like this forever," I whispered to him.

"Same here. But someone has to make food at some point."

"Well, that and feed all the animals. The rest of the time, though?"

I felt Caleb laughing as his body shook against mine. He pulled me closer. "The rest of the time would be spent here, if I had the choice," he whispered in my ear. The warmth of his breath against my skin sent a tingling feeling throughout my body again.

I nestled closer into his chest, pulling the blanket up under my chin, my eyes fluttering shut when I heard Duke growling. I looked at Duke and saw something out of the corner of my eye outside the window. It looked like the shadow of someone standing there. I blinked and it seemed to disappear.

Caleb had picked his head up to look, too, when Duke's growling grew angrier. When he didn't seem bothered by anything, I figured I had seen the shadow of a tree or something, so I relaxed again.

Suddenly, Duke's growling that had subsided became angry again. This time, it was even more angry than before. I looked towards where Duke was staring, and I saw it again. This time, though, it wasn't my imagination.

The air inside my lungs quickly vanished, and it felt like the room was spinning.

I forced myself to take a breath. "He-hey, Ca-Caleb." My voice trembled. "I th-think there's s-someone at the window."

Caleb's body immediately stiffened, and he picked his head up to look in the direction of the window. "I don't see anyone, but Duke doesn't typically just growl for fun. The porch light has a motion sensor on it and it's not on. Was it on when you first saw it?"

"No. I—I'm not crazy. I know I saw someone." My voice sounded frantic. Part of me wondered if he actually believed me, but I pushed that feeling aside. Of course he did.

Caleb was up from the bed, pulling on his jeans. "No, baby. I believe you. Promise." He walked around the bed to kiss me. "I just want to know why the light didn't come on and who the hell is on the porch."

Duke was watching outside still when Caleb went to check that the windows were closed and locked, then shut the curtains. He scratched behind Duke's ears as he praised him for watching out for us.

When Caleb went to the bedroom door, Duke followed him before looking back at me. It was like he was trying to figure out who he needed to protect more.

"No, buddy. You stay with Rae." He knelt and looked into Duke's steel gray eyes "you watch her, boy. Okay?"

As soon as Caleb said that, Duke jumped up on the bed in front of me, facing the door and window, floppy ears up.

"Rae, come lock this door and don't answer it unless you hear my voice." He walked to his side of the bed and grabbed his gun and phone from the nightstand before walking back to the bedroom door. Caleb turned towards me and looked at me with an intensity I had not seen but only once or twice before. "I love you," he said before opening the door.

I could feel my heart racing. Blood pumped in my ears so loud, I felt like I was deafened by it. "I love you, too," my voice squeaked.

I got up and locked the door to our room after he left and then crawled back into the bed, behind Duke.

240

I heard Caleb grabbing the keys to the house and then the front door opening. I wished when I heard the door close and him lock it behind him that it calmed my nerves.

Minutes that felt like hours passed by. I looked at the clock. It had only been five minutes since he walked out of the house.

Ten minutes.

Fifteen minutes.

Seventeen minutes had passed by the time I heard the keys in the front door. I let out a long breath of air, realizing I'd been holding my breath, while waiting for the sound of the keys in the lock.

I waited until I heard him close and lock the front door and then come to our room to get off the bed. "Hey Rae, it's me. You can come unlock the door." I walked to the bedroom door, my legs shaky under me. Duke was right next to me the entire time.

"Did you see anything or anyone?" My voice sounded more panicked than I intended.

"No. I know how they got past the porch light, though. The bulb is shattered. The motion detector is still working, but it can't connect to a light. I can't confirm that someone threw a rock at it since there's rocks all over, but that's the only thing I found among the broken glass."

"But how did we not hear the bulb being hit, or the glass breaking?"

I'm wondering if it was while...well, while we were...distracted."

"Oh gosh." Suddenly the room felt like it was spinning. I reached out for anything to hold on to as I stumbled backwards. "Caleb, he's found me again."

Caleb caught me so I didn't fall and led me to the bed, sitting me down before sitting next to me. "We can't confirm it's him." He ran a hand over his head, and the look on his face told me he was frustrated. "Even though it probably is him, we can't confirm it. I just want you to be aware of that when the cops show up, they can't pin it on him if there's no proof, okay? I texted the sergeant on duty instead of calling, since I didn't want to alert whoever was out there that they're coming. I fully believe it was Ethan, but I also know they can't do anything without proof."

I nodded and hated that we probably wouldn't find any proof that Ethan had been here. I thought more about what he said and then a wave of panic ran through me. "Do you think he was still out there when you went outside?"

He hesitated before he spoke, his face still clouded with frustration. "Probably, but not close enough where I could find him. He probably snuck away when I was closing the curtains and getting my stuff to go out there."

I nodded and a shiver ran through me.

"Rae, I want to apologize to you for something. I should have put up security cameras here, but I didn't. If I had done so, we would possibly have proof of it being him."

I reached for his hand, lacing my fingers with his. "Ranger, you can't beat yourself for this. I never would

242

have guessed that he would be so bold as to come to an officer's home."

"We'll get this guy, Sunshine. I'm going to protect my girl with everything I have in me."

Chapter 47

Caleb

"Alright, babe, what would you like for lunch?" I attempted to sound overly cheerful as I tried to keep her mind off last night. "Rae?" I looked over at her, sitting on the couch, staring out the window.

"I'm sorry, Caleb, I zoned out. What did you ask?"

I walked over to her and held out my hand, encouraging her to move away from the window. "Come on, let's get you some lunch."

"I'm not really hungry."

"You didn't eat breakfast either and I made your favorite, bacon. You have to eat something, Rae." I understood how scared she must be, but I was really concerned about her. Every time she closed her eyes after I'd searched the perimeter of the house, she started to dream within minutes of getting to sleep and woke up screaming. Not even sleeping next to me helped her. I barely slept as well. The first couple times she woke up screaming, I had been able to doze off once she did, but then I woke up with her. After the first couple of times, I was awake and watching her.

"I'm sorry, I—"

I held up my hand. "Do not apologize, please, for something you can't control. This place was your safe place, and someone took it from you last night."

"I'm so tired." She rubbed her eyes and her voice cracked from how tired she was.

"How about you try and get some sleep? I'll sit by the bed, watching over you so you can rest."

Rae nodded. "Can you hold me, though? I want to feel safe."

We walked to the bedroom and crawled into bed, my arm around her, protecting her from whatever may come her way in her sleep.

Rae got two hours of decent sleep and then insisted on me getting sleep as well. Despite trying to sleep more, I was only able to get an hour of broken sleep. Thankfully, Luke and Jenny told me they'd take over everything on the farm today.

"I'm going to walk to get the mail. Would you like to join me?"

She hesitated but nodded and stood, walking to the door.

The sun was warm and Rae stood on the porch for a few moments as she breathed in the fresh air and soaked up the warmth of the sunshine.

"Want to spend a little time on the porch? Get some sunshine?" I asked as we walked to the end of the road leading to the farm to get the mail.

She nodded. "Only if you're there, though."

I took the stack of mail out of the mailbox and smiled at her. "I'll go anywhere with you."

I sorted through the mail as we walked back towards the house. Duke was running up ahead of us, chasing a butterfly. The butterfly landed on Duke's head and back, then flew away, to only return moments later. The sight of it made Rae giggle.

I pulled an envelope from the stack that had my name on it, but nothing else. I carefully opened it and looked inside. What I saw made me stop in my tracks.

"Rae, get inside now." My voice was tense. I hated my tone, but I didn't know where Ethan was at the moment. I didn't know what his plans were, either, but it wasn't worth taking a chance and finding out the hard way if he was still around.

"What? What's wrong?"

"I'll explain inside the house. Now. Inside."

Rae rushed inside the house and I followed closely behind. As soon as the door was locked, I closed all the curtains in the front of the house. This was probably over-kill, but Ethan had been escalating, and I wouldn't put it past him to be watching from somewhere with binoculars or a long-range lens so he could watch her spiral.

I reached for my phone as I passed her the envelope. "I don't even want you to see this, but you're going to hear about it when I call the department, so...just please don't worry."

I kept my arm around her as she opened the enve-lope. "I promise, everything will be okay," I said before I called my squad sergeant. I watched her closely, keeping a firm hold around her waist. She pulled out a note that read "I miss you" and two printed photos. The sudden re-alization showed on her face. Her hands began to shake.

246

The photos were of her and I in the bedroom, last night, before Duke started growling.

"Sarge, I can't talk, but he struck again. My house. Now."

Rae dropped the note and photos before she ran to the spare bathroom. I heard the toilet lid opening and as I walked in the doorway, she threw herself on the ground in front of it.

I walked up behind her and held her hair as she threw up. "Caleb," she sobbed as nausea took over her entire body and caused her to shake more.

"I know, baby. I know. My squad is on the way here."

"I don't want them to see the photos," she cried.

"I know, but they have to take them into evidence so they have more to pin on him. I'll have Santana be the one to take them, if that would make you more comfortable."

She nodded but threw up again while I rubbed her back.

Rae leaned against the wall as soon as she was done. We sat there for a few minutes while she caught her breath. She continued to sob as I rubbed her back and wished that I could make everything better.

"Can I help you stand up so you can wash your face? That may help you feel better."

She nodded, so I helped her up and to the sink. She was shaky, so as soon as she was done washing her face, I picked her up and carried her to the front room, settling her on the couch under a blanket.

When my squad arrived moments later, she sat on the couch, staring at the wall.

My heart broke for her. I had seen tears in her eyes threatening to fall while I told them everything, but they didn't until I had to give the photos to Santana. I hated that Ethan made her feel this way. I knew she was embarrassed, and it broke my heart.

Santana walked over to Rae and sat on the couch next to her. Rae looked at her but didn't say a word. "I will make sure that I am the only one that processes these, along with the girls in Evidence." Rae gave Santana a strained half smile and nodded.

As her fragile smile faded, I knew the road ahead would be a long one, but something else I knew for sure: she wouldn't be facing it alone.

Chapter 48

Rae

"This is so stressful. I just want this to be done with—" I excused myself to the spare bathroom once Santana took the photos, and now I was hiding out, listening to Caleb talk to his squad.

I couldn't hear everything, but hearing Caleb say it was stressful caused my heart to break a bit.

I sat on the edge of the tub, leaning over, with my head in my hands. I was wearing one of Caleb's hoodies, and the sleeves were damp with tears.

I hated this. Not just the fear and not just the memories. I hated Ethan. I hated myself.

Why would Caleb even want to stay with me after this? He'd probably be better off with someone who doesn't bring this much chaos into his life. I'd dragged Caleb into this mess. Into the chaos of my past. The creepy messages and sleepless nights. Or the way I second-guessed everything and didn't know how to stop falling apart. He had already done more than anyone had ever done for me, and now I'd brought chaos to his home, too.

What if Ethan tried something? What if he came here again, and what if Caleb got hurt just because he cared?

My eyes burned and my chest ached like it had been ripped out and stomped on. I hated crying this much, but Caleb said it was a normal trauma response and I was healing. I missed the old me, though. Caleb called me Sunshine for a reason, but I have not felt like her recently.

I slid from the edge of the tub to the bathmat and pressed my forehead to my knees, letting out a shaky breath. "You're selfish," I whispered to myself. "You should've never stayed."

A quiet knock broke the silence. "Rae?" Caleb's voice was soft on the other side of the door. "You okay?"

I didn't answer at first. My lips were too tight, and I was afraid I'd break if I spoke. After a moment, I stood, wiped my face, and cracked open the door. He stood there in a worn T-shirt and flannel pants, barefoot and backlit by the dim hallway light. His brows pulled together the second he saw my face. *Gosh, I've caused him to worry too much.* I opened the bathroom door and stared at him for a moment, fighting back tears. Duke stood at his feet, looking up at me.

"Hey." He reached for me, but I stepped out and gently pushed past him, heading toward the kitchen, needing space—needing to get out what I needed to say before I chickened out.

He followed me.

I stopped at the edge of the counter, hands gripping it, back to him. *Spit it out, Rae.*

"I need to go." It felt like the air in the room became so thin once I said it. Silence stretched behind me.

"I should've left sooner," I said, my voice barely steady. "This was a mistake. Being here, staying here. You've already done so much for me, and now I've dragged you into something possibly dangerous. This isn't fair to you. I'm so sorry."

"I'm not trying to be controlling, but you're not leaving."

I turned, startled by the firmness in his voice. He looked apologetic for his tone since it wasn't how he ever spoke to me. I could tell he wasn't angry, but he was serious.

"Caleb—"

"No." He walked up to me slowly. "You don't get to decide what's fair for me. You don't get to protect me by walking away like none of this matters. Like we don't matter."

My chin quivered. "I heard you, Caleb. I heard you say it's stressful, and I caused that, Caleb. I caused your stress. Ethan doesn't let go. He won't. I tried to get away for a long time and I couldn't. He hurt me when I tried. If he comes here, if he tries something to hurt you because you're protecting me..."

"Then I'll be ready." He stepped closer. "Rae, I don't care how crazy it gets. What you heard me say about stress was...Yes, I am stressed. However, it's because I want you to feel safe. I don't know how to fix this for you, the girl I love, and that's all I want to do. Besides the things we do know, we can't prove that he's involved in everything that has happened, and that is stressful."

"Exactly, and what if that never ends?" Tears were flowing steadily now.

"It will." He held his finger up to tell me to hold on a minute, when I tried to argue again. "But if it doesn't, then that is okay with me, too. I don't care if I have to look over my shoulder for the rest of my life. What I do care about is you. I care that you're safe, that you feel safe. I will fight for you, for us, until he is no longer tormenting you. When the next hurdles come, I will fight for us *then*, too."

"But I don't want to ruin your life," I choked.

"You're not ruining it." His hand found mine. "You're the best damn thing that's happened to me in a long time."

My gaze fell from his eyes to our hands, then the floor. He stepped in again, this time lifting my chin with the gentlest touch. "Look at me."

I did.

"I want you here," he said. "Even with the hard stuff. Even when it's messy. I want every piece of you, Rae. Not just the sunshine. I want the storm, too."

Tears welled again in my eyes. "You don't have to say that."

"I know I don't." His thumb brushed my cheek. "But I mean it. You stay here. With me. No more talk about leaving. Please. I can't lose you again."

My breath caught at the sound of his voice cracking.

"I need you to believe," he added, voice low and steady, "that loving you isn't a burden. It's a choice I'm making every day. And I'm not going anywhere."

My chest felt like it cracked open under the weight of his words. My whole body trembled as I stepped into his arms, leaning my head against his shoulder. His arms came around me like they always did: strong, warm, safe.

The fear that had been holding its grip on me loosened a bit, letting me breathe, in the safety of his arms.

252

Chapter 49

Rae

A couple of days passed with nothing from Ethan. There had been no calls or texts, and none of the officers at the department had seen him around. I didn't know if that made me more nervous or relieved. Caleb and I were sitting outside on the porch so I could enjoy the sunshine while he put up the cameras he'd ordered. I'd chosen to sit on the porch steps, and Duke joined me, laying his head in my lap.

"How many do you have to put up?"

"Just two. The others won't be here for a few days, sadly." He had tried to buy them in town, but no one had them in stock, so he'd had to order them.

"It's oka—" His phone ringing cut off my voice. I froze like I had every time his phone rang the last few days. Different officers from the department had been calling daily with updates on if they'd found anything.

"Don't worry. It's not work, but please don't be mad at me."

I gave him a confused look and tried to figure out why he would be making that request.

He answered the call. "This is Caleb. Yup. Yeah, can you hold on a few minutes?" When he looked at me, I saw a flash of nerves cross his face. He hit the mute button on the phone and walked to the porch swing. "I have a surprise for you."

I walked over to the swing and sat next to him. "Who is on the phone?" I asked nervously.

"You were sleeping yesterday, and I had a thought, so I looked at your phone to see if I was right."

I didn't care if he looked through my phone, so why did he look so nervous? He seemed genuinely worried that I would be upset with him.

"Did you know you had a spam call and text section on your phone?" He reached for my hand and I linked my fingers with his.

I shook my head.

"I found a text from Cierra. She had texted you a few times per month." My jaw dropped. "Rae, the last time she texted you was a week ago. Ethan sent all her texts and calls to the spam inbox."

I was facing Caleb, but I was not looking at him anymore. I was shocked. She *had* continued reaching out even after I wasn't allowed to talk to her?

"Is that...?" I pointed towards his phone which sat behind him. Excitement and nerves swirled in my mind. Caleb nodded. *"Really?"* I asked, trying to wrap my brain around what he'd just told me.

"I know you said you would like to try and reach out to her if I was involved, so I hope it's okay that I called her when I saw the text."

I was smiling so much my cheeks hurt and I quickly wrapped my arms around him. "You just did the sweetest thing for me, so of course it's okay!"

"She's been waiting for a few minutes, though. Do you want to talk to her now, or should I tell her you'll call her later?"

"Now, please, but only if you stay with me." I twisted my hands nervously as Caleb reached for the phone. He noticed and held one of my hands as he took the call off mute.

"Cierra? Hey, it's Caleb…"

It was amazing hearing one of my best friend's voices again, especially since I never thought I would hear from her again. The conversation consisted mostly of her telling me about her kids and all they are doing now. I could tell we were getting close to talking about my life recently, though, and nerves were bubbling to the surface.

"So, Rae, tell me…is that *the* Caleb from high school?" I could hear the smile on her face as she asked me that.

Caleb had been holding my hand and gave it a gentle squeeze as his eyebrows raised a bit. I giggled at the look he gave me. "Yup. He's *that* Caleb. I wish you could meet him, Cierra."

"I feel like I know him already…" There was a long pause, but I could tell she wanted to say something. "I will say, though, when I got a call from your number and a guy was on the other end, it made me curious… Listen, Rae. You do not have to tell me anything if you don't want to. Obviously, something happened, and I have a feeling that it was far from good. I only think that because it was unlike you to not answer when I reached out, and the conversations I had with Ethan were…interesting."

Caleb sat up straighter than he had been.

Cierra continued. "If you want to tell me anything, you can, but either way, there are no hard feelings." She let out a deep breath before continuing. "All I want to know is...are you safe and happy?"

I looked at Caleb and smiled before scooting closer to him and leaning my head on his shoulder. "Thank you, Cierra. I am safe now, and I'm happy. I'm happier now than I have been in a long time."

Caleb pulled me close to him but still seemed restless. I knew it was about her bringing up Ethan. I glanced up at him, and he motioned to the phone and then back to himself, mouthing the words "Can I talk to her?"

"Cierra, can Caleb ask you something really quick? It's about what you said, about Ethan."

She agreed.

Caleb's face turned serious. "Hey, Cierra. When you said the conversations were interesting, what did you mean by that? I'm not only Rae's boyfriend, but I'm also a cop. I have seen and heard a lot of things in my career, suspects using people close to their victims, stuff like that. And I was just curious about what he said to you."

"Oh! So, at one point, Ethan reached out to me from his phone and told me to stop calling Rae. He'd told me that she didn't want to talk to me anymore, but he didn't give a reason. I had my husband go by her old house on his way home. I was too scared to go by myself because something felt off, but we had the kids, so we couldn't go together. Ethan was moving around inside, and my husband could see him through the window, but he didn't answer the door. We had called the cops to do a wellness check on Rae…"

I gasped.

"I'm so sorry if that caused issues, Rae. I was so worried."

I reassured her that nothing came of that. What I didn't tell her is because he was afraid that if he did anything, the cops would find out since we were already on their radar because of her call. I remembered that day easily because it was one of the few good days I had.

"The cops called me back and said that Rae had come to the door with Ethan, and they both seemed fine. A few weeks ago, I called your work number, but they told me you hadn't come in, so I called Ethan to check on you. Ethan said you ran away but then corrected himself and said you'd left him. It all felt off, until he said something right before he hung up."

I had no idea what she was about to say, but my blood ran cold. My entire body was freezing despite the warmth the sun brought.

"Caleb, Ethan said that when he caught up to Rae, she won't have anything to say to anyone because she'll regret leaving him. When I asked what he meant, he said something about her missing time with him and making up for lost time. I called the non-emergency number and told them about what he'd said and mentioned the wellness check. The only problem is, he wasn't at the house anytime they went by."

"That was probably around the time he came out here," Caleb said as we heard one of Cierra's kids crying in the background.

"Oh gosh. I'm so sorry, you guys. I have to go, but I do want to talk again really soon. Is that okay? Also, Caleb, I really only know what I just told you, but if there's anything I need to do, let me know. I don't know everything, but I know he did something to make my best friend leave, and if you are asking as a cop and boyfriend, then it seems serious."

Before the call ended, Caleb thanked her for the information, and I agreed to talk to her again, so she said she would text me.

I didn't care about the crazy information Cierra gave us as much as I cared about kissing Caleb right now. I also didn't care that the porch swing would move as I shifted until I was straddling his lap.

"Ranger, that was the sweetest thing you could have done. Thank you," I said before kissing him deeply. My hands moved across his shoulders and up to the smooth skin on his head before pulling him even closer.

"Anything for you, Sunshine. Anything to see that smile on your face."

The world around us seemed to fade away as Caleb wrapped his arms around me, holding me tight as he kissed me.

Somehow, Caleb always knew exactly what I needed.

Chapter 50

Rae

Another couple days passed without any sign of Ethan, and I was going stir crazy sitting in the house. Jenny and Luke had come by for dinner last night, and Cierra and I had texted and talked a couple of times, but other than that, we had been hanging out around the house and the barn. I loved being around Caleb, but I needed to be outside of the house—off the property. I knew Ethan had been escalating, but I made Caleb promise me that I could start work in a couple of days if we hadn't heard from him. I made him a promise that I wouldn't leave the department unless he was with me, and I also reminded him that he could look for Ethan while he was on duty. He agreed and called his sergeant and my boss to let them know our plan.

A part of me felt guilty for wanting that. I knew it was for my safety since Ethan had escalated, and everyone was on high alert. I knew what he had done, and if he ever got his chance again, I didn't know what he would do as a punishment. However, I also wanted to not have to hide from him the rest of my life.

Caleb and I had been lounging around on the couch for a bit and Duke was lying on my feet when a phone rang. I sat up, instantly thinking the worst but hoping for the best. Caleb reached for his phone and told me it was Jenny.

"Hey, Jenny. Yeah, that's no problem. I know Rae is dying to do something, so we would love to help." He shot me a smile. "Okay, we will get ready and head that way."

Caleb hung up the phone and smiled at me again. "How would you like to go to Jenny's house with me? She said there were some paint cans and smaller tool items that had been dropped off a few days ago, but they were not there when Luke went to pick them up later. The company told her that she needs to have the items signed for this time if she wants the stuff sent out again at no charge. The problem is, as she was finishing up in the barn, she got called into work. I know we are still worried Ethan is out there, but I also know you're itching to do something."

"I would love to go!" I jumped up and ran to put my boots on, then ran towards the front door. My excitement made him laugh.

We made the short drive to Jenny's house. The tree line that stretched between the two houses was covered in bright green leaves, the branches swaying gently in the breeze. Caleb took a right turn off the main road onto a smaller one that led to her place. The gravel crunching under the truck's tires was a welcome sound since I hadn't really left the house while hiding at Caleb's from Ethan.

Caleb stopped the truck in front of the house. I hadn't seen Jenny's house since I was a teen, and the sight made me sad because of the state it was in. While it hadn't suffered too much damage, the sight of the scorched siding made my chest tighten.

I got out and started to wander towards the front porch, but Caleb put his hand out to stop me. "Wait. We can't go in right now due to the structural damage. Luke has hard hats we can use if you want to see inside later."

I nodded. The crunch of gravel came from behind us, and we turned to see a truck driving towards us. Caleb positioned himself between me and the truck as it came to a stop in front of us.

"How's it going? You Caleb?" An older gentleman stepped out of the truck.

Caleb nodded and walked towards him. "Fine, thank you. Thanks for letting me step in to sign for the delivery."

I watched the two of them exchange small talk as the man loaded up the delivery into Caleb's truck. A warm breeze blew my hair around my face and I turned into it, my gaze drifting back towards the house.

For a moment, I could have sworn something moved in the window. I squinted, focusing on the window, a prickling feeling on the back of my neck. I took a couple of steps toward the house, scanning from one window to the next, seeing no movement.

"What are you looking at?" Caleb said, walking up behind me, placing a hand on the small of my back. I looked back where the trucks had been parked next to each other and realized the guy who had brought the delivery out here had left.

"I could have sworn I just saw something moving inside the house."

"Really? Luke's truck isn't out here. He and Jenny are both at work. Where did you see it?"

I pointed at the window. "It could have been a reflection, or even my imagination. I just had a weird feeling."

"Hold on," Caleb said as he walked towards the house. I watched as he stepped carefully up on the porch and checked the front door, before moving to the window. Another small breeze blew through the front yard, ruffling my hair a little, as Caleb looked through all the windows at the front of the house. "Hey, Sunshine, I'm going to go around the back and check the doors there. Can you get in the truck and lock the doors?"

I nodded and hopped in the truck as I watched him walk out of sight.

It was warm in the truck, but not unbearable. I was also able to watch the front of the house better without my hair blowing into my face.

Caleb was back within a couple of minutes and smiled at me as he hopped in the truck. "Did you see anything or am I going crazy?"

He let out a little laugh before leaning in and kissing me on the temple. "Baby, you're not crazy. I didn't see anything in the house, but I couldn't go inside. Luke made sure to get all new doors and replace the damaged windows before doing repairs inside, so he wouldn't have critters or squatters living in there. The only thing I saw that raised some level of concern was the back porch door. The latch was a little loose, but the door was locked. I tried to turn the knob and it didn't open."

"So…"

"I'm thinking it was a reflection from something outside the house, but I am going to ask Luke and Jenny to let me know when they come back here. I'll come with them to just check everything out."

262

I nodded, trying to not feel crazy for thinking I had seen something inside of the house. But a small part of me was still not quite convinced.

♥

After returning from Jenny's house, Caleb and I put the items from the delivery in the barn. Bandit stuck his face out of the stall to say hello, so I walked over to him to return the greeting.

"Hey, Caleb… Can—can I be honest about something?"

"Of course. Always."

"I feel really weird for thinking about this. Selfish, almost. I'm still kind of bummed that I haven't been able to start work. I can't even go to the grocery store without worrying." I let out a long sigh as I ran my hand down Bandit's soft nose. "I love being here at the house and could be wrapped up in your arms all day…" I paused as he started to walk towards me, a sweet smile on his face. He stood in front of me, so close we were almost touching.

"But the sense of normalcy was taken away because of this—because of him? The fact that you can't freely choose to go out, for fear he's out there?" His voice had a gravelly sound to it. The sound of his voice, mixed with how close we were at the moment, sent heat throughout my entire body.

"Yeah, it sounds silly now that it's been said out loud, especially considering how scared I still am. I do still want to go to work in a couple of days, if things seem okay…It's confusing." I let out a breathy laugh, giving away the fact that how close he was made me nervous, but not in a bad way—just in the way that only he could make me feel.

"No, it doesn't sound silly. How about this? We go to dinner at the new bar and grill a buddy of mine opened, and then we get a few things at the grocery store. As long as you promise me you won't leave my side."

He still hadn't touched me, and the lack of contact was making it impossible to think clearly.

"*That* won't be a problem."

"My gosh, dinner was so good. Thank you for bringing me here!" I reached out and took his hand, our eyes lingering on each other's, saying more than words ever could.

Rhett, the owner of the restaurant, walked up to us with a plate in his hand. "Dessert is on the house tonight. I heard you tell the waitress that dairy makes you sick, so I figured you may be one of the first people to try our new dairy-free desserts. That is, if you both don't mind."

"Rhett, are you trying to show off in front of my girl?" Caleb laughed as he helped Rhett make room for the dessert plates.

"No." He let out a warm laugh. "As if I would even have a chance with the way she looks at you. Enjoy, you guys."

My face heated at what Rhett had said, and I gave Caleb a smile. He winked at me, causing my face to feel even hotter than before.

I took a bite of the slice of cake that Rhett had given us, and it melted in my mouth. The vanilla icing was

264

perfect. Caleb chuckled as he moved to take a bite of it as well, and I gave him a curious look. "You did it again—your happy dance you do when something tastes good."

I took another bite of the cake, closed my eyes, and wiggled my shoulders on purpose this time. When I opened my eyes, Caleb was matching my shoulder shimmy with one of his own. Laughter bubbled up out of both of us. Caleb reached his hand across the table, and I placed mine in his without thinking. We both finished the desserts in front of us, hand in hand.

When we were done and the bill was paid, we stepped out of the restaurant, into the warm spring air. Caleb led the way down the street to the crosswalk, making sure he was walking closest to the street the entire way. When we paused at the crosswalk, he slid behind me, arms wrapping around my waist. He leaned down just enough to murmur near my ear, voice low and smooth.

"Do you want to know what my favorite part of tonight was?"

I smiled, leaning back into him. "What?"

His lips brushed lightly against my cheek, kissing it gently before answering. His voice was rich with that slow, teasing drawl that always got to me. "Getting to show you off as my girl." He pressed a kiss just beneath my ear. "Walking with your hand in mine, getting to introduce you to my friend, kissing you in front of anyone watching...letting the whole world know you're my girl."

My breath caught, and he gave a knowing little grin.

"But what we do in private?" He leaned around to meet my eyes, one brow lifted. "Now that's even better."

He winked, and my stomach flipped.

"You don't say." I giggled, leaning into his warm body more.

"Mhm. Getting to love you the way you deserve, having you trust me entirely with not just your heart but your body as well, it's...intoxicating." He kissed me deeply, and a needy sound escaped my lips before I could stop it. "Let's get to the grocery store before I say we should just forget it and go home."

I giggled and covered my face with my hand as I laughed. Loving Caleb and being loved by him was the most simple and...intoxicating thing I'd ever done, and it made me feel alive.

Caleb took my hand and led me across the street to the grocery store. It was quiet besides the sounds of the employees restocking shelves. The combination of the harsh lights and the silence gave off an eerie feeling.

"I don't know if I have ever seen this place this quiet before," I told Caleb, my voice low because I felt like I had to whisper.

"It's almost 8 p.m., so I guess the rush just came and went already since they close soon."

I nodded and continued to walk with him. We picked up the items we'd needed, including my favorite bottle of wine and apples for the horses, and began walking towards the registers.

Caleb stopped in the middle of the aisle. "One last thing. Do you want to pick out a bag of treats for Duke?" The smile I gave him was enough of an answer before he began walking to the next aisle over.

266

We picked out the treats for Duke and headed in the direction of the registers again. As I rounded the corner of the aisle, I felt a pin-prickling feeling on the back of my neck like I was being watched. I turned around, suddenly feeling very vulnerable and not safe like moments before. I looked at the space around me, not sure what I was looking for, but also not sure why I felt a sudden shift.

Caleb noticed the change. "Hey, what's wrong?"

I reached for his arm and looped mine around his. "Nothing, I think? I just had the weirdest feeling—" I touched the back of my neck, and a shiver ran through my body. Nothing stood out to me, so I turned back around and smiled at him.

"Let's go home, Ranger."

Chapter 51

Caleb

I opened the truck door for Rae and helped her out before I grabbed the groceries from the back of the truck. I hadn't been lying when I told her that I loved getting to show her off to anyone who had been around. Seeing her interact with people, now that she felt comfortable again, did something to me in a way I didn't expect. We walked to the house, and she gave me a silly look before shooing me away from the door when I attempted to open it with an armful of groceries.

"Thank you," I said with a smile before we walked to the kitchen to start putting away the groceries. She stopped to greet Duke whose tail hit her leg as he excitedly spun in circles while she was petting him.

"Do you want to watch a movie tonight? We can have popcorn." I lifted the box and showed it to her.

She smiled and took the box, setting it on the counter. "Sure! That sounds…" Her whole body went rigid.

"Rae, what's wrong?"

"I—I'm not sure. I had this weird feeling in the grocery store, and even earlier today at Jenny's—pin-pricks on the back of my neck. I kind of felt like I was being watched or something? I'm not sure. Then the feeling went away and I felt fine again, like right now. It's weird." Her face twisted, like she was thinking about what could be causing this feeling. She looked around where she stood, and then at the windows and front door. "I'm obviously safe and there's still enough light we can see outside. There's no one on the porch."

"Maybe a fever? Come here, let me check." I pressed my lips to her forehead. "You feel fine."

Rae shrugged and resumed putting groceries away. "I'm not sure. Just a weird feeling. I'm fine!"

I opened my mouth to say something flirty but my phone rang. She froze again, and I wished for the day she didn't feel that way when the phone rang.

"It's Luke," I told her, hoping to settle her nerves. Luke sounded stressed as he told me that all the horses in my barn got out somehow. I pinched the bridge of my nose, thinking about our time in the barn earlier. Jenny had locked up everything before she left for work, but even if she hadn't, we would have seen it when we went in. "Oh gosh. Okay, I'll be right there as long as Rae's good." Something about this didn't sit right with me, but I would have to figure out what happened later. I needed to help Luke as long as Rae was comfortable with me going to the barn.

As soon as I hung up, I explained, "Luke saw the horses were out as he was leaving Jenny's place, at the back of my property. He was calling to ask for help bringing them all back to the barn. He said a couple of them seem a bit spooked. I'll only go if you feel okay with that."

"Yeah, go! I have the cameras at the front of the house, and I'll make sure the door is locked as soon as you leave. Duke's here with me. Plus, you'll have your phone on you…and you'll be right out there at the barn."

I hesitated but agreed. I walked to our room to grab a blanket, and when I came back, I passed it to Rae with a flirty smile. I watched her reaction as I put on my boots and went to the door. I could see her cheeks turning pink at my subtle suggestion, and she returned the flirty smile I had given.

I turned to Duke who was sitting at our feet. "Duke, you keep an eye on her. Make sure she is safe." Duke huffed as if he understood his assignment. I scratched behind his ear and praised him for being a good boy.

Turning back to Rae, I reached out and tilted her chin up slightly before whispering, "Pour us some wine and pick a movie out for us." I then pressed a gentle kiss to her lips. "...but not one we will need to re-watch please." I winked at her and gave a sly grin. "I love you." When I pulled back, she looked like she was a million miles away, like she was drunk on that kiss.

Rae leaned into me. "Deal. Love you." I wrapped my arms around her and hugged her before reluctantly pulling back and opening the front door. I stepped onto the porch. "You make it hard to leave, even if it is for just a little bit." She laughed and then gave me a flirty wave as she shut and locked the door behind me.

Chapter 52

Rae

I didn't know how long I had before Caleb would be back, so I knew I had to be quick.

I ran toward our room and picked out one of his flannel shirts, a lacy bra and panties, and then headed towards the bathroom.

"Come on, Duke!" I called as I walked into the bathroom and shut the door behind me, locking us in before I turned.

A couple of minutes into my shower, I heard something outside of the glass walls. I peeked my head out and saw Duke staring at the door, ears up. "Is Caleb home, buddy?" I turned the water off so I could listen, but when I didn't hear anything, I continued my shower. Even though my glasses were off, I could still make out Duke standing by the door. It seemed awfully fast for Caleb to be back already, but maybe he came back to get something.

I finished my shower and stepped out onto the bathmat. Duke had not moved from his spot and had not stopped staring at the door. "Buddy, I don't hear anyone out there." I put my ear to the door. "Nope. Nothing. He probably came back to get something and left, bud."

Duke looked at me and sat down.

I got dressed and looked at myself in the mirror. While I still didn't see myself how Caleb saw me, I'd become more confident since I'd been with him which made me smile. I was standing in a flannel with nothing but a bit of lace under it, and I felt good.

My skin was flushed, and my heart sped up at the idea of being with him when he returned from the barn.

I put on my slippers before I opened the door to the bathroom. As soon as I opened the door, Duke jumped up and pushed past me, nearly knocking me over. "Duke! What the heck, bud?"

He went to the bedroom door and waited. When I opened the door, Duke walked out and began searching for something.

I walked past the spare room and saw the door open. I swore I closed it earlier. Maybe Caleb did forget something and came back to get it. I glanced at the front door and pet Duke's head on the way. "Bud, the front door is still locked." I looked out the kitchen window and saw Caleb and Luke near the barn. "Looks like they've got one more horse to lock up before they come back home," I told Duke. He lay in the middle of the living room, facing away from me.

I found the popcorn Caleb had mentioned earlier and put some in a bowl before taking wine glasses out of the cabinet. Setting them on the counter, I went to the refrigerator and opened the door. Our refrigerator was well stocked, and Caleb had put the wine away when we got home. "Where is the wi—oh, there it is!" I reached towards the back to grab the bottle and then read the label to make sure I got the right one.

I jumped when I heard Duke growl and whine. Then a door shut. I stood up to see what had caused that noise since I was sure I was the only one in the house. I didn't know what to expect him to be growling at, but what caused it was the last thing I'd expected.

The world felt like it had started spinning, and I could hear my blood pumping in my ears, my heart was racing so fast.

"Hello, Rae."

Glass shattered as I dropped the wine bottle, and wine splashed everywhere. Duke barked somewhere in the house, but he was no longer in the living room.

"Ethan. H-how did you get in here? Where's Duke?" I asked shakily, backing away from him. His eyes looked as black as the night sky.

"Don't worry, he's not hurt. He's safe. I know you'd never forgive me if I hurt an animal. He's locked in a room. I had to get time alone with you, to convince you to come with me, but I didn't hurt any of the animals."

"Did—were you the reason the horses were out?" The sudden realization hit me. Ethan grinned creepily.

"What are you doing here?" I cleared my throat to try and steady my voice. "I need you to leave."

"Listen, sweetheart, you sound scared. I just want my girl back." Ethan took a few steps forward, and I backed up behind the island, putting space between us.

I gripped the countertop in an attempt to steady myself. "I'm not your girl. I was until you hurt me. Leave." My voice came out forceful despite how shaky I was.

"Okay, I'll leave, but I want you to come with me." He reached out a hand and took another step towards the island.

"I will not be going anywhere with you. Leave. Now. Before I start screaming."

"I don't think you'll be doing that." He pulled a pocket knife off his belt, causing a chill to go up my spine. "Just come with me and we can be in love again. I saw how you were with him. You—"

I cut him off, yelling, in an attempt to sound more angry than scared. "You mean you stalked me, trespassed, and then took photos of him and I naked? That's what you mean."

Duke hadn't stopped growling and barking, and now he was clawing at the door he was locked behind. I was hopeful my raised voice would make him bark louder. Maybe Caleb would hear even though he was still at the barn.

"His fault for leaving the curtains open. I saw a lot more than that. He doesn't know how you like to be touched, Rae. He doesn't know you like I do." He took a couple steps, making his way around the island, glass shards crunching under his shoes as he kicked them out of the way.

I continued to circle the kitchen island as he did, waiting for the perfect moment I could make a run for the front door. Duke's barking had not been heard by Caleb yet.

"He doesn't have your best interest at heart. You've not lost weight since being here. Probably all that wine and pizza." He pointed the knife at my stomach and thighs. I suddenly remembered what I was wearing and wrapped Caleb's flannel tighter around me. "Keeping the

274

curtain open while you sleep is unsafe. Eating processed foods, making you fat… That's not good either."

I've got to keep him talking until Caleb gets back. Come on, Rae. You can do this.

"I actually have lost weight since being here, since I'm working on the farm." I took a shaky breath. "And Caleb loves my curves."

"No he doesn't, Rae. He just knew you were easy and would get in bed with him. I'm the one that loves you, and I'm actually glad I caught you like this." He motioned again to my body. "It will make our reunion that much easier." His voice sounded angrier, and the way he looked at me, in nothing but my undergarments and a flannel, sent chills up my spine. The look in his eyes was worse than the night he hurt me.

I pulled Caleb's flannel tighter around my body, trying to cover as much skin as possible. "Ethan, please. Go. Now. I'm happy here. If you love me, like you say you do, you'll let me stay happy. Here." We'd continued to round the island slowly, and I was hoping something would distract him so I could run to the front door and escape.

Caleb, please come back soon.

As if Caleb read my thoughts, I heard him outside thanking Luke for calling him, and for his help. He was coming back to the house—thank goodness!

Hearing Caleb's voice getting closer, Ethan's expression turned desperate. I looked away just long enough to look at the front door. Ethan came up behind me, wrapping a big hand over my mouth, stifling a scream.

"You're coming with me now or your hillbilly gets his throat cut."

I nodded quickly, fighting the tears that had begun to flood my eyes.

As soon as Caleb's boots hit the front steps, he must have heard Duke's barking and growling, because his footsteps immediately picked up as he ran to the front door.

"Rae! Rae, baby! It's me! Open the door!"

I realized then that he hadn't taken his keys because I should have been able to let him in. None of this should have happened.

Ethan led me to the basement door, and I quickly realized that was how he got in the house. I realized he was probably hiding in the spare room and it wasn't Caleb who opened the door. At the bottom of the basement stairs, I saw the walkout door open. The lock had been tampered with, from the looks of it. Ethan pushed me to the door, his hand still over my mouth, and the knife still at my side on my bare skin.

"Move," he ordered.

I heard Caleb at the front of the house banging on the windows and calling for me. I wanted to call for him, to tell him where I was so he could save me, but I couldn't with Ethan's hand over my mouth and a knife at my side.

I heard a loud noise along with glass shattering. Caleb must have broken one of the windows on the front of the house in an attempt to get inside.

As we exited the basement, Ethan tripped on an uneven spot in the grass, causing the knife to cut my arm and

276

side as we fell. Pain exploded into a ringing that drowned everything else out for a moment. I placed my hand on my side and felt a small bit of blood trickling down my fingers and side. Tears fell from my eyes now. The spots where the knife had cut me burned as I moved, causing me to cry out.

Wait, he's not holding his hand over my mouth. He still hasn't gotten back to me yet! I screamed. I screamed as loud as I possibly could and yelled Caleb's name.

"You stupid bitch." Ethan stood and grabbed me by the arm, yanking me up from the ground. He smacked my face and then stepped closer to me as he said something I couldn't focus on. I could only focus on the pain and wonder where Caleb was.

Ethan spun me around so I was facing away from him, and he pinned my injured arm behind my back, causing the skin around the cuts to pull painfully tight. He pushed me forward slightly, and the pain caused me to feel lightheaded. "Go to the tree line. Now," he ordered, shoving the knife against my side again.

Through the open basement door, I could hear Caleb searching the house, calling for me.

Ethan continued to push me forward, the space around us growing darker the farther we went.

By the time I heard Caleb's voice again, we were already in the shadows. I could see Jenny's trailer a few hundred feet from us, and it pained me to know I was so close, but I couldn't call for Jenny's help either. Ethan turned us slightly to look behind us, and I saw Caleb pacing outside of the basement as he was calling my name.

It had probably only been a few minutes since Ethan had gotten his hands on me, but each minute of him touching me, in any way, felt like an eternity. We were a few feet from the tree line and I froze. I hated the dark, and he knew that. I looked at him with pleading eyes, hoping that there was some part of him that still cared about me. A part of him that remembered, and cared, that I didn't like the dark. He was mostly the reason why it scared me, but I could only hope there was a bit of a soul left in him.

Ethan nudged me again and growled "keep moving" to me. I looked at him and shook my head, hoping he would see the fear in my eyes and his heart would soften even a little. With his hand still around my mouth, he pulled me in, close to his face. "Oh, sweetheart… I remember. I remember how much you hate the dark. So, this—" he poked the wound on my side with the knife, causing me to scream into his hand, that was still over my mouth—"is going to be fun for me. This is because you left me." I could smell his breath, like he hadn't brushed his teeth in a week, and it made me feel like gagging.

He pushed me into the trees and the sounds of Caleb calling for me faded into the night. The brush and weeds scratched at my bare skin, causing more pain than I already felt.

When we made it to the other side of the tree line, I saw a van across the road. *No. Please. This cannot be happening.* I knew the second that I got into the van, the odds of Caleb locating me quickly, or even at all, would slip away.

278

He walked me up to the passenger side door and put the knife up to my throat. "Before I take away my hand to open the door, I want you to know something. Just know, if you try screaming, I will slit your throat immediately. Do you understand?"

I nodded and a whimper sound came out. I couldn't stop the tears from falling now.

"Good girl. See, I just want what's best for you. I wish you could see that. We're going to be so happy now that we're back together." His fingers brushed my ribs, and bile burned the back of my throat. He took his hand off my mouth and I immediately threw up in the dirt.

Ethan opened the passenger side door of the van and sighed. "You done being dramatic?" He tightened his grip on my arm as soon as I was done, and then he shoved me inside and shut the door.

The inside of the van smelled so bad, it made my eyes burn. As he went around to the driver side, I looked in the back and saw a few days' worth of clothes and paper bags from multiple fast-food restaurants. There was also something that looked like white paint dried on the seat and floor.

Has he been watching me for several days? How long has he been here?

Ethan got in the van and looked at me with what I assumed was his attempt at looking lovingly at me. Ethan leaned in, the knife in his hand placed at my stomach. He grabbed my face and kissed my cheek. I pulled away as best as I could, fighting the next wave of nausea that was creeping up on me.

"Fine. You don't want to kiss me yet? You will." Ethan reached into the back seat and picked up some balled-up fabric. He shook it out and I realized what it was—a pillowcase. He was going to blindfold me. "No, Ethan. Please. Please don't do…" He violently threw it over my head, pulling it down hard, before he had the knife at my side again.

The tears wouldn't stop as Ethan started the engine, which made a loud sputtering sound, causing me to jump. He began to drive and switched the knife to his right hand, pressing it to my arm, so I knew not to move.

The next thing he said to me was in such a chilling tone, I knew I would hear it in my nightmares.

"Let's go home, Sweetheart."

Chapter 53

Caleb

I tried to stay levelheaded, but my girl was missing, and I had no idea where to start. Duke sat by my feet and moved with me anytime I moved. I could tell he was stressed, but I didn't know how to help him when I was feeling the same. I had called dispatch and the cops were on their way, but I needed to do more.

Luke and Jenny. That's who I need to call.

"Luke, Rae has been taken by her ex. The cops are on the way, but I need yours and Jenny's help."

We hung up and I went to the porch while I waited. If I went back in the house, I would possibly mess up any kind of evidence, more than I already had, and I needed anything to prove this guy was guilty.

Duke paced back and forth on the porch, whining. "I know, Duke. We'll get our girl back," I promised him, trying to convince myself more than him.

Jenny drove up to the house from the backside of the property, and within seconds, Luke returned as well. Jenny had rushed out in her pajamas, the kind of friend who literally drops everything and rushes to help. I gave them as much of a smile as I could muster right now and thanked them for rushing over.

"Jenny, can you stay with the officers when they get here as they look over the house? I'm going to give my statement and then I'm going to help find my girl. Luke, will you help drive around looking for her?"

They both nodded, and I explained where I wanted Luke to go.

"We'll find your girl, Walker."

I gave my statement, then called my sergeant to ask if he would help in some way. My sergeant had called everyone on our squad, and they all decided to come in on their days off. A part of me felt guilty because I knew it was the night before their shift, when they should all be sleeping. However, I knew they would be mad if they'd found out later and hadn't been called in. I would forever be thankful for this brotherhood I joined.

My squad divided themselves up, between helping with the current scene and canvassing the property to helping out on patrol as this squad was wrapped up in this call.

While talking to the officers at the basement door, I noticed Duke sniffing. He paced, sniffed, watched the tree line, and then looked at me before repeating the actions.

We had discussed where we would drive around while searching for Rae, and Santana decided to follow me in her patrol car, while my sergeant went with Luke. "I need you two to drive down every road leading to her parent's home. Santana, I have an idea. Come with me."

Santana threw me a confused look.

Duke continued to pace and sniff and stare at the back of the property. "Duke, come here boy!" I lifted Duke up into the passenger seat and ran around the front, hopping in without waiting for a response from Santana.

282

I was driving down the road leading away from the farm and Santana called me. I put the phone on speaker and placed it in my lap. "Walker, what's the plan? Where are we going? I'm flying blind here."

"The woods behind my property. The other side of the tree line. I have a feeling about something I need to check out."

"A feeling? Okay, care to explain?"

"Duke. This dog took to her crazy fast. They were best friends immediately."

I turned left, onto the road leading behind my property. Santana followed behind.

"Also, Rae is scared of the dark."

"Okay, care to explain why you're telling me these things?"

"He's trying to scare her, Santana. He's trying to get back at her for leaving him, sleeping with me, for being happy."

"But where would he take her? He wouldn't just stay in the trees."

I sighed as I jerked the wheel to the left, my truck fishtailing due to loose gravel. I was going faster than I should have on this road, but every second mattered at this point.

"I don't know where he'd take her. I don't know. I just know that Duke was staring at the tree line. He wouldn't go far from me, but his eyes were on the trees."

"Rae?"

"Rae."

Chapter 54

Rae

The rocks crunched under my slippers as I walked to where Ethan was leading me. This pillowcase he put over my head smelled as bad as his breath did, and it took everything in me to not throw up. My side and my arm screamed at me with every move I made.

My feet hit something and I fell, my shins colliding with whatever I tripped on next. I let out a small cry and felt Ethan's hand smack the back of my head. "Shut up. While there's no one out here, I would hate to take a chance on someone hearing you scream."

"I tripped, you bastard. I can't see and I'm in pain!!"

Ethan lifted me up and huffed. "There's stairs here. A few of them. Keep going."

I stumbled as I went up the steps, having to trust Ethan, which is something I had not wanted to do for a long time. One of my slippers fell off and the rough wood on the steps hurt my foot. Ethan didn't tell me when there were no more stairs, so I stumbled again, and he laughed. Sick bastard.

We took a couple more steps and then paused before I heard a door opening in front of me. He started to pull me, but I stood there shaking my head. "Please, Ethan. Let me go," I cried. I felt the knife at my side again as he pulled me forward into the building, putting more of a barrier between Caleb and me. If I was to scream for help, would he even be able to hear me?

The door slammed behind me with a hollow thud, the sound echoing through the walls of the house. Ethan ripped the pillowcase off and then reached to lock the door with a deliberate click, turning back to me with a smile that didn't reach his eyes. I took my first breath of what I had hoped would have been fresh air. Instead, what I'd breathed in smelled old and smoky. Hot tears stung my eyes again as I realized that Ethan had brought me to an abandoned house.

How far had we gone? Would Caleb even look here?

Ethan stepped close, the knife still pressed against my ribs. "You might not see it now," he said in a voice so calm it made my skin crawl, "but this could be our place. Quiet. Away from everyone. Just you and me." He reached out and cupped my cheek. His thumb brushed over my skin, wiping away tears that I hadn't meant to cry. I squeezed my eyes and jerked my head away from him. "Somewhere we could start over. Somewhere no one could touch us." His voice sounded a little less calm than it had before.

"You're sick! I know we didn't go far. You can't seriously think that Caleb won't find us." I pulled away as best as I could, but he caught my wrist and pulled me against his chest. A small whimper escaped my lips as he moved me. I tried to hide the pain that radiated from the cuts on my arm and side, but they burned with every movement.

His fingers wrapped tightly around my wrist. "You think you get to say no? Not this time." His smile was cold and his eyes looked soulless. "You'll learn to love me again—one way or another."

He moved us farther into the house and turned on a dim light that only lit up a portion of the room. "This is where you'll stay. Where no one can find you." He looked behind him at something and sighed. "I'm going to let go of you now because I have to grab something. Do not move. Okay?" He pointed the knife at my face, and I nodded quickly.

While he wasn't towering over me, I was able to look at the house he had brought me to. It looked like a skeleton of what it used to be. The walls looked dark, like they'd been burned. In one corner, a sleeping bag lay crumpled on the floor. A filthy blanket. A bag. Rope.

I was already afraid, but seeing the rope and the bag, with whatever was in that, scared me to death. *Don't go there, Rae. Think.*

Ethan looked at me with a look like he dared me to try and run.

I needed to look for something I could use as a weapon. The flooring was covered in some plastic drop cloths, and there were some tools, a tarp covering a box, and a bit of wood not far from where Ethan was standing. Perfect, besides him standing right next to it. What was he doing?

I continued to look around but saw nothing close enough that would work as a weapon. I tried to picture what the house might've looked like before whatever caused this damage, before it became a hiding place for something this ugly. Something felt familiar about this place, and I couldn't figure out what it was.

I needed to try and distract him, or something, so I could get to the tools.

"You've been staying here?" I asked, my voice sounding small, but I forced it to be steady.

Ethan didn't look at me. "It's quiet. For now."

He made a sound like he'd found what he had been looking for, and then he turned and gave me a slow, dark look—one that said exactly what was coming next. He held up a pair of handcuffs.

"You're out of your mind."

Crap, if looks could kill. That made him angry. He spun on me so fast I barely had time to take a step back before the knife was pressed to my stomach again. My back hit the wall. The air in the room seemed to vanish.

"Don't push me, Rae," he hissed. "You think I won't do it? That cowboy of yours can't save you. No one's gonna hear you scream."

My heart thudded. I kept my eyes on his, forcing myself to not give him the satisfaction of fear on my face, even if it was eating me alive inside.

"You already did your worst to me," I said quietly, with a bite to my tone. "And I'm still here." I spit on his face.

His expression flickered—rage, disbelief, something ugly—and then he turned away. He started pacing. Back and forth. Mumbling. Talking to himself more than me.

"You ruined everything! You told him! You made me into some kind of monster, like you weren't begging for it back then, like you didn't know how lucky you were."

My stomach twisted. I thought he was angry before, but this was so much worse.

"I didn't beg," I said. "I was scared. And you..."

He turned and shoved me again, harder this time, the flannel falling from my shoulder. My back slammed into the wall. and a large piece of splintered wood pierced through my skin, close to my spine. I screamed in pain and he threw me down on the ground. My hands shot out for balance, my breath knocked from my chest.

"Shut up! You don't get to talk like that. Not to me."

I was too far from the tools, but I tried to crawl towards them. He grabbed my hair and pulled me back. I struggled, twisting my body, but he wrenched my arm behind me again. He twisted my skin so tight that it felt like my wound ripped open more.

Keep fighting, Rae.

I kicked at his shin and caught part of it. The knife clattered to the floor. He let out a yell but didn't release me. He straightened up, picking up the knife as he stood, and dragged me a few feet to the sleeping bag by my hair. I screamed in pain as it felt like every nerve in my body was on fire. He straddled my hips and I thrashed beneath him, but he grabbed the handcuffs and yanked my arms back, handcuffing my wrists together. He then picked up the rope and proceeded to tie up my legs. My skin burned as the fibers scratched and tightened around my legs and ankles.

288

My throat felt like it was closing. I couldn't take a complete breath.

"I oughta teach you a lesson for what you did, what lies you said about me. Make sure you understand what happens when you lie about a man like that," he growled.

Tears stung my eyes, but not just from fear. From fury. From the unfairness of all of this. From the way his voice sounded like it always had right before he hurt me.

He cut off the flannel shirt and stared at me with an evil grin. I thought I had been afraid before, but I was wrong. Now I was paralyzed by fear.

Chapter 55

Caleb

Santana and I got to the part of the road behind my property where there was a straight shot through the trees to my house. I jumped out of my truck and picked up Duke to set him on the ground so he could help. I left the truck engine running with the headlights shining on the road in front of us. The only sounds out here, other than the truck, were coming from birds and crickets.

I walked to the opposite side of the road, shining my flashlight into the trees, and Duke followed close behind me. I had hoped I would catch them hiding in the trees but saw nothing.

Santana jumped out of her car and began walking around the opposite side of the road, shining her flashlight into the trees.

"See anything?" I asked with an urgent tone. She looked at me and just shook her head.

I walked farther away from our vehicles, Duke on my heels. I'd trained him to stay right by my side, or just very close to me, but I wished right now he would run somewhere with a possible direction for us. It would take too long for us to get one of our K9s out here.

Duke had his nose to the ground and kept looking at me as he sniffed, every muscle tuned in on whatever he'd found. I'd not trained him to search for anything other than a treat, but I also knew that if Rae had been out here, he'd know it.

"I think we found something!" I rasped as Duke led me along the side of the road we'd parked on. Santana ran over to where we were, and I showed her where Duke led me to. "There's what looks to be a set of footprints here. They're bigger shoes, so not Rae's." I angled my flashlight at the spot in the road where the gravel had been disturbed. They were not obvious, but they were definitely footprints. I walked the way they were angled and saw the next worst thing in this nightmare: tire tracks. Duke wouldn't be able to smell her if she'd gotten into a vehicle. My heart sank and I forced myself to not panic.

I walked in silence with Santana as we walked around the area the tire tracks were in. "Walker, what type of shoes was she wearing?" Santana asked me with more hope in her voice than I felt.

"I'm not sure." I spat out, sounding more frustrated than I meant to. *Crap.* "Sorry…" I would have to apologize properly later, but right now, we needed to hurry.

She waved off the apology with a small smile, and I was thankful she was the one that was out here with me. We'd seen a bunch of ugly things in this world together, and she'd seen me at my worst. I took a deep breath. "I went outside to put the horses back in the barn, so I'm not sure what she'd changed into. When I was searching the house for her, I noticed her shirt hanging out of the hamper, and the shower water had been turned on recently. So, maybe she was barefoot or wearing her slippers?"

"Come look at this." She shined her flashlight on the ground near where she stood.

I looked down at prints that resembled slippers. There were no deep treads in the prints. Next to one of the shoeprints was a footprint. "This has to be her. She could have been wearing her slippers and her foot got stuck in the mud, here"—she pointed her flashlight at a deeper divot in the mud—"and then it got stuck in the mud here, too."

I heard Duke sniffing something, and Santana and I looked at what he'd focused on. "Is that puke?" Santana confirmed it and my world started spinning again. "Santana, she threw up. He could have hurt her, she could have a head injury…"

"Caleb Walker, snap out of it!" Santana hissed as she smacked me upside the head. "Rae needs you right now and you need to be in cop mode. I like her and I need you to focus right now. Do not make me call Sarge and have you benched."

She was right. Rae needed me, and I had to focus. I nodded to let Santana know I was good.

She pointed her flashlight at the ground behind me and walked towards where it shined, patting me on the shoulder as she passed by. "The tire marks are over here, too, possibly leading away from town.

I followed her without a word.

We ran along the road until the tire tracks turned.

"What's back in this direction, Walker? Isn't it just a couple of houses?"

I stood still. Thinking. The sudden realization hit me. It had been so obvious but I had been too close to see it.

"Santana, we need to go back to the cars. *Now*. I know where they are."

I ran back to my truck with Duke, and Santana to her car. "Where? One of the houses?"

"Not just any house. Jenny's."

Chapter 56

Rae

I thrashed around, attempting to break free from Ethan's grasp, my wrists and legs ached because of being re-strained and my lungs burned from screaming. He was heavy, fueled by whatever sick adrenaline was pumping through him, and I could feel the shift in his intent—darker, meaner, final.

"Stop fighting me," he growled, pinning me to the sleeping bag. With his free hand, he picked up the knife again and flicked open the blade, putting it at my throat. "I gave you a chance to be good."

I spat in his face again. I couldn't stop fighting. I knew what he had done to me, what he could do again. It wasn't brave; it was desperate.

His hand cracked across my cheek. Stars exploded behind my eyes, and I choked on the sob that crawled up my throat. He leaned closer, breath hot and sharp with rage, and that knife glinted again as he angled it closer to my jaw. He waved it beside my face like a promise—a promise of what was to come if I didn't behave.

"You think you can hurt me and get away with it?" he hissed. "You think that cowboy of yours is gonna show up and save you like some damn hero?" He hit me again and it made me so dizzy, I had to stop fighting.

I saw the evil smile on his face as he realized he finally got what he wanted. Ethan looked at my body and began to drag the tip of the knife down my side while holding my shoulder in place. I tried to tell him to stop, but my head was still spinning. He traced the tip of the knife up my stomach and my chest as he reached for my bra strap.

Be brave Rae. Caleb will be here soon. He'll figure out where you are.

Ethan started to pull my strap down when we heard something. The house creaked.

Footsteps?

He froze.

My heart pounded so loud, it echoed in my ears. I told myself to stay still and not scream. Ethan was so focused on whatever made that sound that he'd stopped worrying about me for a moment.

Another creak.

"Shit," Ethan hissed.

He stood up fast, yanking me roughly up with him. The rope around my legs had started to loosen just enough that I stumbled on the tarp covering the box in the corner of the room, next to the tools. The tarp fell away from what it covered and I saw a couple cans of white paint, among a few other items in the box. I gasped, realizing where I was. *Ethan was the reason Jenny's delivery went missing.* I was in Jenny's house.

Ethan jerked me around, causing me to lose my footing, and I realized the ropes around my legs had come mostly undone. Ethan didn't notice this and he hauled me in front of him, jerking me back against his chest like a shield. The knife pressed into my ribs again. His breath came hot and fast over my shoulder.

"I swear, if it's him…" he began.

The sounds of wood splintering filled the house.

"Hands up! Drop the weapon!"

A sense of relief washed over me when I saw Caleb and Santana.

The sound of his voice nearly undid me right then—firm, controlled, but full of fire. He was here. He'd found me.

I heard Duke bark somewhere, but I didn't see him.

Ethan tightened his grip on me, jerking me a step back toward the kitchen. "I'll kill her!" he shouted. "Don't think I won't!"

"Try it," came Santana's voice behind Caleb, calm but sharp as steel.

"I will!" Ethan screamed as he stepped backwards. "I will if you take another step…"

The knife had fallen away enough, that it wasn't right at my throat anymore, and I could tell he was nervous. He knew it was over. With a burst of desperation, I snapped my head back. The back of my head connected with his face. His curses tore through the house, and his hold on me loosened. My legs were now completely out of the ropes, and I brought my knee up in front of me, before sending my foot back into whatever part of him I could kick. I kicked fast and hard, landing square against his thigh. He cried out, stumbling backward.

"Rae, I got you! Move!" I heard Caleb shout, and I tried to move away from Ethan.

296

I tried to scramble backward when I saw Ethan attempting to reach for me again, but with my wrists bound tightly behind me, I couldn't steady myself. My foot caught on loose floorboards, and I pitched forward.

Unable to catch myself, I fell into the wall and to the floor. Pain exploded behind my eyes as stars swirled in my vision. The world spun wildly, and my body went limp against the cold floor.

Voices echoed faintly, and I felt pressure around my ankle before my body was being pulled. Was Ethan pulling me back towards him? Santana yelled, and Caleb shouted my name. Everything hurt and I couldn't move.

Then…A gunshot. Just one. Loud. Final. Everything went still.

My ears rang. I couldn't focus. Dark spots flooded my vision, and I felt something warm on my face. I thought I saw something red on the floor, or the wall—I couldn't tell. Something warm slid down my cheek. *Blood?* I couldn't lift my hand to check if it was mine.

Someone collapsed.

But who?

I blinked, trying to focus enough to find out. My head swam. The ceiling spun above me like it didn't want to stay still. I tried to sit up, but my body wouldn't work.

Someone was crying out. *Was that Caleb or Santana?* I tried to call for them, but I couldn't make a sound.

I felt so tired and closed my eyes. *Maybe if I close them, for just a moment, it will help.*

I heard a heavy thud coming towards me and opened my eyes just enough to see what looked like boots walking towards me. Someone knelt next to me.

My eyes closed once more. I tried to fight it, but I was so tired.

I tried to stay awake. I didn't know who had been shot. I needed to know if Caleb was okay.

Am I safe? I didn't know anything at all except that I was slipping under.

Chapter 57

Rae

A steady, rhythmic beep pulled me from the haze. My eyelids fluttered, heavy and reluctant, feeling as if they had weights pulling them down. The world around me was blurry, distant, like a half-remembered dream. A dull ache throbbed behind my temples, and my body felt unresponsive, like I was moving through thick fog.

Slowly, I was able to open my eyes. Glancing around, I saw the sterile white ceiling and blinding hospital lights.

Where am I? What happened?

After a moment, I tried to reach up and rub the blurry feeling away from my eyes, but I felt a weight resting lightly on my hand. Feeling dazed still, I turned my head to see Caleb in the chair beside my bed. His head rested against the back of the chair, eyes closed. His hand was holding mine.

I watched his chest rise, slow and steady, with every breath he took. I tried to speak, to let Caleb know I was awake, but my throat was so dry. A small raspy sound came out, quieter than a whisper.

I gave his hand a faint squeeze and felt how sore my arm was. A small crease of a smile softened his face in sleep.

The monitors beeped steadily around us, filling the quiet room with their calm rhythm.

Tears threatened to fall from my eyes, not just from the dull ache inside my head, but from the hope I felt in this moment.

I was awake. I was alive. Caleb was here. That meant I was safe again.

A dull soreness tugged at my upper arm and side as I moved. There was a constant pulsing ache with every heartbeat—the sting from the wound Ethan had inflicted, now bandaged and protected. I shifted uncomfortably, the sheets cool beneath my skin.

My mind swirled with confusion. Memories of what happened, and how I got here, felt distant.

How long had I been here and was it over?

Answers felt just beyond reach, and I began feeling antsy. I needed Caleb to wake up.

I squeezed Caleb's hand a bit more and his chair creaked as he stirred. His eyes blinked open, hazy at first, then focused as they found mine. "Rae?" His voice was rough, hoarse but filled with relief.

I tried to answer, but my throat still felt raw and dry. I started to tear up again. I wanted to talk to him but couldn't, so instead, I gave his hand another weak squeeze.

"I'm here, Sunshine," Caleb said softly, shifting closer. "You're safe."

I blinked back the tears, the knot in my chest loosening just a little. "Caleb…" My voice was barely more than a whisper.

He reached up slowly, brushing a stray strand of hair from my forehead. Then he reached behind him and picked something up. "When you fell, your glasses broke. I had Santana go to my house to pick up your spares," he said as he unfolded them and placed them on my face.

I mouthed "thank you" to him, and he smiled at me with tears in his eyes. "I thought I lost you," he confessed, voice thick with emotion.

I swallowed, the fog in my mind clearing a bit more, and the aches in my body were now more obvious. I tried to clear my throat, and it felt like a desert.

"Oh, you're probably thirsty. Here. The nurse brought this in a bit ago since they thought you may be waking up soon." Caleb picked up a cup with a straw and held it out so I could take a sip.

"I…I didn't know…" My words faltered.

"Sshhh…You're okay," he said firmly. "Neither of us knew. You're awake, and that's what matters. I am so sorry I left you to go outside."

I blinked up at him, slightly shaking my head, which I regretted instantly. I closed my eyes, feeling dizzy from just that little bit of motion. After a moment, I was able to open my eyes again. I looked back at Caleb, searching his face for answers. "What…What happened to Ethan?" My voice came out shaky and small, but I was happy I could finally speak.

Caleb's jaw tightened and he stared into my eyes more intensely than before. "He's not going to hurt you anymore."

My heart pounded, every muscle tensing. There was an intensity in his eyes that I had not seen before. "Is he…?"

Caleb nodded. "He's dead, Rae. The moment he tried to hurt you again, Santana stopped him."

My breath caught. The room spun for a moment, and I didn't know whether to feel relief or numbness—or both. Tears spilled down my cheeks, but this time the tears were different—softer, a mix of grief and relief. I was so relieved, but I was sad for the loss of life. It was a very confusing mix of emotions.

He squeezed my hand gently. "You're safe now. I promise."

I leaned back, letting the weight of the truth settle. I was safe. For the first time since opening my eyes, I felt something steadier than pain or fear—hope. I squeezed Caleb's hand and closed my eyes focusing on the weight of his hand on mine, and the feeling of hope I now had.

And for now, that was enough.

Chapter 58

Caleb

Rae had spent a couple of days in the hospital after being rescued so they could monitor her healing. Her doctor told us she was lucky she had only a minor concussion and that she would need a few days to heal, but that she would be fine soon. When she was released, Rae seemed nervous about going home, so I had offered the idea of staying at her parents' place until she was ready.

"You doing okay?" I asked after I extended my arm towards her and saw her wince slightly. She pressed her hand gently on her side as she linked her fingers in mine.

Ten days had passed. She'd been cleared by her doctor regarding the concussion she had, and she had started to act like herself again. The only limitations she had were because of the cuts on her side and arm. Nightmares had flooded her dreams during the first few nights after she was released from the hospital, so I never pushed the idea of going home.

Work had been so understanding about me not returning, and Rae not starting, when we thought we would have. Thankfully, I had plenty of vacation time saved up since I rarely took time off.

When Rae had woken up this morning, she told me she was ready to go home, and the smile on her face showed her excitement. We missed Duke, but because she needed time to heal, Santana, Luke, and Jenny took care of him and the farm while Rae recovered.

"I love you, Ranger," she said to me as she tightened her grip on my hand.

"I love you, too, Sunshine."

I watched Rae from where I sat in the truck. She was staring out the window, looking at the spring flowers that speckled the sides of the road leading to my house. I rolled her window down for her, and she smiled at me before she closed her eyes and soaked up the sunshine.

I pulled up to the house, close enough that Rae wouldn't have to walk far. Thankfully, Rae was just achy now and no longer dizzy. However, that didn't stop me from worrying.

I put the truck in park and looked over at my girl. "Stay here," I requested with a gentle hand on her arm. I sweetly smiled at her, and she answered with a small "okay," her voice barely above a whisper. I could tell she was nervous to step back inside the house, but she hadn't said as much.

I opened the truck door and was met by a warm breeze.

Maybe Rae would want to sit outside for a bit today since it's so nice out.

I rounded the front of the truck, thinking about how to make her comfortable, both with the aches she still felt but also with the memories the house would now bring. When I looked at her door, I saw her looking at me with a smile on her face, waiting like she always had.

Gosh, this girl will forever be my undoing. I opened the truck door and rested my hand on her knee, "How do you want to do this? Want me to carry you? Support you as you walk? Let you do it?" I looked up as she giggled.

"Ranger…" She reached out and touched my cheek. "I'm okay. I'm safe. I'm…"

"Sore and going to let me take care of you." I attempted to sound stern, but I couldn't. Not with her.

She giggled again.

I reached up and lifted her up out of the truck, then set her on the ground, waiting to remove my hands only after I saw she was steady.

I reached in and grabbed the bag that Jenny and Santana had packed for her once the police had cleared from the house. Throwing it over my shoulder, I looked at her for a long moment. I knew the doctor said she was cleared after her concussion, and there were no broken bones; she was just sore. However, that didn't mean I wasn't going to take care of my girl—for the rest of our lives. "Don't hate me."

She opened her mouth, probably to ask what I meant, but before she could say anything, I scooped her up in my arms and began walking to the front door. Giggles erupted from her body.

I walked with her in my arms up the steps at the front of the house, her arms wrapped around my neck. If anything hurt her, she hadn't said a word, and smiled through the pain.

When we got to the door she stilled "Caleb..." Her breathing stuttered and her body became tense.

"I know, Sunshine. Just remember, he's gone and can't hurt you anymore. Plus, I'm right here and we'll take it one step at a time." I kept my voice soft, soothing, trying to calm her nerves. "Oh, and Duke is waiting inside for you."

Rae's mouth drew into a tight smile, and she nodded. "I am excited to see Duke. Thank you for being there for me, too. I couldn't do this without you." She gave me a light kiss, and it felt like fireworks going off in my body. I could tell her nerves were still present but could also feel her relax as I returned her kiss.

"Let's get you inside before we do unspeakable things to each other on this porch," I groaned as I kissed her.

Rae laughed immediately with her head thrown back.

I carried her inside the house, grateful that the danger was over and she was finally home where she belonged.

Chapter 59

Rae

The air inside the house was warm, but I had light goose-bumps prickling my skin. After a super happy greeting from Duke, Caleb could see me start to focus on the memories that being back here brought. The last time I'd seen Duke, I didn't know if Ethan had hurt him or not. I only knew he said he was safe, but I didn't know if I could believe him. The last time I stood in this area of the house, I was hoping to spend a quiet, intimate evening with Caleb. There were no traces of glass or wine on the ground thanks to Santana, Luke, and Jenny.

Caleb stood by me, his hand placed gently but firmly on the small of my back, grounding me, proving to me that he would be with me through every step we would take. My breathing was slow and even as I looked around the front of the house. I couldn't explain it, but I didn't feel frightened. I looked at Caleb. "It's not as scary being back here as I thought it would be. Sure, I'm aware of what happened, but knowing I'm safe again, that I survived it, too, it helps."

Caleb stared at me and smiled.

"What?" I giggled.

"It was like I saw a fire in your eyes just now, coming back for the first time in a long time." He gently touched my cheek and leaned in to kiss me. I leaned into the kiss, pressing my body against his, and I felt him smile, which made me smile.

"Well, I need to get freshened up. I think I'm going to shower," I said with a playfulness in my voice.

"I'll go pick out some clothes for you to change into and set them on the bathroom counter for you."

"Or… you could just join me." I grabbed his hand as I started to back away from him, leading him to the bathroom.

Caleb's brows lifted just slightly, but his lips curved into a slow smile. "But Rae, baby, you're sore."

"Then be gentle, Ranger." I winked at him.

He told Duke to stay and then let me guide him through the hallway, our fingers still entwined. I turned the bathroom light on, and it cast a soft glow around the room. I moved with quiet purpose, swaying my hips, despite the achiness I felt—just enough to tease him and bring a smile to his face.

I reached for the hem of my shirt, but he stepped forward and caught my wrist. "Wait," he said softly. "Let me wrap your arm and side first."

I paused then nodded as I watched him grab the first-aid kit under the sink. When I first woke up in the hospital, he'd told me that our friends had made sure everything would be ready for us when he brought me home. When they found out I wasn't ready to come home, they'd picked up extra medical supplies and brought them to my parent's home. They'd taken turns staying with Duke and had even made dinners for us in case I'd needed Caleb to help me more. I would never take for granted the friends that I had, or the man standing in front of me who would move heaven and earth if it meant I was safe and happy.

308

Caleb stood in front of me and cradled my arm carefully in his hands. The stitches were neat but stark against my skin, a reminder of everything I'd survived. He wrapped it with waterproof wrapping, pressing gently on the adhesive that secured it to my arm. I tried so hard not to react when it hurt, and I knew I wouldn't be able to stop it when he moved to my side. The cut there was worse than the one on my arm because at the end of everything, all the thrashing around I'd done had opened the wound more. He gently helped remove my shirt so it didn't catch on any of the stitches.

"Real sexy," I chuckled as he pulled out another waterproof strip.

"Yeah, you are," he said with a wink as he centered my bandaged stitches under the waterproof wrapping. I took a couple of deep breaths as he pressed the adhesive down. The skin around it was so tender, but Caleb's movements were as gentle as possible. He finished pressing down the adhesive, but his hand stayed at my side. He leaned in and pressed a gentle kiss to my lips. "That should hold."

"Thank you." My voice was quiet.

Caleb traced my jaw and down my neck with his fingertips as he kissed me. I tried to reach behind me to unhook my bra, but I couldn't with one hand.

"Allow me," Caleb whispered in my ear, sending shivers up my spine. He helped me out of the straps, and I tugged him towards me and kissed him deeply. I stepped back, breathless, and slid my sweatpants down, stepping out of them with a quiet, breathless laugh as the fabric tugged at my sore hips.

Caleb undressed, too, his eyes never leaving me as I continued to undress. There was no hesitation now, no questions—just the silent language between us that had always meant more than words.

I stepped into the shower first, reaching to turn the water on. As it poured down over my shoulders, I sighed, feeling content in the warm water. Caleb followed, sliding in behind me and pulling the glass door closed.

The water was hot, slowly filling the space with steam. I stood close to the wall, my body relaxed, shoulders easing as the warm water soothed my skin.

Caleb moved in close, chest brushing against my back. He started by washing my hair for me. I hadn't been able to wash my hair by myself since the hospital, so this had become a routine thing for him to help me with. He reached for the soap, lathered it slowly on the loofah, and began running it over my skin, starting at my neck. He worked down my shoulders, my arms, carefully avoiding the bandages.

The moment he moved lower, heat rushed through me in a way that had nothing to do with the water. Every slow drag of his hand and the loofah along my hips, and the backs of my thighs, had my body reacting before my mind could catch up.

"Caleb…" My voice shook. Every part of me needed him.

He stood up behind me, the heat of his chest brushing my back, his breath warm on my ear. "I know," he

310

whispered, his lips grazing my damp skin. "I feel it, too. You're still sore, though, are you…?"

"Caleb, I *need* you. Right now."

His touch turned confident but still unbearably gentle. He never went near the stitches under my ribs, never pushed or pulled in a way that made my breath catch for the wrong reason. The way he touched me was a mix of gentleness and heat that made my entire body react.

"You are so beautiful, Sunshine," he said, making me blush.

When his fingers slid lower, he teased me slowly until my knees threatened to give out. I tried to brace myself on the wall, forgetting about my stitches, and the ache caused me to wince. He steadied me with a firm hand on my hip.

"Easy," he said, his breath warm against my neck. "Just lean on me."

I leaned against him, his body feeling like fire against mine. I gasped when his mouth found my shoulder. The combination of his lips, the heat of the water, and the careful way he touched me, I felt myself reacting to him in an instant.

"Turn around," he whispered.

I was aware of him watching me as I turned, with that look that made my entire body warm. When I faced him, the hunger in his eyes nearly undid me. He kissed me the second my hands touched him, slow at first, then deeper, hungrier. His hands stayed low on my hips, drawing me closer to him, making my breath stutter.

I could barely think straight with the steam curling around us as we kissed each other while letting our hands wander. I wanted him so badly it hurt.

Like he could read my thoughts, he pressed his forehead to mine, his voice a rough whisper. "Tell me if anything hurts."

"Only if you stop," I breathed.

His quiet groan vibrated against my lips. His hands slid beneath my thighs and he lifted me, settling my back against the cool tile wall as my legs wrapped around his waist. He moved with me—slow, deep, devastating in the best possible way. Our bodies fit together, and I gasped at the connection. Every shift of his body was controlled, careful, but the tension underneath that restraint made it hotter. He kissed down my neck, his hands guiding my hips exactly how I needed while keeping the weight off my injured side.

I clung to his shoulders, my nails in his skin, my body trembling as the heat built fast and sharp. My head fell back, water running over my skin as his voice found my ear.

"I've got you," he whispered, low and certain. "Let go for me, Sunshine."

I didn't stand a chance. The ache in my arm and side had been forgotten about. The pleasure hit hard, shaking through me in waves that pulled a helpless sound from my chest. Caleb held me through all of it, saying my name as he came apart with me.

When I finally melted against him, shaking and breathless, he wrapped his arms around me carefully, keeping pressure off every tender place. He kissed me again, brushing a few wet strands of hair out of my eyes.

We lingered in the steam and water, hearts beating as one, my head leaning against his.

"I love you, Sunshine."

"I love you, too, Ranger."

After a moment, Caleb murmured against my ear, "Babe, will you move in with me, permanently?"

I lifted my head slightly, to look at him. "Permanently?" I asked, breathless and smiling.

He nodded. "Permanently."

I smiled and then kissed him deeply.

We stayed under the water until it began to cool, then stepped out wrapped in towels and quiet smiles. Caleb dried me gently, starting at my shoulders and arms, then patting my legs.

"You just like touching me," I teased softly.

"Guilty." He grinned.

I wrapped the towel around me and stepped in front of the mirror, picking up my hairbrush, attempting to brush out the tangles.

Caleb stepped behind me, placing one hand on my waist, his other hand tracing circles on my shoulder. "You look like home."

I leaned back into him, reaching up to touch his cheek. "Good," I whispered. "This... this is where I'm meant to be."

He kissed me again like he was reminding me I was safe, loved, wanted, and his.

Two people, finally whole again—together.

Rae

I was in the kitchen mixing the salad for the end of the summer bonfire night we'd decided to host. We had invited Jenny and Luke, our coworkers, our families, friends from in town, and even Cierra.

Caleb walked in after setting up the canopy and the table for the food. Duke followed close behind him. "Everything you guys made looks great. Thank you for doing all of this while I set up the bonfire."

I smiled at him and kissed him as he passed by to wash his hands. "Of course, and I know I have said this before, but you were right about Sage. She's amazing. I couldn't have done all of that by myself."

My boss had been here for most of the morning helping prepare food and only left to pick up her family to bring them back. She had insisted on helping the second we asked her to join us. Caleb had been right about me liking her, and I'd forever be grateful for this job and our friendship.

We had been preparing food all morning and I hadn't gotten ready yet. "Caleb, I need to get cleaned up. Everyone will be arriving soon. Can you take over chopping the last of the salad mix-ins?" I asked as I reached for the bow on the apron. I'd tied it too tight and couldn't get it undone.

Caleb stepped behind me and loosened the knot, helping me lift the apron over my head and kissing me in the process. "Of course, Sunshine. Unless you would like some help?" He winked at me as he picked up the tomato and knife, knowing we didn't have time for what he was hinting at.

I giggled and blushed. "Maybe later. If I say yes now, we won't make it to the bonfire by the time everyone gets there." I playfully swatted his arm.

"True, so you better get in there fast before I decide I don't care if we are late."

I turned and walked to our room, laughing.

I pulled a towel from the linen closet and walked into the bathroom.

I quickly showered and dried off, then stepped up to the counter as I began to wrap the towel around myself. In the mirror, I caught a glimpse at the scar on my waist and my arm. They were both bright red now due to the warm shower, but that would fade to a pink tone soon, making them a bit less obvious. My scars reminded me of everything I'd gone through and how far I had come—how Caleb saved me.

I stared at the scars, thinking about the memories they brought, until I heard Caleb talking to someone out in the front room. I knew I had to hurry. I walked to the drawers, opened one, and pulled out fresh undergarments. After putting those on, I quickly walked to the closet to pull out my jeans and a T-shirt. I decided to pull out a flannel just in case it was cool later this evening. The weather had been tricking us and acting like fall was starting early so I figured a flannel would be a good idea. I decided to bring a flannel for Caleb as well, so I grabbed an extra one.

I set the flannels on the end of the bed so I could put my jeans on and heard a soft noise like something hit the footboard. Curious, I picked up the flannels again and set them on the bed again, hearing the same noise.

I picked up each flannel and inspected it, trying to figure out what would have made that noise.

Picking up the second one, I found a small box in the pocket. My hands stilled as I sat on the edge of the bed, eyes wide, staring at the box in my hands. I didn't dare open it, but I couldn't stop staring at it.

This is a ring box. This is a freaking ring box! Was Caleb going to propose at some point? My mind was going a million miles a minute.

"Hey, Rae, everyone is here and they took the food. You almost ready, Babe?" I blinked. The sound of Caleb's voice pulled me back to the present, and I shoved the box under the flannel in case he peeked his head in the room.

"Yeah, I will be out in a minute!" I realized I was speaking so fast. *Calm down, Rae.* "I'm just finishing up getting dressed."

"Okay, I'll get the truck started and get Duke loaded up." I heard him walk away from the door and let out the breath I had been holding for far too long.

I quickly stashed the box back in the flannel and hung the flannel back up, smiling as I did so.

Oh my gosh. A freaking ring! Oh my gosh he can't know that I know. Calm down, Rae.

I took a few deep breaths to calm myself as I continued to get dressed.

When I was ready, I ran to the truck with only one flannel in hand. I leaned into the truck window. "Do you want a flannel or something in case it gets cool?"

"Baby, if I need to get warm, I won't be using a flannel." He gave me a grin and a wink that sent chills all over my body.

"Oh, you are on one today!" I laughed as I hopped in and closed my door.

"Oh, hold on. I forgot something." He hopped out of the truck and ran back into the house, reappearing seconds later. He was so fast, not giving me enough time to steady my heart rate.

"Okay, sorry about that, I had to grab the salad tongs. I forgot to give them to Jenny." He said as he passed them to me.

He reached out and took my hand as he drove to us in the direction of where we would have the bonfire.

I sat on the tailgate, flannel on, sipping a glass of wine Caleb had brought me. Duke sat next to me with his head in my lap, and we people watched together. I watched my friends, new and old, talk, laugh, and sing by the fire while roasting marshmallows. This bonfire night to celebrate the end of summer was a great idea that Caleb had. The friendships I'd made over the last couple of months, and reconnecting with friends from my past, was just what my heart had needed, and now it felt like we were celebrating.

I spotted Caleb on the other side of the bonfire talking to my parents. While they didn't know all of what happened to me, they knew enough to be grateful for Caleb saving me. I watched Caleb when he spoke with them, respectful but comfortable, like he was talking to his own parents. I wished his parents could be here. They would be so proud of him for everything he'd accomplished.

When Caleb noticed me watching him, his blue eyes lit up and a smile crossed his face. He looked so handsome with the gorgeous sunset behind him as he walked over to me.

"What are you doing over here by yourself?" he asked as he stepped between my knees, placing his hands on my hips.

"Just taking it all in. I'm so happy here, with you, with our friends, with Duke." I scratched under Duke's chin.

Caleb looked at me with such loving intensity. "Come here for a second." He took my hand in his and helped me off the tailgate.

"Hey everyone, can you all come over here for a minute?"

As soon as everyone was gathered around, Caleb cleared his throat. "Rae and I want to thank you for coming here tonight. You all are important people in our lives. No matter how long we have known you. Which is why I wanted you to be here for this." He turned toward me and Santana passed him something. I quickly realized what was in his hand.

Caleb reached for my hand and knelt in front of me. The group of friends began chattering quietly in hushed but happy sounding tones.

"Rae, you know I love you, right?"

I nodded with tears in my eyes.

"Sunshine, I have loved you since high school, and I let you get away back then. I never want to let you go again. Will you marry me?"

Tears began to fall steadily down my cheeks as I smiled and nodded. Caleb stood and I threw myself into his arms. "Yes, I will marry you, Ranger!"

Cheers erupted from the crowd of our friends and family as we stood there kissing, not even noticing anything going on around us, only focusing on each other.

Caleb and I sat on the tailgate together, watching the fire die down, after everyone left for the evening. We held hands, but we were silent. No words were needed.

I looked down at the ring he had given me, a beautiful princess cut diamond on a white gold band—the perfect ring.

The fire had died down now, and I expected Caleb to pack up so we could head back to the house. Instead, he moved farther into the bed of the truck and lay down. "Come look at the stars with me." I moved to where he was and lay next to him, pressed against the warmth of his body with my hand on his chest. Duke shifted from where he had been on the tailgate and curled up next to my feet.

Caleb gently rubbed circles on my arm as he whispered to me, "I love you, Sunshine."

I whispered back "I love you too, Ranger."

A few minutes later, I noticed Caleb's hand had stilled, and he had lightly begun snoring.

How is this my life? How is any of this real?

I smiled to myself as I snuggled closer to Caleb. In the warmth of his arms, I soon fell asleep, too, happy and safe.

He's got me, always. The best part is, I've got him, too.

Acknowledgements

Writing my debut novel was somewhat terrifying, but I could not have done it without the unwavering support of a few special people.

Forever and always, the first thank you goes to my husband. Thank you for supporting this crazy adventure. From giving your opinion when I was stuck on which sentence sounded better, looking at the cover photo a million times even though barely anything was changed, making dinner *so many* times so I could focus, and starting research on certain book publishing topics when I focused on writing, you helped out more than you know and I could *not* have done this without you.

To my editor, Megan Harris, you are a *godsend.* From the moment I got my first email from you, I knew I wanted you in my corner. From your edits to the advice you gave along the way, *thank you.* I don't know what I would have done without you!

To my beta reader and dear friend, Sarah, I am so unbelievably thankful for you. The constant support you have shown, asking questions and letting me know someone cares, helping look at the cover art a thousand times and giving your opinion on it, taking the time to text me updates as you read my book, and more…thank you from the bottom of my heart.

To my work family, my in-laws, and the friends who showed up and supported me through this process—thank you. Your encouragement, patience, and belief in me meant more than I can put into words.

About the Author

Danielle Redman is a Missouri-based writer who creates romance stories centered around healing, safety in love, and finding home in the people who make you feel safe and seen. When she isn't writing, she works full-time and enjoys traveling, reading, and spending time with her husband and her dog. She is the author of the Oak River County series.

You can find her at: danielleredmanauthor.com